I0571506

SHOOTING STARS
TRAVELING CIRCUS

BOOKS BY KIM BLACK

Little Black Dress, The LBD Project, Book 1
Red Heels, The LBD Project, Book 2
Bare Essentials, The LBD Project, Book 3

By Kimberly Black

Lydia, Woman of Purple
Her Most Precious Gift

Children's Books

Pockets
Sophie Louise Will Not Say CHEESE

For more, including short stories and anthologies,
visit www.kimblackink.com

SHOOTING STARS TRAVELING CIRCUS

KIM BLACK

Steepledog
Productions

© 2019 by Kim Black
Published by Steepledog Productions
PO Box 50814
Amarillo, TX 79159
www.kimblackink.com

Printed in the United States of America

All rights reserved. No part of this publication may be reproduced, stored in a retrieval system, or transmitted in any form or by any means—for example, electronic, photocopy, recording—without the prior written permission of the publisher and author. The only exception may be brief quotations in printed reviews.

This is a work of fiction. Names, characters, dialogs, and incidents are products of the author's imagination, and shall not be construed as real. Any resemblance to actual events or persons, either living or dead, is entirely coincidental.

Cover design by Samuel and Sean Black

ISBN 978-1-946846-12-9 Print

ISBN 978-1-946846-13-6 Ebook

DEDICATION

To Rebecca,

Happy 21!
You are an incredible young woman,
and an inspiration to everyone who knows you.
Live your best every day.
Love you to the stars and back!

ACKNOWLEDGMENTS

Heartfelt thanks to all who helped to bring this story to life.

To James D. Quiggle for your editing
expertise and encouragement.
To Brandi, Donna, and Suzi, my Lone Star Women of Letters,
for your love and never-ending support.
To Tammie for listening and talking me off those pesky ledges.
To Emily, for being one of the first to love this story.
To Samuel and Sean, for lending your
incredible talent to all my worlds.
And to Riley, for everything.

EPISODE 1

I'll Fly Away

The man with the badge on his shoulder growled as he read. "Charlotte Annice Birchfield." He stood tall and broad as he looked down into his data-com. The dusky orange sunset at the end of the driveway created a glow around him, transforming him into a chiseled black silhouette in uniform. "As a representative of the United North American Territories, I request that you submit your property to a voluntary search."

Annie clenched her jaw. Nobody called her *Charlotte*. *Charlotte* was her mother's name. She was *Annie* Birchfield. *Annie.* She tightened her grip on her daddy's old cattle prod until her knuckles turned white. She stood guard in front of her family home, wearing a pair of ragged blue jeans, a faded tee-shirt, and a worn pair of work boots. She knew she looked no more threatening than a hissing cat, but she intended to make her hiss count.

"No, sir, I won't," she spat. "My parents don't like having folks here when they're out." She raised her voice loud enough to cover the fifty feet of gravel that separated them.

She wished her brother was home. He'd know how to handle this guy. Cody would be back anytime. But for now, she'd have to stand her ground like Daddy had taught her.

Authority took a step away from his vehicle and tapped the device in his palm. "Charlotte Annice Birchfield: seventeen," he read again. "Mother: deceased three years. Father: deceased one year. Resides with brother, Cody Alan Birchfield: twenty-three." He recited her personal stats to serve as a challenge.

"All I said was they ain't here." Annie squared her shoulders and took a step toward Authority. "But that don't change the fact that you're not welcome."

He gritted his teeth. "Charlotte..."

"Just stop." She thrust the electrified pole forward. "Do you have a warrant of compulsion?" If he wanted to use the law to threaten her, then she would do the same.

The man took a deep breath. "I do not. I have a request for voluntary compliance."

Annie took a few steps closer, raising her weapon to shoulder-height of her petite five-foot-three frame. "I don't much feel like volunteering, and it's fixin' to get dark. Why don't you just tell me what you're lookin' for?"

The man's eyes formed black slits under his thick brow. He glanced down at his device. "You have a quarter horse in your possession, registration number 1138-AA-23. I would like to inspect that animal."

Annie's heart slammed in her chest. She had been expecting a call for over a month since the news reported that all registered horses would be seized. *Just like daddy predicted.* Just like when the government took their cattle all those years ago—for the health and safety of the country.

She pressed her lips together into a thin, tight line. "My horse died last month. It's too dark already at the barn, and we don't have good electricity out there. Why don't you just go back to town and see if you can get a warrant tomorrow? That'll give me a chance to talk to my brother about what to do with you." It would also give her the opportunity to hide her horses. They knew about Jefferson, but they didn't know she had three others.

Authority tucked his device into the nylon pouch on his belt and crossed his thick arms over his chest. "Miss Birchfield, I would advise you to comply with my request now. As it stands, I could charge you with attempted assault on an officer. I don't want to do that. If I have to get a warrant, I will add as many charges as the law allows."

"Well, right now, the law don't require me to let you on my land." Annie squeezed the trigger on the grip of the cattle prod until she could feel the vibration of the rod. She could hear it hum through the quiet of twilight. "And if you come back here without a warrant, you can save yourself the trouble of adding the word *attempted* to the assault charge. I'll do you in."

"Threatening an officer is not becoming, Miss Birchfield."

"I suppose it's a good thing I don't much care what you think."

The man sighed. "I had hoped you would be reasonable about this matter. We just want to inspect the animal to see if it is healthy. There have been reports of some kind of outbreak..."

"I guess since he's dead and buried, an outbreak won't bother him much." She hated being dishonest, but she knew he was lying, too. Authority had only brought a sedan. He couldn't carry a horse back with him, healthy or otherwise. He was here to kill her horse. She extended her narrow chin and glared. "You need to leave now."

Annie silently prayed that he would get into his car and go. She had never had to use the cattle prod before, and she didn't want to use it on a lawman, even to defend what was rightfully hers. Annie held her breath and waited.

"I will return tomorrow, Miss Birchfield. I'll have my warrant for the search—and for your arrest." He looked her over once more and then shook his head as if disappointed.

Annie refused to give an inch, leaving Authority no choice but to go. She watched him back into the road and then stared after him until he was out of sight. When she finally lowered the cattle prod, her arms began to shake.

Another set of headlights appeared down the road, and she raised the weapon again. A wave of relief washed over her when she recognized the rust and green-chipped paint of her brother's battered pick-up. She stepped aside to let him drive to the time-weathered farmhouse. As she followed the cloud of dust, she turned her head back to look over her shoulder, fearing the lawman might return.

"Annie, we don't have much time," Cody hollered as he hurried from the cab of the truck, followed closely by Buffalo, Annie's blue heeler puppy.

"Authority was just here," she said, interrupting. "He asked to see Jefferson. Make sure he's healthy. Prob'ly to kill him," she scoffed, following her brother into the house.

Buffalo jumped up onto the couch, and Annie scratched his lopsided ears for a minute. She watched as Cody rushed around the room, pulling out their parents' most prized possessions and arranging them on the kitchen table.

"What're you doing?" she finally asked.

"The law passed, Annie. I just heard it in town this afternoon."

Cody's pale blue eyes looked wild with excitement. Annie imagined hers matched his right about now.

"What're we supposed to do?" she asked.

"If you want to keep your horses—if we want to keep anything—we have to leave." Cody walked to her side, and his nearness helped to calm her. He inhaled deeply and raked his fingers through his sand-colored hair. He started again, but this time his voice sounded softer. "I made arrangements for us. I found a small ship that has enough room for us and our animals. The pilot agreed to carry us off-planet at dawn."

"Suits me," Annie said. "I hate to leave Momma's house, but I am *not* lettin' anyone take my horses." She glanced around the room at everything for which her parents had worked themselves to death. She knew if they left earth, the Authorities would torch it all, but right now, she didn't care. "The man that came said he'd be back tomorrow with a warrant," she added.

Cody grabbed her hands. "He's coming back tomorrow? That's what he said?"

"Yeah." Annie shrugged. "Said he'd arrest me, too."

An instant sweat broke over Cody's brow. "Shoot, Annie, we gotta move. He's likely to show up here at midnight, and he probably won't be alone. We only have a couple of hours to get out. I hope Dhabi won't be mad if we show up early."

"Dhabi?"

"Dhabi Ramal. The guy with the ship," Cody explained. "I'm sure he'll be just thrilled if we show up with the law on our tail."

Annie's thoughts raced. Would Authority actually come at midnight? Could they possibly get anything packed so quickly? How could she prepare her horses for a jump out of the atmosphere in just a few hours? "Will the horses be okay? Can you give them something?"

Cody nodded. "Once we get them into the ship's hold, I can sedate them. They should be okay. But we have to hurry. You can't take everything. Just bare minimum."

She looked down into Buffalo's enormous brown eyes. "Yes, you can come," she said, more for her own sake than for the dog.

"I'll get the horses into the trailer, and as much of my med gear as I can carry," Cody said as he headed to the back door. "You get a bag of clothes for each of us, and all of Dad's guns and Momma's jewelry. Pack the trunk with whatever you can fit."

"I'll get the cash from Daddy's box," she said.

"I already did. I had to pay for our trip upfront. Just get the rest."

Annie watched as Cody left for the stable. She clicked her tongue, and Buffalo followed her down the hall to Momma's bedroom. Annie flipped the switch and looked around the room for one last good-bye. Momma's voice seemed to echo off the walls. *Take care of the homestead. Take care of each other.*

Annie reached up to the small wooden box on the dresser and snapped the brass latch closed. All of her mother's jewelry— what little there was—now rattled about in the case in her hand.

She pulled a lace pillowcase loose from the bed and wrapped the box in it. Dropping to her knees, she slid a long case from beneath the bed and found her father's collection of firearms. Once she had both boxes in her arms, she went back to the hall and stacked them at the arch to the main room.

Buffalo trotted behind her as she hurried to Cody's room

for his clothes. She smiled as she culled through the shirts she hated and packed only the clothes she liked best. She held up a short green jacket and frowned. "This is why you still don't have a girlfriend," she said, tossing it to his closet floor.

Annie rolled the clothes up and packed them into the gray duffle he kept on the lowest shelf. As she closed his bedroom door, she tossed the bag to the end of the hall with the other things. Now to her treasures.

Annie prided herself on a simple life. Her wardrobe was modest. Mostly work clothes and just two dresses for parties and church. She only had one weakness…her boots. She looked at the dirty work boots on her feet and kicked them off quickly. She'd have to choose carefully, and these didn't make the cut. After a few moments, she had narrowed down her selection to five pairs of cowgirl boots, all in brilliant hues of quality-dyed alligator. Annie pulled on the chocolate brown boots and lined the other four down the side of her bed.

Grabbing her clothes, she began rolling the pieces up and shoving them into her boots. "This will help save space," she explained to Buffalo, who watched with a doubtful tilt of his head. She took the stuffed boots and carefully laid them across her bed quilt, forming a compact square. She tied the quilt corners together over the whole pile. "Good enough."

Annie dragged the large bundle down the hall, snapping off all the lights as she left each room and closed each door. She tossed toothbrushes, combs, and anything else she thought might be a necessity into a towel and made another smaller bundle with that.

Back in the main room, she found her father's trunk and filled it with their personal papers, the jewelry box, and the last family photograph that hung over the mantle. She picked up her grandmother's Bible and a few other books from the shelf and arranged them into the gaps in the trunk. Nothing more would fit. Her father's gun case went on top.

"The horses are in the trailer, and the truck is running," Cody said, bursting through the front door.

Annie jumped, startled at the sudden break in the quiet of the house she was deserting.

Cody glanced up at the mantle clock. "We don't have time for much else. I'll load the cab, and you grab whatever foodstuff you want."

"I'm taking my bike," she said. It wasn't a question.

Cody gasped and shook his head. "You don't have time to get it ready. And there's no room for it on the trailer—not with all four horses."

"I'll ride it out to the ship," she said. Annie knew she was probably selfish to insist they take her motorcycle, but she rationalized the necessity. "We don't know what conditions we'll find ourselves in. We may need something small. And it's too valuable to leave. If nothing else, we can sell it for cash."

Cody grabbed the trunk and his duffle bag. "I'm loading this stuff, and then I'm leaving."

Annie hauled her bundle of boots and clothing over her shoulder and followed him out to the truck. "It won't take me five minutes to get it going. I'll follow you out." She dumped the pack in the bed of the truck. You go through the house and make sure I didn't miss anything important. I'll get the bike and pull it around front."

"And if it doesn't start right off?" he asked.

"Then I'll leave it." She probably wouldn't, but that's the response she knew he wanted.

She ran to the lean-to at the back of the house and rolled out her antique Indian motorcycle. It was her baby, apart from Buffalo and her horses. She checked it over and nodded. As she closed the door to the shed, she remembered one last thing she needed. She took a step inside and climbed up on the narrow bench against the long wall. She stretched to reach the ledge at the top of the wall, and her hands found the blue steel sawed-off shotgun her daddy had placed there for safekeeping.

"You're coming with us," she whispered, slipping the gun into the loops on the side of her bike. She pulled her dark brown hair into a low ponytail and straddled the bike. With a quick flick of the kickstand, she had it started and rolling around to the front of the house.

Cody whistled for Buffalo to join him in the cab of the truck. The spotted dog turned his head from brother to sister and back. Annie smiled and whistled, patting the little stretch of the seat in front of her. Buffalo sprinted to the bike and jumped into place, propping his front paws on the handlebars. Cody shrugged and got into the truck. "I'll see you at the loading dock. Dhabi's ship is at the far end of row six."

Annie saluted as Cody and everything they possessed rolled toward the back road away from the only home they'd ever known. Annie made a short turn around in front of the house before she noticed a pair of headlights turning into the driveway from the road out front. As the bright white beams caught her, Annie looked over her shoulder, making sure Cody was away. She left her bike running, but propped on its stand, and pulled the shotgun from the loops on the side.

A red and blue light flickered from the hood of the automobile, and Annie knew for sure the lawman was back. As he opened his door and got out, Annie raised her weapon.

"Miss Birchfield," the now-familiar voice growled. "I don't want to hurt you," he said.

"That's a lie." Her voice revealed a tremor of fear, which triggered a fierce stream of barking from Buffalo. The dog jumped down from the bike and charged Authority.

"Call off your dog," he ordered.

"I told you not to come back."

"It's now past midnight, Miss Birchfield," he said, looking sideways at Buffalo. "I have my warrant of compulsion, as well as your arrest orders." He took a step in her direction. "I can rightfully seize any animal on your property."

"I'm warning you to leave now while you still can." Annie leveled the gun on her shoulder and aimed the business end toward Authority. "Get back, Buffalo," she whispered.

"You name your animals." The lawman raised his brow and grinned. "We advise against that, you know." With a flick of his wrist, he raised his right arm and fired a bright blast from a small weapon in his hand. A blue-white fireball shot forward and hit Buffalo in the shoulder.

"NOOO!" Annie screamed.

Buffalo let out a single yelp and was down. Still and silent at Annie's feet.

Not allowing another second to tick away, Annie fired her daddy's antique shotgun. A full load of rock salt flew and spread and made a thousand tiny bee-stings in the face of Authority. The lawman went down.

Annie didn't wait to see what he would do next. She scooped up her lifeless pup and jumped onto her bike. With blinding tears in her eyes, Annie sped away down the back road of her home place. She raced to the shipyard, finding row six only after pausing to ask directions from a working girl at the corner.

She slowed enough so that she didn't draw attention to herself. Most of the ships and bays were dark and quiet, but at the end of the row, she found her brother arguing with a square-shouldered man of Indian descent. The cargo ship behind them was lit up like Christmas and looked much larger than Annie expected. Down one side of the weathered blue hull was the license number and name: *CT04-Nightingale.*

"You were going to take my money and run?" Cody yelled.

"I wasn't leaving you," Dhabi pleaded. "I was conducting an engine check. You want to be able to take off without any trouble, don't you?"

Annie drove her bike into the middle of their disagreement. "Authority is after us." She held up Buffalo for Cody to see. "He shot my dog. We have to leave now."

Cody looked over the puppy and nodded. "Give him to me, quickly," he said. Cody carefully took the dog in his arms and hurried to the cab of the pick-up truck.

Dhabi sent Annie a suspicious glance.

"My brother is a vet—a doctor for animals," she explained. "We have to get away right now. The law is coming."

"I didn't agree to carry fugitives," Dhabi complained. "I have to think about this."

"No time," Cody called out through the window, driving the truck and trailer into the ship's hold. "You can return our payment or take us off-planet *now*."

Dhabi shrugged and looked Annie over from head to toe. "Get on, then," he said, pitching his thumb over his shoulder. "We can be off in twenty minutes."

Annie's bike engine roared inside the hollow of the ship. "Make it five minutes. I shot a lawman."

"I won't take a murderer," Dhabi said. "I won't."

"I didn't kill him," Annie said. "But I might kill you."

Dhabi raised his brow and hit the switch for the bay door. He waved his arms wildly when he saw the train of flashing lights at the other end of the shipyard. "Get your gear secured. Liftoff in five."

Dhabi disappeared behind a door labeled CREW. Annie strapped her motorcycle to the rail on the wall and raced to the back of the horse trailer. She led out her four horses to the rail and helped them settle down even as the ship's engines began to thunder around them. Cody came about the front of the truck carrying his LS, life support, pod.

"I don't know if I can save your dog," he said. "I put Buffalo in my oxygen pod. He's in a coma. He'll stay that way for now. I'll do what I can."

Annie took the metal pod from her brother. "I'll hold him while you sedate the horses."

The ship lurched, and the horses reared and neighed. Cody opened his medical bag, and within just a few minutes, he had each of the four horses calmed and secured.

"Strap in, folks," Dhabi's voice called out from a speaker overhead. "Less than one minute, and we'll be pulling G's."

Annie followed Cody to the jump seats and strapped in. She'd never been off-planet before, but Cody told her all about his three trips to First Station, where he studied the effects of prolonged orbit on varying sizes of animals.

"Go ahead and scream or laugh or whatever when you feel your stomach start to rise," he reminded her. "It helps to keep your abdominals taut. Less likely to vomit."

Before he could say anything else, Annie felt the pull of home, and she began to cry. As the tears flooded over her cheeks, a fury burned in her stomach. Home was gone.

She took a deep breath between sobs and dared herself to look Cody in the eye. She felt sorry that her devotion to her animals cost him so much—his livelihood, his home, his friends. When her gaze met his, she saw the shimmer of emotion in his eyes. It was almost more than she could bear.

She hugged the LS pod, wishing...

Cody reached out his hand and squeezed her shoulder as the force of acceleration shook the whole ship. "I'm here for you," his voice assured her. "I don't know where we're going, but as long as we're together, we'll be all right."

"Cleared the atmosphere," Dhabi's voice said with an air of control. "We have about forty minutes to figure out our destination, so as soon as you have your legs under you, please join me in the cockpit, Dr. Birchfield."

Annie was no longer crying. It took only a second for her to realize the ship's artificial gravity system had kicked in. Inhaling deeply, she loosened her grip on the pod and let it rest on her knees. She stared through the glass window at her beloved pup. Buffalo's white-ticked fur was speckled with blood and scorched around the wound in his side. The small digital screen at the end of the pod showed four blinking lights. One glowed a pale green, one blue, and two yellow.

Cody loosened his straps and stood. "Is Buffalo going to be okay?" Annie asked.

"Little sister, we should say a prayer for all of us tonight."

EPISODE 2

Bless the Broken Road

"That's why I was checking the engines," Dhabi yelled.

Cody shook his finger in the captain's face. "You were on your way into space. If we hadn't arrived when we did, you'd have been long gone with all our money."

Annie stepped between the two men, closed her eyes, and shook her head. "Just stop arguing now. What's done is done, Cody. We *did* arrive in time. We're safe on board. If you two keep up the squabbling, the horses will get upset."

The men both took a step back from her. They each drew a breath of calm. Annie gave them a sharp glare. "Cody, I shouldn't have to remind you what a mess a distraught horse can make."

Dhabi's face showed a worried frown. "This may be too much for my little ship to take. I'm not sure I shouldn't hand you back over to the law."

"This is what I'm worried about, Annie," Cody said. "He can't be trusted. I gave him every bit of our savings — every dime. I told him what we were doing. I told him we had to get off-planet to save our animals. He's just looking for an excuse to dump us and pick up a reward."

"Reward?" Dhabi asked.

Annie watched as Cody's face flushed red. "See?" her brother yelled.

She held up her index finger to her brother, something she'd seen her daddy do on many occasions. "Ten seconds of silence." She whirled around to face Dhabi and swallowed hard, hoping to sound reasonable.

"We're not *really* criminals," she began. "I'm sure there ain't any reward for us at all. We are just moving our animals off-planet to save their lives. Authority wants to seize them and have them slaughtered."

Dhabi tried to stare her down, but couldn't help but blink in the intentional chill of her icy blue gaze. "I'm a law-abiding citizen. I only want to do what's right."

Annie allowed her full pink lips to curl until Dhabi looked away. "Our animals are our responsibility. We just want to take care of them the best we can. It's the same thing the government did with the cattle years ago."

"They had to control the methane gasses. And then they were protecting us from the Mad Cow outbreak," the captain complained. "Authority explained it very thoroughly."

"My dad's cows weren't sick at all," Annie continued in low tones. "But Authority took them and slaughtered them anyway. Said they would genetically engineer the cattle to be disease-resistant. Look what happened after that. No cows. They all went the way of the lions, giraffes, and bears. Like the dinosaurs. All extinct now."

"You don't know anything about that." Dhabi scoffed at her. "What? You might be sixteen years old?"

"I'm seventeen," she said as if the additional twelve months made any difference. "But I listened to my parents and my grandparents. They told me what happened. Earth wasn't always as it is now. People used to live useful lives into their seventies and eighties. My grandma said that her grandmother lived to be a hundred and six."

"That's not true." Dhabi shook his head.

"It is. I know that's not what you hear on the digital, but the digital only says what the government wants you to know." Annie reached out and gently took the man's arm, vaguely aware that by touching Dhabi, she was fueling her brother's ire. "I'm trying to save my horses."

Dhabi pulled his arm out of her reach. "You're selfish. Why

do you even have horses? Do you know how many people four horses could feed? Maybe the government is trying to take care of the people. Have you ever thought of that?"

Cody shook his head and rejoined the conversation, this time with a controlled temper. "I'm an animal doctor. I happen to know that the government has cloned enough sheep to feed everyone in the world for decades." He suddenly stopped. Annie realized he was waiting for his emotions to subside. "The reason so many people are starving is that it's how the Authority can keep the population in check. I have personally seen the documents. Too many poor? Let them starve; problem solved."

Annie led Dhabi to the horses. She gestured to her quarter horse. "This is Jefferson. He's the one that was registered. He's the author of this little adventure."

Dhabi looked into the huge dark eyes of the slim brown horse. "You named him?"

"Of course, we named him," she chirped. "We name all our animals."

Dhabi blinked and chewed on his lip. "You're not supposed to, you know?"

"And in a few years, the government will pass a law that you aren't supposed to name your children because you'll get too attached to them." Annie raised her brow. "They already fine you if you have more than one child. It's crazy. Just one more way for them to control us."

Cody rubbed the nose of the painted pony next to Jefferson. "This is Stubbs. Mama named him after George Stubbs, a famous horse painter from the nineteenth century."

Annie watched the disbelief settle into Dhabi's expression. She couldn't tell if he felt admiration for their bold rebellion against the "rules" or a sense of complete betrayal and confusion about what he should do with them. The young woman just smiled and stepped in between the other two horses. She stroked the mane of the largest horse—a black one with a white star on his forehead. "This one is Cody's. His name is Nero, and what an emperor he is. He is the kind of horse that would have won prizes in the old days."

"Well," Dhabi began as he looked the creature over, "These days, a beast like this could feed a large family for a month."

Annie shot a harsh glare at the man. "You're the beast." She patted Nero's neck and turned to face the smallest horse. "This little buckskin is Liza Jane. I shouldn't even introduce you to her. She's very sensitive, and you'll just hurt her feelings."

But as she spoke, Annie noticed something change in Dhabi's appearance. A softness filled his eyes, and his shoulders dropped and rounded. He took a step toward the horse and raised his hand to her nose.

"Liza Jane?" he whispered. "That's something." Dhabi blinked rapidly as if he had dust in his eye that he was trying to remove discreetly.

"What is it?" Cody had seen the difference, too.

"Nothing...just odd."

"What's odd?" Annie asked. She could see that Liza Jane liked Dhabi.

"When I was young, my family lived in an apartment in the Indian Projects. My father had the choice to homogenize our culture, which would have meant divorcing my mother to receive financial benefits. He refused. We got to keep our heritage, but of course, that meant we were fairly confined to our sector. The little girl across the hall from me was named Liza Jane." He stared into the horse's big black eyes. "We were friends. I remember how she used to draw pictures of horses—hundreds of them—for hours and hours. She used to say that one day she would have a whole stable of ponies."

Annie took a step into his bubble of memories. "What happened to your Liza Jane?"

"Gone." Dhabi sighed with a sorrowful breath. "She caught the cough as so many kids do. Especially in the projects. She went to the hospital and never came home. Her mother gave me one of her drawings to help me remember her."

Annie smiled through shimmering eyes. "Do you still have the picture?"

Suddenly Dhabi snapped back to the present and dropped his hand back to his side. He whirled away from the horses and hurried back to the bridge door. "Of course not," he barked. "I have responsibilities instead." He disappeared down the hall.

Annie and Cody shrugged and tended to their horses in silence. After another minute, Dhabi's voice filtered through the com. "Dr. Birchfield, join me, please."

"Why don't you come with me?" Cody asked.

"Do you think Dhabi will mind?"

"What's he going to do? He's already planning to turn us over to the law."

Annie kissed Liza Jane on the forehead. "Do you think so?"

Cody nodded, opening the door for his little sister. "He's probably scanning all the digitals for information about us. Seeing who might offer him the best deal for our heads."

They marched down the hall to the small cockpit, and Dhabi waved them in. "Good, you're both here."

"What's wrong?" Cody asked. Annie noticed her brother skimming over the instrument panel for indications of trouble.

"Everything." Dhabi gestured for Cody to sit in the co-pilot's seat. "If we try to dock at First Station, we'll all be arrested immediately, and all of our cargo will be confiscated. It seems Authority believes I was the initiator of this flight."

"What are our options?" Cody asked. "I don't want you to suffer for our problems."

Annie's anger surged. Why was Cody trying to be nice to this guy? Barely an hour ago, he was ready to strangle him for taking their money and running. They couldn't trust him, could they?

Dhabi brought up a map display of ports labeled with numbered codes. "The only neutral station I can get to on the fuel we have is the Mackenzie."

"Mackenzie is neutral now?" Cody asked, rubbing the back of his neck.

"As of last month," Dhabi responded. He nodded and clicked his tongue. "When the sin taxes doubled, Mackenzie declared itself independent. We can refuel and grab a ferry from there. I can take you one jump, and from the next port, you can find other means of transportation, or whatever."

"I don't want to go to a sin station." Annie had heard from friends with siblings in the military about what went on at sin stations. "Our parents would have a fit."

Cody shook his head. "Annie, we don't have a choice. If we go to First, our trip ends right now. If we go on a little further, we have a chance to save our animals."

Annie gestured to Dhabi. "How do we know he won't just turn us in?"

Before Cody had a chance to reply, Dhabi nodded and began. "You don't know that. I could call Authority and have them waiting for us wherever we dock. I can do that anyway. But even if I tried to cut a deal ahead of time, I have no way of knowing if they will honor it. I'm not ignorant."

Cody raised his brows as if he was pleading with Annie for trust.

She relented. "Okay, but how are folks on the stations? Are they any better than the law?"

Dhabi rolled his eyes. "For what *you're* wanting, yes. Most of the people on the stations are looking for fast money *and* a way to subvert the law. They will take either-or, but if they can do both, all the better."

Cody reached for Annie's elbow. "We'll make the best of the situation. Once we can ferry to an outer colony, I can get a job, and we won't have to worry about Authority."

Dhabi chuckled and rolled his eyes.

"What's funny?" Annie asked. She propped her hands on her hips and glared into the captain's eyes.

"My mother used to say to me, 'A man who has nothing should never complain of the scraps he is thrown.'" He sighed when they didn't respond. "You are frightened to go to a place filled with people just like you. What did you think leaving earth would be like? Everyone out here is running from something, too."

Annie wanted to spit out some witty reply, but as her brain searched for words, she realized that Dhabi was right. She knew she should apologize, but her pride wouldn't allow it. "Why don't y'all work it all out, and I'll go back to the animals. I need to sit and rest a bit."

Cody nodded. "Go on, and I'll be there in a few minutes."

Annie left the cockpit and wandered back down the hall to the hold. The horses rested quietly. She picked up the LS pod and rocked it in her arms. She looked down through the window on the side at her puppy. "Buffalo," she whispered. "I need you to get well and wake up."

She sat on the floor of the hold and stared at the dog. Minutes passed in silence as she daydreamed about the long afternoons she had spent teaching her beloved pup a dozen tricks. Buffalo could not only ride on her bike, but he loved to ride on the horses' backs, too. She'd taught him to do flips and even sit up in the saddle as Stubbs did a few tricks of his own.

She didn't need tricks now; she needed a wet nose burrowing into her neck. She just wanted to see his whip of a tail wagging back and forth. She prayed for him to breathe on his own again.

"*Get along, little doggie, get along, get along,*" she sang softly to Buffalo. "*The whipper-wills a-singing her even-tide song. It's time for the doggies to find their corral, for the weary ol' rider t'find the arms of his gal.*"

Cody cleared his throat behind her, and Annie straightened her back and wiped the tears from her cheeks. She placed the pod with her things and stood to face the men. "Plans all made, then?"

Cody nodded.

Dhabi smiled and reached out toward Annie. "That was quite beautiful. Your voice, I mean."

Cody grinned at the captain. "Our mother taught her a whole lot of songs. But that sort of thing is frowned upon."

Dhabi shook his head. "Maybe on Earth, but not out here. Out here, people are hungry for music—the real kind with words and voices. Not the digitally generated, mathematically correct sequences approved by Authority for mental stimulation. You were singing."

Cody shook his head. His eyes displayed obvious concern. "Look, she's just a kid. She was singing to her dog. Don't make a big deal out of it. It wasn't some subversive act or anything."

"Yes, it was," Dhabi replied. "It was entirely subversive—and perfect."

Annie lowered her chin and let her arms fall limp at her side. On Earth, she could be charged for an unapproved performance. She looked up and shrugged.

Dhabi stared at Cody. "Haven't you been off-planet before?"

"I've been to First Station several times."

Dhabi scoffed. "That hardly counts." He laughed and gestured to Annie. "You were made for this, little girl. You two could be set for life."

"What're you talking about?" Annie asked.

"Your brother and I have just spent the last half hour trying to figure out how to make enough money for a ferry jump. My dear, you have just rendered that whole conversation irrelevant." Dhabi walked a tight circle around Annie, studying every inch of her. "What kind of clothes do you have? Is a dress too much to ask?"

Annie looked wounded. "I got a dress. I go to church."

Dhabi laughed. "Of course you go to church. Every Sunday, I'll wager. And during the week, you raise horses, sing, and shoot lawmen. What a perfect little Christian you are."

Annie's face flushed red with indignation. "It says in the Good Book we are to lift our voices and make a joyful noise unto the Lord. It also says we're to be faithful stewards of the abundant blessings He has bestowed."

Dhabi let out a deep belly-laugh. "I love it. I absolutely love it."

Cody caught Dhabi's arm and growled. "You can stop right now. If you say another word...if you mock my sister again..."

"Mock? I'm not mocking her, Dr. Birchfield. I adore her. When we reach McKenzie, I can make a few calls, and if she's willing to sing, you will have all the money you'll need for a ferry. You have no idea what people will pay for this. For her."

Annie shook her head and pushed her thumbs into her front pockets. "I don't sing in front of people." Just the idea of allowing people to watch her sing made her stomach turn.

Dhabi turned to Cody and ignored Annie's refusal. "I've been going off-planet since I was ten years old. I'm telling you plainly; this is what outpost residents want. They love people who snub the law. They are all about making cash in the most devious ways. But what they truly long for—what they can't get enough of—is real entertainment. A dozen years ago, I made a small fortune playing my sitar. That's how I bought my ship. I still play on occasion when I need some extra money."

Annie focused on her brother. She saw that Cody listened carefully, glancing at her every time Dhabi took a breath.

The captain continued. "I can play a little. I know a few songs. But man, she can sing. That's priceless out here, do you understand?"

Annie crossed her arms and stood solid. "I don't..."

Cody stopped her. "Annie, let's hear him out. We're in a tight spot."

"There must be another way," she insisted.

Dhabi raised his eyebrows and gestured to Cody.

Cody sighed and placed his hands on Annie's shoulders. "We were talking, trying to figure out a way to pay for the next leg. Dhabi knows a few people that are willing to pay top dollar for a horse."

"NO!"

"Not to eat, Annie. They can resell it to colony folk and still make real money. I told him we could sell Nero."

"No, Cody. We are not going to sell a horse. There has to be another..."

"What then?" her brother asked. "One of the guns? Momma's jewelry?"

Annie started to nod, but then couldn't bear the thought of parting with any of their parent's things. "What about my bike?"

Dhabi shook his head from the doorway. "Motorcycles are plentiful. Nice ones—not old junkers like yours."

Annie ignored his comment and stared into Cody's eyes. "I can't sing for people. I never have."

"You never shot anyone before. You've never been on the lam before. You've never traveled into space, either. Maybe this is just your day for firsts." Cody wrapped his strong arm around her shoulders and pulled her close. "I know this is too much for you."

She pushed him away. "It's not *too* much. I can handle..." She realized that she'd just given both men exactly what they wanted. "Shoot!" She frowned and kicked at an imaginary rock on the floor. "Fine. I'll sing. Y'all make me sick, ya know."

Dhabi clapped his hands. "I have a few people to contact. Get your dress ready, and decide on a dozen songs or so. You can change in the room through that door over there." He pointed to a door beyond where the horses slept. "Fix your hair, too."

The captain almost skipped as he retreated to his bridge.

Cody smiled, and Annie had the urge to knock him over for it. "How many years did you and Momma and Daddy tell me never to sing in front of others. Now you're practically begging me to do it."

"I *am* begging," Cody answered. "You're a talented singer. And this could help us out of our little predicament."

"The predicament that I caused in the first place," she muttered. "You know I can't let you sell Nero. I'd do anything for our animals."

"You've already done so much. Given up your home and your friends."

Annie laughed. "You are the one with friends, remember. These are my friends," she said, gesturing to the horses. "Only ones in the world who love me. Except you."

"I do love you, sis. I won't let anyone hurt you." He kissed her forehead. "Now, get out your party dress and shine your boots up nice."

"I'll wear my red boots. They're already shined."

Cody looked at the stack of their possessions against the wall. "How many pairs of boots did you bring?"

"Counting the ones I'm wearing?" She knew that any number above two would receive a look of disappointment, but at this moment, she didn't care. She was about to be the hero, and heroes could have as many boots as they wanted. "Five."

"Annie, you're ridiculous." He shook his head. "While you're dressing, be thinking about what songs you want to sing."

She poked her brother in the arm as she passed him. She'd pulled out her black polka-dot party dress and her red boots, along with the bundle of toiletries and Momma's old songbook. "*I'll be ready shortly*," she sang. "*For the skinny and the portly.*"

A light flickered on in the little cabin as Annie walked in. She looked around the room and closed the door. About half the size of her bedroom back home, this compartment included stacked berths on the short wall, a desk and chair opposite that, and an arched opening straight ahead leading to a small bathroom. As she stepped through the portal, a light snapped on overhead. To her right was a toilet within a shower stall, and to her left was a hanging rod for clothes. A tilt-out sink with a mirror above it separated the wet and dry areas.

Annie arranged her dress on the single hanger on the rod and placed her other things on the lower berth in the main room. She undressed quickly and took a quick shower, not lingering long enough for the water to warm. Before realizing there was no towel, a surge of hot air shot out from all around her, scaring her half to death. "That's neat," she said, trying to calm down.

She dressed quickly and brushed out her curls. She pulled a red ribbon from her dress pocket and wrapped it around her head, tying a tidy bow just above her ear. She pinched her cheeks until they turned a rosy pink, and dabbed at her lips with Momma's pink rouge. Lastly, she found her gold locket in her toiletry bag and hooked the chain behind her neck. She smoothed her thumb over the front of the pendant. The worn gold sparkled with the tiny diamond chip set in a starburst design. She popped the latch on the side and smiled at the photo of the red horse within. "Ranger," she whispered.

She turned at the knock on her door. "Almost ready to dock," Cody's voice said.

"Be right out," she called back.

She gathered her belongings and checked the mirror again. "I'd rather have a tooth pulled than sing for folks," she said. "Momma, I'll just sing like you're singing with me, okay?" As soon as she said the words, she realized how much she resembled her mother. She turned away from the mirror and headed back to the cabin door. "Wish you were here, Momma. You, too, Daddy."

She stepped out into the hold, and the cabin lights went out behind her. "All ready," she said, with a tremor in her voice. She handed the songbook to her brother. "Why don't you pick out the songs for me?"

Cody nodded. "Dhabi says that his friends are all ready for you."

Dhabi joined them. "We'll be docking in twenty minutes. We will have time to eat, and then you'll perform. They have a very nice venue. Upscale. You will make a fortune."

"Exactly how will we get paid?" Cody asked. "What price?"

Annie tried to listen, but her nerves took over as the men discussed how difficult it was to book a show with such short notice, and how the attendees would decide what Annie's singing was worth. She heard Dhabi mention percentages, and then her ears stopped working altogether.

She put away her dirty clothes and went to sit in the jump seat on the wall. She picked up Buffalo again and began to hum. She noticed that Dhabi had gone back to his bridge and that Cody was pulling on the straps of her seat belt.

"We're about to dock," he said.

She nodded and fastened herself in the seat. She held

tightly to Buffalo as the ship picked up a shudder. A sudden pull at Annie's stomach told her they were nearly there. She forced herself to swallow several times to keep the bile from creeping up her throat. She wasn't sure if she was nauseous from the landing or the thought of singing. Either way, she was pretty sure she was going to throw up.

Cody patted her hands. "It's okay, Annie. You'll do great."

They unstrapped from the jump seats and hurried to calm the horses.

After another ten minutes, Dhabi joined them in the hold. "Why don't you put your things into the cabin, so we can lock them away?" he suggested. "If I could hide your horses, I would, but we'll just have to take our chances with them."

"What do you mean?" Annie whined. "I'm not singing for fun. I'm singing so that we don't lose any of our horses. I'm not leaving them if there is a chance they'll be taken."

Cody held up his hand to check her threats. "Hang on, Annie." He faced the captain. "Are you saying that someone could break in and steal our animals?"

Dhabi shook his head. "No, the chances of that would be minimal. But there are inspectors at every outpost."

"You assured us that McKenzie would be safe for us," Cody said.

"It will. My friend is sending over one of his security men to watch my ship."

Annie took a deep breath and pushed her jaw out, hoping to look tough, forgetting that she wore a satin ribbon in her hair. "If your friend is so trustworthy, what's the problem?"

"My friend is probably the most honest person on McKenzie. But that doesn't mean I trust him completely." Dhabi shrugged.

Cody nodded. "You mean that when he says things like, 'We'll leave at dawn,' he might be intending to leave right after midnight?"

Dhabi looked down and mumbled. "Something like that. What choice do we have but to trust him?"

Annie watched her brother weigh the options. With that severe expression on his face, he looked just like Daddy. She wished.

"Why don't I stay with the ship?" he asked.

"No," Annie said flatly. "I'm not getting off without you."

Cody pulled her a step away from Dhabi as if they could somehow speak privately. "Listen, you have to go, Annie. If you don't sing tonight, this is all for nothing. Dhabi has to go; he's the one who set it all up. I'm the third wheel. You go and do us all proud. I need to stay with our family. I need to check their vitals and give them a little exercise. And if you promise to go, I'll clean up after the horses for as long as we're on this ship. Promise."

Annie frowned. "How can I sing without you there?"

"Honestly, you'll probably sing best if you pretend *nobody* is there."

Dhabi grimaced. "I'm not sure I trust you on my ship alone. No offense."

Annie took a deep breath. If Dhabi didn't want Cody to stay on board, then she suddenly did. She turned back to face the captain. "I'll only sing if you let my brother stay."

He gritted his teeth and shot a cold stare at Cody and then Annie. "I have to make the arrangements for our dinner. Be ready to go in five minutes, Miss Birchfield."

Cody and Annie exchanged satisfied looks as Dhabi left them. "I don't know if I trust him at all," Cody whispered.

"I don't, either," Annie said. "Do you think I should carry a little something for my protection?"

"Probably a good idea," he said. "Still in Daddy's box?"

She shook her head and pulled her pearl-handled .22 from the custom pocket on the inside of her left boot. "I wouldn't feel right leaving Tillie behind."

Cody and Annie moved their belongings into the cabin, stowing most of it under the lower berth and the table. Annie placed the pod holding Buffalo onto the bed. "Don't let anything happen to him, okay?"

Cody nodded. Annie noticed that he avoided making eye

contact. She knew that he held little hope of reviving the pup. She took a deep breath and ignored the whole idea. Annie needed Buffalo, so there was nothing more to think about. Annie changed the subject and asked what songs Cody suggested. She listened to his list but wasn't sure if she heard him at all.

They returned to the hold at the same time as Dhabi. He was dressed in black from chin to toe, except for a red silk square peeking out from his breast pocket. His shiny black hair was now combed neatly, and Annie detected a hint of patchouli on his clothes.

"Don't look so surprised," he said. "I know how to dress for the occasion."

Annie realized that her mouth was agape and closed it so quickly that her teeth clapped. "You look very handsome," she said.

"I am your manager from here out. If anyone asks you any questions, direct them to me. I will take care of everything. Do you understand?"

Cody shook his head. "That's not…"

Dhabi held out his hands, palms up. "I'm telling you this for her protection. She's young and beautiful. If the wrong person decides that she's unattached, they may try to take her for themselves."

"But, I'm not attached to you," Annie said.

"I understand this. It's all for appearances. You understand that I'm sacrificing a lot with this arrangement, too. I mean, no woman will be approaching me as long as I have you at my side."

Annie almost coughed. She smiled. "Got it." She stood on her tip-toes to kiss her brother's cheek. "We'll bring you back some dinner."

"Do you know what songs you're gonna sing?" Cody asked.

"I remember."

"Then we should go. Barabbas is expecting us." Dhabi pulled a long black case from a small storage compartment near the bay door.

"What is that?" Annie asked.

"It's my sitar. Just in case you need some back-up."

"And how will you know any of the songs I'm gonna sing?" she asked, taking hold of the elbow Dhabi offered. They walked off the ship, Annie's boots noisily clicking down the gangway. She looked over her shoulder at her smiling brother as the bay door closed.

"I'm excellent at improvising, my dear Miss Birchfield."

EPISODE 3

Sing for Your Supper

Annie followed Dhabi through the docking bay. He strode with a long gait as if he owned the whole space station. McKenzie was initially established as a jumping-off base to the rest of the galaxy, much like First Station, but built by civilian contractors. It became known as a sin station, because Authority allowed just about any activity on McKenzie, as long as the appropriate taxes were paid. Annie wondered whether the residents had declared their independence to free themselves of the financial burden or to enjoy even more depravity.

"Is this place far?" She looked all around them as she walked. Ships of every size and shape nested in the different docks of the enormous bay.

"Just inside the main base," Dhabi said with a gesture to the glowing doors ahead. He glanced over his shoulder and nodded, pausing for the girl to catch up to him. "Are you frightened?"

"Not sure what to expect is all," she answered. "I'm just supposed to sing, right?"

"That's all." Dhabi led her to the doors and pulled on the silvery green handle, stepping aside to let her pass. "After you."

"Thanks," she whispered as she stepped through the brilliant glow of the doors and into a grand but dimly lit reception hall.

A long steel desk blocked their way. "Name and business." A young man dressed in a dark green uniform greeted them without looking up from the digital display on his desk.

"Dhabi Ramal and Annie Birchfield. We're expected at the Garden Bistro and then to perform at The Quail afterward." Dhabi held his clean-shaven jaw parallel with the floor, giving him an air of importance.

"Garden Bistro is under quarantine as of fourteen hundred today. All reservations have been canceled. You may proceed to The Quail immediately." The man never made eye-contact but shifted his shoulder a quarter of an inch in a gesture of dismissal. The far end of the steel desk retracted, and a door beyond it slid open.

"Thank you." Annie smiled at the man. He ignored her.

"You don't have to use manners here," Dhabi explained. "It's not expected."

"You held the door opened for me back there."

"It was...I just do that kind of thing. Besides, you don't know where you're going." He gestured ahead of them. "Look at this place."

They peered through the industrial grating that barred entry into the foyer of the Garden Bistro. The vestibule of the restaurant was dark and empty. A sign at the door flashed the notice: *Quarantined for Unknown Bacteria until Further Notice.*

Annie studied the sign and shrugged. "Maybe we're lucky."

"More likely that someone was expecting a payment that they didn't receive."

Annie swallowed hard. "What kind of folks are we dealing with here?"

"Mostly corrupt, some criminally so, others just doing what they must to survive." There wasn't a twinge of judgment in his voice. He held another door open for her. "Just like us."

Annie raised her eyebrows and slowed her pace as she entered the establishment known as The Quail. The dark room was filled with clouds of every odor and color. The lights that flashed from the corners were only for ambiance, providing no direction for newcomers. Annie waited for Dhabi to take the lead, and then grabbed the fabric of his jacket sleeve so she wouldn't lose him in the crowd.

People pressed close from all directions. They smiled and laughed. A few looked her up and down. She felt light tugs at her skirt and her hair. *This was too much*, she thought. She wanted to scream but stifled the urge. *I have to do this. We have no other choice.*

"Dhabi, I don't..." she began but stopped when she realized that he couldn't hear her voice over the din of the electronic music that pulsed through the room like lifeblood.

Looking over Dhabi's shoulder, Annie could see a heavy-set man dressed in a shiny suit coat waving both arms overhead. "My friend!" the stranger called. "Come and sit!"

Dhabi led Annie through a narrow door held open by the other man. When the door closed, a light clicked on above them, and all the noise of the main hall immediately stopped. It took several seconds for Annie's eyes and ears to adjust to normal.

The man with the jacket scooped up Annie's right arm and began shaking her hand vigorously. "My name is Andre Grieg. I am the owner of Quail, and I welcome you, Annie." His accent was different from any she had ever heard before—sharp and bitter sounding.

"It's a pleasure to meet you, sir." Her voice still sounded loud in her ears. "Your place here seems real popular." She figured that was as close as she could come to a compliment without lying."

Dhabi grinned and edged himself between the other two. "Andre, old friend, I have brought you a treasure in this girl. I hope that you can accommodate our needs."

By the tilt of Dhabi's head, Annie could deduce he was negotiating for payment. She clasped her hands behind her back and stared at the bare concrete floor.

Andre smiled, trying to keep the upper hand. "Would I let you down? Sit, both of you. The Garden closed temporarily this afternoon, but I managed to get a tray sent over for you. You must be hungry." He directed Annie to a metal chair in front of a white plastic table covered with fruits and bread. "Eat; sit and eat."

Annie started toward the food, but Dhabi held her back. "When I see payment, we'll eat. I don't want to be beholden to you for even a crust of bread."

"Dhabi, you injure me." Andre fixed a sad frown on his thick lips. "I have your payment here." Andre pulled a translucent green envelope from his inner breast pocket and slipped it to Dhabi.

Dhabi counted the money. "Wait." He pulled Annie another half-step back. "This is not what we agreed upon."

Andre shrugged. "I thought you would like this better." He raised his palms.

"This is only half, Andre. Why would I prefer half?"

"I give you half now." A bead of sweat formed just below Andre's hairline. "Then, after the performance, we get tips from the audience. I split them with you, fifty-fifty."

"And what if the tips don't match our agreement? I don't like uncertainty." Dhabi slapped the envelope in his palm. "I like guarantees."

"My patrons are generous." Andre smiled at Annie. "And of course, they will love her. She is good, no?"

Dhabi nodded. "Yes, she is exquisite."

Andre shrugged.

Annie watched Dhabi consider the proposition for a few seconds. He held a firm grip on her arm and then conceded. "I will agree...so long as the split is seventy-thirty to us."

Andre raised his chin, expecting a counter-offer. "What if you take the portion of the tips to match this amount," he said, tapping on the envelope, "and I will keep the rest?"

Dhabi and Annie exchanged a glance, knowing that Andre had already foreseen this offer. Dhabi scoffed. "I think I would prefer seventy-thirty."

"But with my offer, you have your precious guarantee. I promise to make up the difference if it falls short." Andre chewed on his bottom lip.

Without thinking, Annie blurted out, "What if we split

the tips three ways? That'll give me plenty of motivation to sing my best for everyone?"

Dhabi scowled. "I am the manager, Andre."

Andre smiled and nodded. "Perhaps you are, my friend, but she is the talent. Her suggestion is almost as you say: sixty-six to you two and thirty-three to me. I will even give you the extra one percent if you like."

Dhabi exhaled sharply, and Annie could feel his laser stare boring into the side of her head. After several seconds of tense silence, he offered his hand to Andre. "I accept your offer."

Andre laughed and slapped him on the back, causing Dhabi to release her arm. Annie moved swiftly to the table and snatched up a wedge of melon and a slice of brown bread.

"Don't make yourself sick before you sing," Dhabi warned.

"Promise I won't. I just need a little something to keep my stomach from rattling." Annie slurped the juice from the melon as she bit down.

Andre smiled and pointed to the food. "Eat as much as you like. You will perform in fifteen minutes. Whatever you don't finish, I will send with you after." He nodded to Dhabi, who returned the gesture. The large man bowed to Annie and then left by the same door they entered.

Annie ate quickly and drank a small glass of flavored water. "You're sure you can accompany me?" she asked between swallows.

"I can." Dhabi sounded confident. "You just begin, and I will follow."

When Annie had eaten as much as she wanted, she stood and brushed away any crumbs from her dress. She raked her slim fingers through her hair and squared her shoulders, forcing herself to take long, slow breaths.

"Don't throw up. That's the big rule out there."

Annie tried to decide whether Dhabi said that out loud, or if she had manifested the instructions with her imagination. When he laughed, she decided he had actually spoken.

"No vomit, no passing out." She smiled and nodded.

Both of them jumped at the sudden knock at the door. "You're up," a voice called.

Annie opened the door and followed a lanky man from the quiet room to a raised platform in a nearby corner. There was a tall stool centered on the stage, with a spotlight shining straight down upon it. The intense pulse of music from before had softened to a dull hum. The atmosphere had cleared to a light haze, and Annie had no difficulty seeing her way through the crowd.

The slim man helped her up the steps and directed her to stand in front of the stool. The Quail's patrons hushed and turned to face her. Dhabi joined her and set his case to the side.

"Do we need to plug anything in?" he asked.

The thin man shook his head. "The whole stage will be amplified. I'll run it from down here." He pointed to a small desk at the base of the steps. "If you're not good, I'll turn you off, too." He didn't smile. He faced the audience and took Annie's hand, raising it above her head as if he introduced a winning prize-fighter.

A green light appeared at the front edge of the dais, and the man raised his voice. "Ladies and gentlemen," he announced with a sarcastic laugh. "It is with great pride that The Quail presents the talents of Miss Ann."

Annie took a split second to process the introduction, long enough for Dhabi to sit on the floor and position his sitar. The crowd clapped, but Annie recognized it as a purely obligatory reaction, without enthusiasm.

"Thank y'all so much." She cleared her throat and stretched tall, trying to keep down the acid that slowly climbed her esophagus. "My first song is one that my momma taught me when I was a baby..."

"Don't talk. Just sing," a voice yelled from somewhere in the back of the room.

Annie smiled and nodded. "Yessir." She looked into the darkness of the room, able to make out almost nothing beyond the tip of her nose illuminated by the bright light overhead. She drew a deep breath and began.

> *"She was just a little girl,*
> *Not more than three years old.*
> *When Daddy took her out to meet*
> *The newborn baby foal,*
> *She held her hand out to the horse,*
> *And touched his furry side.*
> *Said, 'Daddy, he'll be my best friend,*
> *Together we will ride.*
>
> *And she said, "Let's go, Ranger, let's go.*
> *Let's find a path to call our own,*
> *Somewhere among the trees,*
> *We'll find a quiet waterfall,*
> *And listen to the breeze.*
> *Let's go, Ranger, Let's go..."*

Annie was only vaguely aware of the sitar playing behind her as she sang two more verses. As the last phrase of the song faded into the silence, she could hear her own heartbeat thump a few times before the applause began. In just a few seconds, the clapping had swelled into a storm. She felt another surge of nerves overtake her, and she reached behind her for the support of the stool. As she took a deep breath, the crowd immediately quieted, anticipating the next song.

Annie sang a dozen more tunes that she had learned as a child. Each was simple but roused a bigger ovation than the last. She finally turned to Dhabi and shrugged, "What else?" she whispered.

Dhabi smiled and shrugged back. "Pick anything. They love you."

Annie tried to think of another song, but her mind went blank. As the crowd grew silent again, she struggled for anything. Like a flash, one last song sparked into her brain. She tried to push it down, knowing it was not appropriate for this crowd. It was Momma's favorite hymn. She'd be laughed at. She'd undo whatever tip she might have earned so far.

The harder she tried to suppress the song, the louder it sounded in her ears. She couldn't help it.

"Amazing grace, how sweet the sound,
That saved a wretch like me."

The audience was utterly silent. Dhabi didn't even play his instrument. Annie could hear her breath wheeze as she started the next phrase.

"I once was lost, but now I'm found,
Was blind, but now I see."

As she sang the last three verses, she noticed something strange. The front row of listeners slowly stood, and she saw the men clutching their hats over their hearts. As she sang, she grew brave and dared to look the people in their eyes. She could see the glisten of tears. As she came to the end of the song, the crowd didn't move. No clapping. No yelling. Silence.

She swallowed hard, trying to manage a smile through her own emotions. Dhabi stood behind her, his sitar already packed away, and he whispered into her ear. "Sing it again."

She took another breath and began, *"Amazing grace…"*

This time the crowd sang with her, their voice drowning out hers. They sang as if it was the anthem of their people. They swayed and cheered and sang with their whole collective heart.

As she began the hymn for the third time, Annie noticed Andre passing a bucket through the crowd. Audience members barely looked down as they poured whatever they had into the coffer. As the final verse ended, everyone in the room cheered.

One by one, people lined up to come and shake Annie's hand. A few dared to hug her, but Dhabi discouraged such close contact. Andre finished his collection and gestured for Annie and Dhabi to join him in the small room again.

"Genius!" was all he said as they all crowded around the white plastic table. Andre and Dhabi quickly divided the money into three portions.

Annie had finally caught her breath enough to ask, "Are we done for the evening?"

Dhabi nodded. "Yes, we have enough to…"

Andre interrupted. "But when can you come back? This is the best show I've had here in over a year. We should make this a regular event."

Dhabi shot Annie a sharp glance, which was unnecessary; she wasn't going to make any trouble.

"We can't do that, yet, I'm afraid. Our little company has an itinerary to keep." Dhabi took the time to go through the money and turn all the bills in the same direction. "But I do know that you are a man with many connections, friend. If you gave me some names, we might be inclined to contact them— giving you due credit, of course."

Andre considered the proposal. "I think I could arrange that, Dhabi. But most of my associates will want a bigger show than just a girl with a sweet voice." He regarded Annie with a smile. "Of course you are lovely, my dear, but many of my friends have venues more like coliseums. They will expect more."

At this, Annie smiled and nodded. "Do you mean a show with animals and tricks and such?"

"You know where you can get animals? That would be a big show. What kind of animals?" Andre leaned close and raised his brows.

Before Annie could answer, Dhabi interrupted. "She's just asking if that's the type of show you mean? It's not as though we have any animals."

Andre nodded with enthusiasm. "If you can produce a show with animals—dogs, sheep, whatever you can manage—I can find you an audience."

Dhabi carefully handed Annie her share of the money, and discretely slipped his portion into a wallet. "Annie, would you like me to carry yours, only until we get back to the ship? I would hate for you to be accosted."

Annie shook her head and dropped her share into her boot. "Don't have to worry about me. I ain't never been accosted yet."

Andre laughed. "She's a bright girl, Dhabi. You watch her carefully. She's got brains."

"I know."

Andre gave Annie the container of leftovers, and then she offered her hand to him. "It was real good to meet you, Mr. Grieg. If I'm ever back on McKenzie, you'll be the first person I look for."

Andre hugged her shoulder, as Dhabi watched with feigned scorn. "We are friends now. You call me Andre."

Annie smiled and nodded. Dhabi took her arm. "We have to go, Andre, but I'll contact you tomorrow before we catch the ferry out. I would appreciate some names."

Andre agreed. "Where are you going next? I can call ahead for you."

"No need. I can make all the arrangements necessary. I promise not to forget you," Dhabi assured him.

Annie followed the men back through the almost empty club. She said goodbye to Andre, and she and Dhabi headed back to the ship.

"What a night." Dhabi sounded exhausted. "I just hope nobody tries to turn us in to Authority before we can jump tomorrow."

Annie grimaced. "I think the audience liked the show. If anyone was thinking about turning us in, that went out the window by the end of the last song, don't you think?"

Dhabi shrugged as he opened the bay door on his vessel. Cody was waiting for their return. Dhabi patted Annie's shoulder. "It was a good show. You did well. But it 's hard to read these people."

"Which people?" Cody asked.

"The people who stood and sang *Amazing Grace* with me at the end of the set. The ones with tears streaming down their cheeks, with their hands over their hearts." Annie stretched her arms over her head.

Dhabi raised his brow and nodded. "Yes, those people."

Cody smiled broadly and hugged his sister. "Sounds to me like you had a good night."

Annie took a deep breath. "We did. And I didn't throw up. Not even a little in my mouth."

Dhabi cringed. "Your sister has the strangest manners."

Cody led the others inside as the door closed. "You got manners?" His tone teased.

Annie punched him in the arm. "We got some news, too. Andre is sending us some names of his friends who will host us for shows at our other stops."

Cody shook his head. "Sis, we're not making a tour of this. We have to get away and keep our heads low for a while. At the very least until we're no longer wanted by Authority. And besides," he added. "Dhabi wants to dump us as quickly as he can. He doesn't want to escort us all over the universe."

Dhabi pulled out his stack of cash and waited for Annie to do the same. Cody raised his brows when he saw the amount they each waved in front of him.

"This is just sixty-seven percent of our take. Well, not even that if you consider we got paid half upfront, and we each made more than double that amount in tips." Dhabi held up the green envelope too. "I'm beginning to think that the best place for all of us to hide is in plain sight. If we put together a show...a big show...like what Andre talked about, we could make enough to pay off Authority and still buy each of us our own colony."

Cody shook his head. "We don't live like that. I can't let you use my baby sister to..."

"I'm not a baby anymore, and I think a big show could be good for us. I did real good out there tonight. And I had fun."

Dhabi nodded. "She did very well."

"And you don't have to speak for me, either." She turned on Dhabi in a fever of emotion. "I'm goin' to bed. Y'all can hash this out however you want. But I want to put on a show. My horses and my dog..." she suddenly realized that she was speaking about Buffalo. She glared at both men and stopped, as a lump of sadness swelled her throat closed. She threw the stack of money at them and ran to the small cabin across the hold.

"I'm sure glad you're a mature woman about this," Cody called after her.

Annie went inside and closed the door behind her, as loudly as she could. She picked up the LS pod and gazed in at her puppy and sighed. "Buffalo, you look like you're just sleepin' in there. I half-wish I could curl up and join you. Nobody's making you do things you don't want. Nobody's bothering you at all, huh?" She kicked off her boots and stretched out over the small berth. "Funny, though. I thought I'd hate singing for others. Turns out, I like it. Turns out, the audience liked me. Folks are funny, I guess. They pay for the silliest things." She hugged the tube tightly and wished.

After a few minutes, Cody joined her. "Your horses are fine, by the way." She could hear the grudge in his voice.

"Thank you for looking after them."

"I'm not trying to stifle you, Annie."

"Then don't."

He paced the tiny floor space. "I don't trust Dhabi. I don't know this Andre character, so I don't trust him, either. It's my job to take care of you. I spent this whole night wondering if I would ever see you again."

"I can take care of myself. I'm not a child." Annie sat up on the narrow bed, barefoot, clinging to her dog like a baby with a teddy bear. She looked very much like the child she denied herself to be.

"We can't put on a show." He assumed the rugged stance of their father, with his feet planted firmly on the floor and his hands on his hips. "I'm in charge of you, and I say no."

Annie stared into her brother's eyes without flinching. He tried to return the cold gaze, but Annie knew she had the upper hand in this duel. As the seconds ticked away, Cody broke the eye contact and huffed in anger.

"I'm sleeping with the horses," he said and marched out.

Annie pulled the ribbon from her hair and focused her attention back to her dog. "Buffalo, we're gonna be famous."

EPISODE 4

Take the Money and Run

"Get everything in order," Dhabi barked as he marched through the hold of his vessel. "Before we are allowed to dock with the ferry, an inspector has to make a visual check of our cargo. He'll want documents ready. He'll want to see your animals. He'll review our food and fuel inventories."

"Should I hide Buffalo?" Annie asked, unsure if Dhabi was suggesting they needed to be upfront or secretive.

"No. Put him on the berth in the cabin. And make sure he's on the list. The inspectors are looking for anything that's not on the list. If it's not here in writing," Dhabi said, tapping on his hand-held, "it's fair game for them to take."

Cody nodded to his sister. "Make sure everything is on the list."

Dhabi sighed and rolled his eyes. "No, make sure *everything you want to keep* is on the list. If you have anything that you can part with—anything at all—leave it out in plain sight and leave it off the list."

"This is confusing, you know?" Annie whined.

Cody scratched his chin and raised his brow. "No, I get it." He faced Annie and squared his shoulders. "It's like a bribe."

Dhabi shook his head and waved his hands at his passengers. "Not a bribe! Don't use that word at all. It's a peace-offering. It's an incentive to help us on our way."

Annie shrugged. "Okay. It's *not* a bribe. But it sounds like a bribe."

She spent the next half hour working frantically with Cody and Dhabi to get the hold perfectly staged for inspection. As she centered a small plate filled with fruit they had carried back from The Quail on a crate near the door of the sleeping cabin, a chime sounded the inspector's arrival.

Dhabi set his hand-held into the locked mode and opened the bay door. A thin red-headed woman in a dark green jumpsuit stood outside. She uncrossed her arms and threw her shoulders back as she strode aboard. Dhabi stepped forward and offered her the digital inventory. She nodded and scanned the hand-held with a stylus from her breast pocket.

"Any declarations?" she asked without flourish.

"I believe it's all there," Dhabi replied.

Annie noticed that he stood taller and held his chin level with the floor. He suddenly looked like a military officer. She almost laughed.

Dhabi held out his hand to the others. "I have two passengers, as noted, and their animals also noted. We intend to take the ferry jump to Seventh Station, and then out to one of the colonies near there." He gestured around the hold. "Please feel free to review the ship at your leisure. If you have any questions, please ask."

The woman nodded again and began her tour. Annie watched as she stared at the plate of fruit. Checked the inventory and then shot a look of disgust at Dhabi. "I am not one to accept bribes, Captain Ramal. McKenzie is not run by corrupt Authority. It is a private facility. We take care of our residents here."

"Of course," he said.

Annie and Cody kept their distance as the inspector followed Dhabi up to the bridge and then back through the cargo area. She opened the door to the cabin and peered in, but didn't go inside. She ended her evaluation at the horses.

"These are your animals?" she asked, directing her attention to Cody.

"They belong to my sister and me, yes."

"And you will affirm they are healthy?" She shifted her

eyes from Cody back to the horses.

"Yes, ma'am. They're in prime condition," he said.

The woman smiled. "You have had them checked recently?

Cody dipped his chin. "I'm a vet. A veterinarian. That's what I do, ma'am."

She raised her perfectly sculpted brow and turned to face Cody squarely. "A doctor?"

"Yes, ma'am," he said again. "For animals."

Annie knew that the inspector was impressed. She watched her brother relax his stance as he took half a step closer to the woman. She had seen him charm dozens of girls with his "aw-shucks" grin and a glimmer in his eye.

"Would you like to meet the horses?" he asked.

She stiffened slightly. "That's not necessary." She turned her eyes back to the inventory. "I can see them just fine."

Cody smiled. Annie knew he was in his element. "They won't hurt you. Let me show you." He held out his hand, and the inspector took a deep breath and then a step toward the horses.

Annie exchanged a glance with Dhabi as Cody and the Inspector spent the next few minutes with Nero and the others. Annie edged quietly to Dhabi's side.

"We're all good," she whispered to him. "Won't take nothing, and she'll be eating outa his hand. I've seen it plenty before."

"I hope you're right."

Cody walked the woman to the bay door again. "I believe Nero has taken a shine to you, Gwen."

The woman smiled. "He's such a big animal. I had no idea he would be so gentle."

"Horses are very respectful animals," Cody assured her.

"Like a southern gentleman?"

"Yes, ma'am." Cody cocked his head to one side and was about to spread a little more charm, but Gwen held up an index finger to stop him.

She touched her left ear and paused for a second.

Annie and the others realized she was listening to an official announcement in her earpiece.

She shot them a distressed look. "I don't know what your little band has done, but McKenzie's security has just been served a request by Planet Authority to detain your ship and the crew for interrogation."

Annie's heart began to pound against her ribs, and her stomach twisted with worry. "Oh, no. They're gonna take them."

Dhabi immediately took action and began to offer the inspector anything and everything.

"I'm sorry," Gwen said with a sincere softness in her voice. "I'm obligated to hold you here. There's nothing I can do."

Cody took Gwen's hand in his and led her back to Nero's side. "The reason they want us is the horses. They want to slaughter our animals. There's not a thing wrong with them, but they want to kill them anyway."

She looked into the big black horse's eyes. "The notice didn't say anything about the horses."

"No. It wouldn't. Authority knows the value that Independents place on animals. They wouldn't risk tipping their hand. They know your security teams would let us go if they did."

Gwen released a tense breath and shook her head. "I don't know. I've not heard of anyone slaughtering horses."

Annie raced into the cabin and grabbed the pod and ran back to join the others. She held her dog up for Gwen to see. "He shot my dog—right in front of me." Tears glistened in her eyes. "I'm telling you truly; my horses are next."

Gwen looked into the pod at Buffalo's sweet face and singed fur. "They did this?"

"Yes," Annie whispered. "He was just trying to protect me, and the lawman shot him." Annie hugged the pod and sniffed.

Gwen looked around the hold and shook her head. She looked down into Annie's eyes, then back up to Cody. He matched the uncertain expression on her face with his own.

"Please," he whispered.

Gwen drew a deep breath and focused her attention on her digital. She tapped away for a second and then barked at Dhabi. "Captain Ramal, you are to report immediately to..." She studied the flight schedules. "Go to docking bay 94, Ferry 327. You'll have to hurry, though. It has to be clear of the McKenzie space pad to make room for the Authority transport arriving within the hour."

Cody seemed to melt with appreciation. Annie jumped in place and blew a kiss at the kind-hearted Inspector. "Thank you much, Miss Gwen. You're saving all our lives."

"You need to go now." Gwen's expression seemed to plead for them to hurry. "I've cleared you for docking, but if anyone intercepts you, there won't be anything I can do."

Cody nodded and walked the woman to the bay door. He took her hand, and then it appeared to Annie that he changed his mind and then kissed Gwen's cheek. "We're truly indebted."

Gwen smiled as she left the ship. "Then get out of here and get away safely, so that you can pay me back someday."

As the door sealed shut, Dhabi began yelling. "Get strapped in! If we don't get docked in time, we've had it."

He raced to the bridge, and his strained voice thundered through the speakers over the engine roar. "My read-out shows Ferry 327 departing McKenzie in eighteen minutes. It's going to take a full-fledged miracle."

Annie began to pray, holding tightly to Buffalo. "Lord and Father, creator of this whole universe, please hear and help us in our time of most desperate need. We thank you for the kindness of Miss Gwen, and for the generosity of all the folks we've met on this journ..."

Her prayer was interrupted by a series of Dhabi's most creative swears pulsing over the com. Annie was grateful when the ship's engine finally drowned out his poetic profanities, and she could continue. "And Lord, please forgive Dhabi's language. I'm sure he doesn't mean it." She paused. "But even if he does, Lord, please forgive him, because we really need him right now, and it'd be awfully inconvenient if he got smited before we got clear. Amen."

The small ship lurched, and Annie shot a worried glance to Cody.

"It's going to be all right," he assured her.

"I know." She swallowed hard and closed her eyes.

They sat in relative silence for a few seconds as the vessel's maneuvers steadied.

Dhabi's voice emerged again. "Dr. Birchfield, join me on the bridge. Leave your sister in the hold. We may need her to keep the horses calm while we dock with the ferry."

Cody released his harness and nodded to his sister as he hurried to the bridge door. "Stay sharp."

"Yessir," she said.

***

"I could do it myself under normal conditions, but we're strapped for time." Dhabi's gaze danced around the cockpit, and his arms reached from one switch to another. "I'll need an extra body to get our fuel off-loaded."

"What do you mean?" Cody studied the digital panels that lined the front of the console in front of Dhabi.

"Before we can dock with the ferry, we have to transfer the contents of our main fuel cell over to the dock cells. Call it a surcharge, whatever. It takes about seven minutes to empty ours." Dhabi gestured to a read-out on his left. "This shows our fuel levels here." The monitor glowed pale orange. "When that turns dark red, we're empty and can dock with the ferry. You keep your eye on that and let me know as soon as it starts blinking. Blinking means we can go. You'll have to throw that toggle below to close the valve while I start us back up."

Cody stared at the orange light. His heart pounded in his chest. "It's getting darker."

"Not dark enough."

Dhabi focused on the read-outs on his right side and typed furiously. "I have to get our manifest and itinerary sent to the ferry captain."

"We have to be empty?" Cody didn't move his attention

away from the light as he asked.

"We keep our auxiliary cell. That's enough for emergencies. It's the Ferry System's way of making sure we buy fuel when we reach our destination."

"And if…"

"No 'if's,' my friend. Ferry caps are not flexible human beings. Lots of rules. If our manifest or itinerary doesn't match perfectly with what your red-headed beauty sent them—we don't get a ride. If we aren't fully docked when their schedule says to leave, we don't ride. If they discover we held anything back in our fuel cell, they eject us during the warp jump." Dhabi shook his head but never looked up from his work.

"What would that do to us?"

"Flash of light, instant vaporization, that sort of thing."

Cody swallowed hard and stared at the darkening orange glow. "Right."

Dhabi finished his typing and watched his monitor for a few quiet seconds. He sighed as a message appeared on the screen ahead. "Good. We're approved for docking as soon as the fuel cells are empty. We have two minutes before warp departure."

Cody's breath clipped short as the seconds ticked, almost audibly in his ear. "We're not going to make it."

"Probably not."

"Still dark orange." Cody's finger touched the toggle switch, and he could feel his pulse throb in his fingertip.

"The second it turns red and blinks," Dhabi said with a slight tremor in his voice.

"Come on," Cody whispered to himself.

A bold yellow message flashed on Dhabi's monitor. "They've sent the docking code. As soon as we're empty…"

Cody willed the light to turn red. He refused to let his eyes shift away or close for even a split second. The light darkened a little more. And then more. And then it began blinking.

"Red and blinking," Cody yelled as he flipped the toggle.

"Fifty seconds to departure," Dhabi barked. "Get back to

your seat."

"I'm staying up here."

"Then grab a strap and hold on to your head." Dhabi worked frantically to get the ship moving and positioned alongside the ferry. "Entering docking code." His fingers moved over the keypad in with a fever. "Shutting down the main engine in three...two...one."

The sound of the ship's engine powering down pulled at Cody's heart as the roar turned to a low hum. He knew they were completely vulnerable.

An alert flashed across Dhabi's monitor, accompanied by a loud beeping tone. Cody's blood pressure raced as he read the message.

PLANET AUTHORITY WARNING...ALL FERRIES GROUNDED FOR INSPECTION UNTIL FURTHER NOTICE... PLANET AUTHORITY WARNING.

"We're sunk." Dhabi leaned forward in his chair. "No way is this ferry cap going to defy Authority."

Cody exhaled and slumped his shoulders. The bridge lights all flashed in unison, and everything shook and pulled at once. Before he knew what was happening, Cody found himself on the floor, his hands clutching instinctively at anything stable. "What's happening?"

"He did it!" Dhabi yelled with a whoop. "We're off. Get back to your feet and look at this!"

Cody reached up to grab Dhabi's arm and then steadied himself on the back of the captain's chair. He stared at the digital read-outs in wonder. He pointed to a white point of light moving smoothly across a grid. "What is that?"

Dhabi smiled and tapped at a blue light in the far corner of the grid. "The blue one is McKenzie Station, my friend. The white one is us. We're away."

A wave of cooling relief swept through Cody's bones, and he discovered that he could finally breathe again. "I guess my sister and I are in a pretty good heap of trouble."

Dhabi stood at his side and laughed. He slapped Cody's

shoulder. "I guess we all are."

EPISODE 5

Show Me the Way

"So, now what?" Annie brushed at Liza Jane's mane to calm the skittish horse. "Do we just hunker down and keep a low profile?"

Dhabi checked the inventory to be sure the manifest matched his digital records. "No, we are going to be on this ferry for days. We can't hide away in the ship. We have to get out and meet some people. If we don't make some connections while we're aboard here, we won't be able to arrange any more shows."

Cody stood between Nero and Stubbs, checking their vitals and assessing their nerves. "There's more than enough to do here for a while. And I'm still not sold on the idea of Annie singing for strangers while we're wanted by the law."

Annie kissed Liza Jane on the nose and turned her attention to Jefferson, her prized quarter horse. "Well, I think you're both right." She decided to go with the honey approach. "Cody, I think you should stay here and take care of the animals while Dhabi and I check out the place and see what kind of opportunities are available."

Cody shook his head. "Absolutely not. I don't want you off gallivanting all over this ferry. If anyone is going out, it should be me."

Annie smiled. She was determined to stay in her brother's good graces, but she was still sure she could have her way. "Okay, you and Dhabi get out and see what's going on. I'll stay here with the horses. Even with their pared-down diet, there's plenty of manure to shovel, and they are *my* horses."

She watched as Cody's mouth twisted to one side and then the other. "You can't stay here alone."

Annie struck a pose between the two smaller horses. "Do I look like I'm alone? Besides, I have my shotgun loaded with salt, and I know how to shoot. You can't call me helpless."

"I ain't ever called you helpless. But if someone boards us and gets after the animals, I have credentials. It may not prevent them from commandeering them, but it would go a little further than rock salt." Cody turned to Dhabi. "You promise to look after my sister?"

Annie pressed her lips together to suppress an ear-to-ear grin.

"I won't let her out of my sight." Dhabi shook his head as he glanced at Annie. "Put on something nice. Like what you would wear for a show."

Annie kissed Jefferson and then her brother. "Thank you, Cody. The shovel is hanging right over there." She bounced into her quarters and quickly changed into her polka-dot dress and her red cowgirl boots. As she tied her hair ribbon and linked her locket chain, she stared at Buffalo in his pod. The lights still blinked yellow. "I need you back, Buff." She hugged the cylinder and placed it carefully back on her berth. In half an hour, she was at the hatch door.

"I'm setting a message notice for anyone who might drop by, but I don't expect to have company for a while." Dhabi punched at a panel by the main exit. "If anyone does call, I'll know about it immediately, and we'll head back right away."

Cody faced the captain with squared shoulders and a quiet but stern voice. "Are you sure there aren't folks waiting to turn us in?"

Annie stepped to Dhabi's side and placed her hand on Cody's shoulder. "Brother, he can't make that kind of promise. But we'll be fine."

He frowned at his sister. "You can't know that."

Dhabi offered his most confident smile. "When the ferry

master defied Authority and approved our passage, he put himself in the same column as us. That tells me a little something about our fellow passengers, too."

Cody shifted his gaze to Annie. "Yeah, that no one on board can be trusted."

Annie nodded and shrugged. "Just like us, right?"

Dhabi and Annie left Cody with the horses and headed through the hatch toward the ferry's main facilities.

"It's like its own city," Annie said with a gasp of wonderment. "I had no idea."

Dhabi gestured toward a map display on the wall. "We need to get our bearings first. Have you never been on a ferry?"

Annie shook her head. "I ain't never been off Earth before. Cody's been to First Station a few times, but I hadn't ever breached the borders of Texas before this week." She studied the map and determined their ship was docked on Ring 14, Section J. She looked over the mazes in the diagrams. Blue rectangles were shops, orange squares were food and beverage establishments, pink were hotels, gray were medical facilities, and green diamonds were law. She saw small red dots placed in the corners of various rectangles but couldn't find the corresponding explanation in the legend.

"What do the red dots mean?"

Dhabi laughed. "Red dots are entertainment." He looked right and left from where they stood and then went back to studying the map.

"So, we need to go to one of those places to set up a show, right?" Annie tried to see what Dhabi was looking for on the legend.

"Not that type of entertainment, dear." He shook his head. "You keep your clothes on while you sing."

A hot blush spread over her face and down her neck. "Oh. Yes, well, then not those places." She took a deep breath and looked around. Hundreds of people walked all around, but no one seemed to see them. "Have you been on a ferry before?"

Dhabi took a step back and offered Annie his elbow. "Yes.

Not this one, but others. You should stay close to me, and don't talk to anyone. I know where we're going."

Annie walked at Dhabi's side from the map kiosk to a mezzanine overlooking an open shop area crowded with travelers. At the entrance to the lift stood a dozen men and women, eyeing the pair as they descended. Annie smiled, but Dhabi scowled.

"Who are they?" she asked.

"They're employables. They hang out, looking for jobs. They had enough money to get on the ferry, but not enough to get any farther. They trade work for travel." Dhabi sounded as though the explanation left a bitter taste in his mouth.

"That's okay, though. Right?" Annie glanced back over her shoulder. The employables were already staring at the next person on the lift.

Dhabi wrinkled his nose. "Most of them are cons. They get aboard your ship and then steal from you, or worse. I've heard of groups who say they need passage, but then once you're out on the edge of space, they mutiny and take everything. It's not a good idea to hire more than one person at a time. I wouldn't even do that."

Annie raised her eyebrows and sighed. "I guess I got a lot to learn out here. I'm sure glad you know what's what."

Dhabi gestured to the pair of doors just ahead of them. "Let's try this one."

Annie followed him into the lobby of what Annie guessed was some type of casino. Just beyond a wide archway were rows of tables, each circled by six or eight people doing something she couldn't make out. Dhabi approached a cheerful-looking woman at a desk.

"Good day, Miss." He winked at the woman and offered his hand.

Her mood seemed to sour. "No soliciting." Her voice was flat. She didn't move to take his hand.

"You misunderstand. We are performers. We are looking for..."

"All employables must wait at the designated areas near the lifts." The woman made a motion with her hand as though she were shooing a fly.

"Oh, no, my dear. We are not looking for passage. We are here to speak to your stage manager. This young lady has the voice of an angel, and she would like to offer her services while we travel." Dhabi smiled at the woman and made a flourish over Annie's head. "Her last station performance brought the audience to tears. In all the right ways."

Annie smiled at the woman, who leaned over her desk to take a closer look. "Are you all right, sweetie? Is this man forcing you to do things against your will?"

Annie almost laughed. "No, ma'am. He's right honest. I'm a singer."

The woman cast a suspicious glare and then sat back in her seat. "We aren't looking for entertainers at the moment, but I know of a place that is." She ran her finger over a panel on the desk, and a contact card appeared on the plexi-display in front of Dhabi. "This is a reputable stage I'm sending you to. If you aren't on the ups, don't bother calling. Do you understand?"

Dhabi quickly grabbed the info with his data-com. "We're much obliged, Miss...?"

The woman twisted her lips from side to side. "My name is Loretta, and you can tell Bartholomew I sent you. He'll give you a fair wage for your talent." She looked at Annie and back to Dhabi. "And if you aren't on the ups, he'll have you in a cell before you can sing a note."

Annie reached out and took Loretta's hand from the desk. "Thank you, ma'am. Thank you. You're a real blessing to me."

Dhabi nodded and led Annie back out into the market area. "Looks like this Bartholomew is at the other end."

As they walked the length of the bazaar, Annie studied the faces of the people she passed. Most carried a look of exhaustion or sorrow or both. What was out here that wearied and worried them so? Mothers held their children as though everyone else was a predator. Couples walked single-file with their heads down as much as possible. Everyone seemed to avoid eye-contact. Annie felt sad just seeing them.

They reached the end of the market but didn't see anything that looked like a theater. Dhabi asked a man about Bartholomew. He pointed overhead.

Annie looked up to see a blinking sign on the side of the mezzanine above. *Bart's.*

"Upper level," was all that Dhabi said as they maneuvered through the crowd to the nearest lift.

Annie could see another group of employables at the head of the lift. She started to look away, but then she noticed that Dhabi was staring at one of them. The woman was blond, probably in her mid to late twenties, beautiful, slim, and svelte, as Annie's daddy liked to say. She wasn't sure what *svelte* meant, but from the looks of the women Daddy had labeled with the word, she assumed that it meant tough enough to knock any man over.

Not only was Dhabi staring at the woman, but the woman was staring back. And both of them were smiling.

Annie expected Dhabi to stop and speak to her, but he just kept walking to Bart's. He glanced back as they went inside.

Bartholomew was a short man with slick black hair and sideburns that curved and pointed to the center of each cheek. He wore a pale blue suit with a darker blue scarf at his neck, and Annie noticed that his eyes matched the silk knot precisely. The man studied Annie from head to toe, squinting as he looked down at her polished red boots.

"Loretta said you would come." He raised both hands over his head and motioned with his fingertips for them to follow him. "What is your name?"

"My name is Dhabi Ramal."

The man turned around so fast that Dhabi almost ran into him. "Are you the one with the angel's voice?"

Dhabi shook his head and regarded Annie.

"Then she is the one I want to hear."

Annie smiled and blushed. "I'm Annie Birchfield, sir. Miss

Loretta spoke mighty highly of you and your place here."

Bartholomew's face crackled with a thousand creases that merged into one big smile. "And what do you sing, my darling? Opera? Calliope?"

"No, sir, just songs."

Bartholomew and Dhabi both laughed at her, and she couldn't decide whether to laugh with them or be offended. She figured it was always best to laugh if she could.

"Charming." Bart turned to Dhabi. "I assume she is the little girl who performed at The Quail this week?"

"I'm not a little girl."

Bartholomew's smile grew broader, and Annie wondered if that was even possible, as it now seemed to extend beyond his face. "And when can she audition? I assume you manage her."

Dhabi nodded. "She can sing for you tonight if we can come to an agreement."

Bartholomew raised a brow. "I have a standard contract for all of my players. It's a simple scale for every individual on stage. I only need the name of each performer. That's agreeable to you both?"

Dhabi nodded. "For how many nights?"

Bart turned to face Annie. "Sing something for me, dear."

Annie blinked at the man and took a deep breath. "Umm. *I once was lost, but now I'm found, was blind, but now I see.*"

Bart's expression turned serious. "Hymns. Well, your voice is lovely, yes. We'll try you for one night and see how it goes. If you can get the audience to their feet, I'll guarantee you a second. Do you play anything or dance? My crowds like a show with energy."

Dhabi grinned. "I accompany her. And she can certainly dance as she sings. You won't be disappointed."

"I hope not. My stage is known for the finest performers on the circuit." The man took Annie's hand and patted it. He and Dhabi worked out the details, and they were soon heading back to the ship, with one quick stop.

"I need to speak to this woman for just a moment." Dhabi

gestured to the employable blond goddess who was already moving toward them.

Annie almost laughed. "I thought you said that you never hired them."

Dhabi shot her a warning glance as he offered the woman his hand. "I am Captain Ramal. What is your name?"

"I am Ingrid. It's a pleasure to meet you, Captain." Her emerald green eyes never shifted from their entrancing gaze.

Annie admired the woman's confidence and poise as she spoke with Dhabi. Her honey-blonde hair was pulled straight back into a tight knot at the nape of her neck. She wore a simple white dress with no sleeves or embellishments. The only notable thing about the sheath was the way it fit her body. It flattered her well-proportioned curves without a hint of tightness. Everything about her was straightforward and elegant.

Annie looked at the other employables, who dressed in layers of clothes that didn't particularly go together at all. Ingrid didn't belong with any of them.

"You're a cook?" Dhabi looked surprised. "Well, my ship is in great need of a cook. And where is your final destination?"

Ingrid moved her sculpted shoulders a fraction of an inch in what Annie assumed was meant to be a shrug. "I have no particular destination, Captain. I enjoy the journey. I do not expect compensation. Just a place on your ship, and a share of the adventure."

Annie worried that Dhabi would mock the poor girl for saying something so silly. But he didn't. Instead, he offered his hand again. "Well, Ingrid, I believe you're just what we're looking for. Gather up your things, and I'll escort you back to my ship."

The woman went back to the wall behind the others and picked up a traveler bag. Without looking back, she took Dhabi's other elbow, and the threesome made their way to the ship. Ingrid asked several questions about the vessel and the other passengers. Annie kept thinking that the woman would run away with each answer.

They were on the run from the law. The ship's hold carried

four contraband animals. They were all but broke. But it seemed to Annie that the more honest Dhabi was with her, the more excited she became about joining them.

Annie didn't know what to think. Dhabi had warned her not to speak to strangers. Not to even look at them. And then he goes and brings one home with him. Annie wanted to dislike Ingrid. She was cool and beautiful. Polished in every way. *The opposite of me, she thought.*

Annie remembered that Mama had always told her to make friends whenever she could. As they reached the hatch door, Annie turned and offered her hand. "I'm Annie." She looked into Ingrid's eyes, expecting the green jewels to be cold and shallow. Instead, she saw a depth of peace that Annie had only seen once before, in her grandmother's eyes, just before she passed.

"Ingrid," she answered. The woman grasped Annie's hand and squeezed firmly. "I think we'll be great friends."

Annie stared too long, and Ingrid released her grip and followed Dhabi into the hold. Cody raised his eyebrows at the addition to their party.

"This is Ingrid." Dhabi's introduction sounded grand to Annie, but Cody seemed less impressed.

He nodded. "I'm Annie's brother, Cody." He went back to his business of cleaning and straightening the cargo netting, which formed the make-shift horse stalls. "Are you inspecting?"

Before Ingrid had a chance to reply, Dhabi positioned himself between Cody and the woman. "Ingrid is our new cook. We should all make her welcome."

Cody shrugged and kept to his task. "I didn't realize we had..." He stopped short. He glared at Dhabi and then shot a pointed smile in Ingrid's direction. "Welcome, Miss Ingrid." He went back to work.

Annie could see that Ingrid was not offended by Cody's attitude. She watched as the blonde instead walked into Nero's stall and began to whisper to the horse. Annie couldn't make out what she was saying, but by the look in his eyes, the stallion liked her.

"Be careful where you step, Miss. I haven't finished cleaning out Nero's space." Cody's warning sounded insincere to his sister.

"Nero, what a perfect name." Ingrid turned to face Cody as though she floated on an invisible cloud. "You're right to be suspicious of me. You don't know me, and you're trying to protect your animals and your sister, as well as yourself. You have every right to question me and anyone else who turns up." She paused until he stopped his work and looked up into her eyes. Annie watched, wondering if Ingrid's magical gaze would work on her brother. "I will do my best to earn your trust, Mr. Birchfield."

Annie saw that there was some reaction when Cody made eye-contact with her. He smiled. It wasn't his aw-shucks grin. It wasn't his contented curve. Annie recognized his I-know-a-secret lip curl, and it confused the daylights out of her.

"It's Doctor Birchfield." When Cody said it, Ingrid turned away quickly. "You have lovely green eyes," he added.

Dhabi took Ingrid's hand and led her to the other end of the hold. "I'll show you the mess. Though once you take over, we'll hardly be able to call it that anymore."

The two of them disappeared down the hall to the common area.

Annie grabbed a brush from the basket on the work table and began smoothing Stubbs's mane. "She's sure pretty. And she seems to like Dhabi enough. 'Least he sure likes her."

"How long will that last?" Cody muttered as he tossed his cleaning tools into the basket. He held out a shovel toward Annie. "Trade you."

Annie shook her head. "Can't. I gotta get myself shined pretty soon. I'm auditioning for a sweet little man named Bartholomew in a few hours. He heard about my show on McKenzie."

Cody scowled. "Can you trust him?"

Annie shrugged. She didn't know if she could trust anyone

beyond her brother and her animals. "I suppose we can trust him about the same as we can trust Ingrid." She liked them both, but she knew that either one might turn them all over to the law if the reward was good enough.

Cody laughed and took the brush from his sister. "Don't worry about Ingrid. We can trust her."

"How do you know that?"

"You can always trust a woman with green eyes." Cody motioned toward Annie's quarters. "Get to shining, then. I think I'll go see this audition tonight."

EPISODE 6

Tall Dark Stranger

Annie dressed as quickly as she could. She put on her navy blue dress with her glossy teal boots. Opening her mama's jewelry box, she found the pair of turquoise and silver earrings under a little fluff of cotton. She pinned them through her earlobes and then twisted a few more curls into her dark brown hair. She tucked her pendant into her neckline, blew a kiss to Buffalo, and then she was ready to go.

Everyone else waited for her at the door. Dhabi had his sitar case in his hand. He and Cody were all shined up as well.

"Mr. Bartholomew is sure gonna be impressed." Annie took Cody's elbow. "I'm glad we're all going."

Ingrid smiled and nodded. "Break a leg tonight. I'm staying here to keep watch over the horses."

In another half hour, Annie stood on the massive stage at Bart's. Cody sat on the front row with Bartholomew, and Dhabi sat at Annie's feet with his instrument. She sang a few songs and even shuffled in time with the music when it was appropriate. The Quail's platform had been small and cozy for the two of them. Bart's stage seemed to swallow her in its enormity.

"You're quite charming, my dear. You do harken the sound of angels." Bartholomew stood and poised his hands on his hips. "But I think it needs more. The whole thing needs to be bigger." He turned around and shrugged toward a dark corner. "Ideas, Mr. Stewart?"

Annie squinted to see who Bartholomew was addressing.

After a second, a tall, slim man with square shoulders and a long gait stepped into the dim light of the auditorium.

"More movement, more people on stage, more music. All of it." The man took his time walking up to the stage.

The word *ambling* popped into Annie's mind. And then she saw Mr. Stewart's face. His skin was tanned, and his nose was just a little bit crooked at the bridge. His jaw had a fringe of a beard that crept up over his lip. His eyes were a dark steel blue that never seemed to wane in their attentiveness. His voice carried a lilting accent that Annie hadn't heard before.

"'Ave you got anything else?" he asked.

Annie's mind went blank. She looked to Cody, and then Dhabi, Bartholomew, and back to Mr. Stewart. "What do you mean?"

The man scoffed and rolled his eyes. "I am speaking English. What else can you do? This little jig isn't enough to call dancing. Do you have a partner with whom you can dance?"

"There's my brother." She pointed to Cody, and he shook his head.

Stewart climbed the steps and stood face to face with her. "I can't see folks scrambling to watch a brother and sister dance pair." He snapped his fingers at Dhabi. "Play something with a quick tempo."

Dhabi obeyed, and before Annie realized what was happening, she found herself in Stewart's arms spinning and skipping around the stage. A few seconds later, she was back in her place. Both Bartholomew and Cody were on their feet, wearing broad grins and clapping.

Annie looked up into Mr. Stewart's eyes, breathless. "I see what you mean."

Mr. Stewart tipped his face forward a fraction of an inch. Still standing only inches from him, Annie realized he was only a few years older than her. She felt a shiver race through her bones.

Bartholomew waved them all down the steps. He took Annie's hand. "I adore you, dear. You will be my star tomorrow night. In the meantime, I'm sending Mr. Stewart back to your ship. He's the most gifted director I've ever known. He will get your show in tip-top shape." He turned to the other men. "I trust this is acceptable to you all?" He didn't wait for a response.

Annie walked back to the ship, still feeling Mr. Stewart's fingers pressing into her lower back. She couldn't remember anything about the music or the dance or the stage. She blinked hard, trying to banish the steel blue from her vision.

"Bart wants the biggest show 'e can get. I want to see everything you've got." Annie heard Stewart's voice but didn't pay any attention to his words.

"Cody, do you play an instrument?" she heard Dhabi ask. More talking behind her. She kept walking. Her stomach felt woozy.

Mr. Stewart was walking right beside her and talking to the others. She liked the sound of his voice. Annie could listen to it all day, though, after a minute of considering that thought, it occurred to her that she wasn't listening to him at all. She had no idea what he was saying or had said for the last several minutes. For all she knew, the man had been speaking directly to her, and she'd been ignoring him. Annie thought she might throw up. She picked up the pace, anxious to get back to her berth.

Dhabi opened the hatch and followed the others inside. Ingrid greeted them and gestured to the common area. "I have dinner ready for you." She regarded Stewart. "There's plenty for all."

"Ingrid, this is Mr. Stewart." Dhabi stood between the two of them during the introduction.

"Welcome. Are you joining the crew, Mr. Stewart?" Ingrid smiled at the man as she nodded toward Annie and ignored Cody.

"Call me Jake, and, no. I am merely here for the evening as a production consultant for the young performer." He reached out to Annie's elbow, and she shifted away from his touch. She was sure that if his fingers made contact with her skin again, it would indeed leave a burn mark.

Jake Stewart froze in place as the others continued toward the dining hall. Annie turned to see a puzzled expression on his face and his hand extending outward like a scarecrow's. "Are those horses?" he asked.

Annie nodded. The others continued through the hall, and she stepped back to his side. "Of course, what did you think?"

"I've never seen horses. In pictures, of course, but not alive. Not in the same room. Why are there horses here?" Jake put his hand down but didn't move his feet at all.

"They belong to Cody and me. Do you want to meet them?" Annie stepped toward Nero, and Jake backed away from the animals.

"No. That isn't necessary. They're enormous."

Annie laughed. "They're exactly the size of horses. C'mon and meet them. They won't hurt you." Without thinking, Annie grabbed Jake's hand and dragged him closer to her animals. She realized her boldness before Jake did, and released his hand once he was near her buckskin. "This is Liza Jane." She regarded the others in turn. "And this is Stubbs, and Jefferson, and Nero. Nero is Cody's horse."

Annie saw the worry on Jake's brow. He pushed his hands into his pockets and looked toward the hall and then back to her. "What are they for?"

She shrugged. "Well, what are people for? Horses just are. In the old days, they had jobs on farms and ranches and such. Nowadays it's a bit tougher for them. People want to eat them. They're getting pretty rare."

Jake squinted and moved toward the hall. "So why do you have them? What do you do with them?"

Annie walked beside him across the hold and down the hall to the mess. "We take care of them. If we hadn't moved them off Earth, they'd be dead now. Authority is slaughtering them for no good reason."

"But what do you do with them? I don't understand."

"Right now, it's hard 'cause they're on a ship. But back home I'd ride them and teach 'em tricks. Jefferson is fast as lightning. Liza and Stubbs can both jump and count and even prance a little. I'm still workin' with Nero. He mostly likes to rear up and look tough." Annie watched Jake's expression grow more excited with each word.

"Are you making this up?" Jake took an empty seat at the end of the table next to Annie. "Your horses can do tricks?"

Cody laughed. "My sister has taught them all sorts of things. Once we get them outside where they can run and jump, they'll be happy and free again."

Dhabi nodded. "And perhaps then we can add them to her act."

"Why not now? This would be just what Bart wants. This would be the biggest show anyone's ever had on a ferry, and Bart would love that distinction." Jake raised his brows, which emphasized his eyes again, causing Annie to lose her train of thought.

Cody shook his head. "Naw, I don't see how to make it work on board. We couldn't even get them to the theater without a scene."

"Yes, a scene." Jake sat forward in his chair and grinned. Annie finally forced herself to pay attention. "Have you ever heard the story of the Pied Piper? Me mum used to tell it over and over. You'd be like that. People would see the horses, and they would follow them. They wouldn't be able to help themselves. The crowds would be fantastic."

Annie leaned back and studied the reactions. Ingrid just smiled. Dhabi nodded with an air of satisfaction. Cody chewed on his lip.

Dhabi spoke up. "We talked about adding animals. Why not now if Mr. Stewart says so?"

Cody shot a glance to Annie and then Dhabi. "Our animals are not...sanctioned by Authority. I'm not sure we want to draw too much attention."

Jake laughed. "You haven't been out here before, have you? People out this way don't care what laws you break. They look for opportunities to snub their noses at Authority. Your show would be a brilliant rebellion, and the people would clamor for it." He took Annie's hand again, and she almost swallowed her tongue. "Convince him, Love." He tapped on the table with his free hand. "And another thing. All of your animals have names. Bart pays scale to each performer with a name. Adding the four horses will increase your pay three times over."

Annie was still recovering from being called *Love* while holding Jake's hand. She shrugged and carefully withdrew her hand from his. "If you think it would be all right."

"Listen to me, Annie. When we're finished eating this delightful dinner, we'll all go back to the hold, and you can show me what tricks you've taught the horses. We can work out a full-fledged program that will knock your beautiful boots off." Then he asked her a question that hit her like a hammer. "Do you trust me?"

Annie swallowed hard and forced a laugh. She reached for her glass and took a long sip of water. When she finished, Annie straightened her spine and, ignoring the gymnastics of her stomach, looked him straight in the eye. "It's not a matter of trust, Mr. Stewart."

"Jake," he corrected.

"It's not a matter of trust, Jake,"

"I beg your pardon, but it is just that." He shifted his chair toward her a fraction of an inch and turned his whole body her way. He reached his arms out for her. "When you taught your animals their tricks, did they learn to do them the first time?"

"No, of course not." Annie kept her hands just beyond his touch.

"And could I teach them a trick? I mean, right now. Could I go in there and have them prancing for me through a hoop in say —fifteen minutes?"

"No."

"And why not, pray tell?"

Everyone else around the table watched their exchange as if they watched a stage play.

"Because they don't know you." Annie realized what he

was telling her. She tried to decide her best response while studying his *I-told-you-so* expression. "And I don't know you, either."

A curve formed on his lips, and he leaned forward. "Then, that is my goal for the rest of the night. I want you to know me. You learn everything you need to know about me until you trust me. And while we're working on our trust, you show me all the splendid things you can do with your magnificent beasts."

He reached out his hand to shake Annie's. She hesitated, afraid of her body's reaction to his touch. She relented and shook his hand. A warm sensation tracked up her arm and into her throat, and she almost laughed. "I hope you know what you're in for."

A full smile parted Jake's lips. "I believe I do, Love."

EPISODE 7

One Trick Pony

After dinner, Cody went to study the pod readings for Buffalo, Ingrid and Dhabi cleaned up the mess area, and Annie led Jake back to the horses. She gathered a few things—some rope, a riding-whip, and a bridle—while Jake found a bench from which he could watch at a safe distance.

"Now, what are all these things for, Love?"

Annie almost laughed. She'd never been around someone who seemed so worldly yet knew so little of her world. "I need all of this to coax the horses into doing their tricks. They're smart but stubborn."

"Sorta like you." Cody sat on the floor of the hold with the LS pod in his lap. He had positioned himself between Jake and Annie.

Jake squinted as he leaned forward, looking at Cody and his gear. "What's all that, then?"

Cody held the pod so that Jake could see inside. "Annie's dog. He's on life support in here."

"Authority shot him." Her words dripped with indignation. She turned to face Jake. "So I shot Authority right back."

"You didn't," Jake said with equal parts statement and question.

Cody nodded. "She did. Had a shotgun full of salt."

Jake laughed. "Remind me to stay on your good side."

"Always wise." Cody punched at some buttons at the end

of the tube for more readings. He looked up at his sister. "He's stable for now. I'm going to need to find a med bay before we run out of nutria-tabs."

Jake nodded. "I can help with that. After the show, I'll speak to a friend of mine. She can get you whatever you need." He turned back to Annie. "Does it always take so long to get set up?"

She tapped her whip against her knee and cocked her head to one side. "When I'm doing it all by myself, yes. It would go a lot faster with help."

Jake smiled. "Take your time. No rush."

Annie pulled Nero forward and bridled him. "He's the biggest, and I haven't worked with him as much as the others."

Ingrid and Dhabi joined Jake to watch.

Annie began by tapping the whip on the floor in front of the enormous black horse. "How old are you, Nero?"

The horse pawed nine times.

"Good boy. What a good boy." Annie rubbed Nero's nose. "May I?" She tapped the whip on his ankle.

The black beast knelt in a graceful bow, and Annie climbed upon his bareback. She clicked her tongue and touched the end of her whip to his chest just above his leg. Nero stood and began a slow march around the hold of the ship.

"There's not much space in here, so galloping is *not* an option. He can trot and dance a little, too, with enough room." When the horse brought her back around, Nero took another bow, and she dismounted.

Jake, Ingrid, and Dhabi stood and clapped. Cody just smiled and nodded.

"That was perfect." Jake took a deep breath. "Do you have any idea what a show like this could do?"

"Make enough money to keep us all safe?" Dhabi asked.

Ingrid shook her head, walked down to Annie's side, and said, "This could inspire a whole generation of people. Nobody realizes the potential of animals these days. I remember..." She cut herself short and shot a quick glance toward Cody.

Annie noticed and looked at Cody as well, not sure what she expected to see. He never looked up, but Annie could see that he was smiling. *What's that about?*

"Can all of your horses perform?" Jake took a timid step in the animals' direction.

"Of course." Annie led Nero back into the stall. "They can all count, bow, march, and prance. Liza is the best dancer—because she's the smallest. Stubbs lets me ride him standing up, and he lets me dismount with a backflip."

Jake raised his brow and shrugged. "What do you mean? Standing up? Backflip?"

Annie sighed as she took the bit and reins from Nero's head. "With a saddle, I can stand up on Stubbs's back while he trots. He can't really trot in here, but I can show you with him standing in place."

Annie drug the saddle out, and with minimal instruction, Ingrid helped her secure it around the painted pony. Cody put Buffalo back into Annie's cabin and returned to help with the other animals. Dhabi and Jake sat back down to watch.

Annie gave the horse his cues, and he counted, bowed, and allowed her up into the saddle. She patted his shoulders, and he reared up on his hind legs in a graceful pose. "Ho." She waited a second. "Alright." He lowered his legs and shook his head with a deep nod. "Good boy."

Annie leaned forward over his red and white mane and whispered into his ears. She flipped her own hair back over her shoulder and kicked off her shiny croc boots. As they clattered on the floor, Annie could see Jake lean forward in his seat. She smiled.

With one smooth, swift motion, Annie stood in the saddle, still holding gently to the reins. She clicked her tongue, and Stubbs walked a small circle in the hold. Annie waved. "I should be holding my hat. That would make for a prettier wave."

As Stubbs brought her back to their beginning position, Annie lowered herself into the saddle, with both of her legs on the opposite side of her audience.

"She should never turn her back to the crowd," Jake whispered to the others.

"Just watch," Cody chided.

Taking a firm hold of the saddle horn, Annie arched her back and faced them, upside-down across the saddle seat. She flipped her legs over her body and landed on her bare feet beside the horse. She made a quick twirl and took a bow at the same time as Stubbs.

All four of the others began to cheer. Jake seemed emboldened by Annie's ability and strode right up to her and the horses. Before he reached her side, Stubbs pushed his nose out between them, and Jake stopped with his hands raised in surrender.

"That was brilliant. That's all I can say." He looked Stubbs in the eye and took a step back again. "And you, sir, were magnificent."

Annie smiled and laughed. "He's a little bit jealous and a lot protective."

"Tell him I'm your friend." Jake tried to walk around the horse, but Stubbs insisted on moving between them.

"Help me take the saddle off. We can brush Stubbs together, and maybe that will help. I can tell him anything you want me to say, but you're gonna have to earn his trust." Annie pulled her boots back on and watched as Jake tried to befriend the animals.

"They are beautiful creatures, aren't they?"

"You never been around animals much, have you?" She slid the saddle from Stubbs's back and took the halter off.

"Only ever seen horses in pictures." Jake shrugged. "Authority doesn't much like people who keep pets anymore."

"I know. Authority discourages relationships between man and animals. They don't understand that there can even be a friendship between species." She gathered all the tack and began putting it away.

Jake handed Annie the whip. "You still use a whip."

"Yeah. But I wouldn't hit my horses with it. I love my

guys." Liza Jane whinnied. "And my gal, too."

"If you can do this—sing, dance, do these tricks and ride— you will be the most famous lass of this generation." He took the horse brush from her and followed her instructions, stroking the pony's neck and shoulders.

"I don't wanna be famous. I mean, that's okay if I am, but that's not all I want. I want to make a difference in how people look at animals. They aren't diseased beasts to be feared and slaughtered. They're beautiful and smart."

"You surprise me, Annie Birchfield." Jake kept brushing as he spoke. "You have this little angel voice, and when I took you for a spin around the stage, I thought you looked a little scared of me."

Annie kept her gaze down, afraid she might confess the truth.

"But, Love, you are fearless, aren't you?"

"I ain't got time to be afraid of much. Too busy for worries. Too busy for fears." She glanced up with her most confident expression, hoping it was convincing.

"That sounds like a song."

"Just something my daddy used to say." She sighed. "I find myself using his words more often when I'm missing him. He's been gone for nearly two years now."

"Never knew my father." Jake seemed to stare at the brush in his hand as he spoke. "Me mum said that he left us to find a job in the UNA territories, but once he got on the plane, she never heard from him again. Don't even know his name."

Annie hunched her shoulders. "Sorry about that." She reached out for his brush and felt the same excited heat at the touch of his fingers on hers. "Where was your home?" She hoped to change the subject.

"I lived in the European Union until six years ago. I got in a scrape and needed to get off-planet. Been on this ferry working with Bart ever since." He helped Annie put the tack away and ease Stubbs back into the stall. "I guess you've never been out of the UNA?"

Annie shook her head. "Ain't never been outta Texas 'til now. But then again, Texas is bigger than the whole EU." She raised her gaze to meet Jake's. "Does everybody over there talk like you?"

He laughed. "No. My accent has a touch of Irish in it. Some carry a brogue. Some are more refined altogether."

"Hmm." She looked around and suddenly realized they were alone in the hold. She took a step back. "What else should we work on for the show?"

"You like my accent? My voice?"

Annie grimaced and turned to face Stubbs, wishing he would push his nose between them again. He didn't. "Should we perform with the horses first? Or sing first? What do you think?"

He took a step closer and reached for her hands. "Because I like your accent—your voice—very much."

"You ain't even listening to me. I'm trying to talk about business." She pulled her hands away from his touch and pushed them into her dress pockets. "I thought you were a businessman."

"Right." He took a step back and nodded. "It's getting late. I should go now." He turned to face the hatch door. "Let me consider everything I've seen tonight, and I'll work up a routine. I'll be back in the morning to pick you up. We'll have breakfast at my favorite little bistro and then do some shopping. The dress you wore earlier is cute enough, but if you're going to be turning yourself upside down, you need something that keeps you covered. This isn't that kind of show." He looked over his shoulder at her with a crooked grin. *"Is it?"*

She raised her eyebrows and planted her fisted hands on her hips. "I should say not!"

He opened the hatch. "Get some rest. I'll be here early. Big day tomorrow."

She watched for a moment as he walked away down the dock before she sealed the hatch behind him. She took a deep breath and held it for a second. When she finally released it with a sigh, it sounded like a moan.

"First love?" Ingrid's voice startled her, and she jumped as she turned around.

"What?"

"Is Jake your first love?" the tall blonde asked again. She stood only a few feet from Annie, with an armful of laundry.

"I'm not in love." Annie shook her head and scoffed as if the whole idea was ridiculous though she couldn't deny the butterflies in her stomach.

"There's nothing wrong with being in love. It's one of the best things in life." Ingrid shrugged. "But if you're not—well, that's okay, too."

Annie pressed her lips into a tight thin line. "I don't know anything about love." She pushed her hands back into her pockets. "I don't think it's love." She picked up a jacket from the bench against the wall. "Have you ever been in love, Ingrid?"

"Oh, yes, I've had many loves in my life. Some were great, others were just hard. When you find someone you love, it will be the most difficult thing you will ever do." She took the jacket from Annie's hand.

"Finding someone?" Annie asked, following her across the hold.

"No. Finding someone to love is easy. The hard part is loving them. At first, it is easy. You see all the good things that they want you to see. But the longer you know someone, the more you see, and it's not always beautiful. Love is a decision to be kind, respectful, and understanding, even when you are faced with the ugly parts you uncover." Ingrid looked at the jacket more closely. "I think this is Jake's. I'll leave it out here, and you can give it back to him in the morning."

Annie shook her head. "I can catch him if I hurry." She took the jacket and opened the hatch. "I'll be right back."

Before Ingrid could stop her, Annie hurried out the door and into the docking hall. There was no sign of Jake. She sped up, her boots clunking on the metal floor grates. *He must have already turned into the common area*, she thought. She slowed her step as she reached the corner, not wanting to get caught up in the crowds that passed. Ferry passengers pay no heed to earth time. No day or night in space. That was for the newcomers.

Annie scanned the packs moving from one place to another. She caught a glimpse of him, she thought, but he held his data-com to his ear, speaking to someone. She remained quiet, not wanting to interrupt his conversation.

"Yeah, that's right." She recognized his voice as she moved closer. It was Jake.

Another group moved between Jake and her, and she almost lost sight of him. She gripped the jacket with both hands.

"They have four horses. And I saw the girl's dog, too. It's in a life-support container."

Annie froze. *Who is he talking to? And why would he mention Buffalo at all?* She continued to listen, keeping out of Jake's line of sight.

"I'm telling you to come and see for yourself." Jake's voice sounded urgent. He seemed to reach for something that wasn't there.

Annie realized he had only just now missed his jacket. She ducked out of sight and hid behind a few people as he passed only inches from her.

"No," he said. Jake's voice carried a bite to it. "I don't know how long they'll be on the ferry. I don't know where they're going. If you want them, you need to get here tomorrow." He paused. "I can't promise you anything more." He lowered the com and shoved it into his pocket.

Annie waited to see where he was going next. Her heart pounded in her ears while she watched him take a step toward the docking hall. He stopped and turned back to the commons again. He looked over his shoulder as if he couldn't decide which plan gave him the greater advantage. The butterflies Annie had felt earlier had turned to rocks in her stomach. She wanted to punch him in that beautiful face of his.

He seemed to decide to wait until morning to retrieve his coat and walked away from the docks. Annie watched for several seconds until she was sure he was gone. She turned back toward her temporary home, with the betrayer's coat tucked under her arm. A few minutes later, and she was back on the ship, tossing the worn leather into a heap on the bench.

"Didn't find him?" Ingrid asked. She regarded the jacket and then faced Annie with a sympathetic frown. "You can return it to him tomorrow."

Annie chewed on her lip, wanting to scream. She didn't know if she should explain what she heard to Ingrid or not. She wasn't even sure what she heard, but her gut told her that Jake was up to no good.

"Oh yeah, I'll sure give it to him in the morning."

EPISODE 8

Blow Up

"You don't look like you got much sleep." Ingrid handed Annie a mug of something black and hot. "You've hardly touched your breakfast."

Annie wrapped her fingers around the plain blue mug and stared at the bowl of protein flakes in front of her. "Too much to think about, I guess."

Cody was already in the hold with the horses, and Dhabi was checking the engine. Annie placed the mug against her lips but didn't drink. After a few more seconds, Ingrid sat down next to her.

"What is it? Are you nervous about performing tonight?" She seemed to study Annie's face.

"I don't know." Annie set the cup down without taking a sip. "How can you tell if someone is honest?"

Ingrid pressed her lips into a thin line, giving Annie the impression that she was hesitant to answer. "There are signs. Some people don't make eye contact. Some stammer or change the subject." She shrugged. "Things like that. Are you worried about someone in particular?"

Annie faced her squarely. "Last night, Jake said something. Well, I think I might'a heard something."

"When you went to give him the jacket?"

"Yes."

"But you're not sure what you heard?"

Annie sighed. "I know what I heard him say, but I don't

know what it means. If it means what I think it means, we could all be in a lot of trouble."

Ingrid took a deep breath and nodded. "But now you think you might have misinterpreted it?"

Annie nodded. "He was on a call, so I only heard his half of the conversation."

Ingrid nudged Annie's cup toward her. "You should drink it while it's hot." She paused until Annie took a sip. "I think you should just ask him about it."

Annie almost spat out the coffee. "I can't do that! He'll know I was listening."

"And that's worse than what you suspect of him?" She handed Annie a napkin.

"No. I don't know. What if it was an innocent remark?" Annie looked at Ingrid, hoping for answers.

"What if it wasn't?" Ingrid stood up and carried the breakfast dishes to the basin to wash. "I don't know what he said, and I don't know what you think it meant. I don't have to. But you have a choice to make. There are consequences whether you confront him or not. Which would you rather face?"

Annie grimaced. The worst thing that could happen if she confronted him and was wrong? He would be angry. Maybe angry enough to cancel their show. If she were right, then they would have it out and be looking for a way to escape. But if she said nothing, well, the more she thought about it, the more she decided that wasn't really an option. Not performing was better than being dragged back to earth, going to prison, and losing her horses.

She looked up at Ingrid, who had been watching her work out her decision. "Thanks. You're great at giving advice, you know?"

"I've had a lot of practice." She smiled and turned back to her work. "And I've made plenty of the wrong decisions in my life. I can spot them from miles away."

Annie laughed. "You don't look like you've made many bad decisions."

Ingrid turned to face her again. "Sometimes it's hard to tell just from looking at someone. That's why I always suggest asking."

"You can ask me anything you like, Love." Jake's voice startled both women as he stepped into the mess. "I'm an open book."

Annie wondered how long he'd been listening from the corridor. "What are you doing here so early?"

Jake shrugged and regarded the leather jacket folded over his arm. "Had to come and get my skin. Seems I left it here last night." He nodded toward Ingrid. "And I thought I might take you both out for a little shopping."

Annie handed Ingrid the rest of the dishes from the table. "Shopping?"

"Like I said, Love, you need some stage clothes. And I thought Ingrid might enjoy coming out with us." He raised his brow.

"You don't need me in your way." Ingrid shook her head.

Annie jumped to her side. "Please," she insisted. She lowered her voice to a whisper. "If you come, I won't chicken out."

Ingrid nodded. "Alright. I'll let these soak for a bit." She turned to face Jake. "Are we leaving right away? Do I have time to speak with the captain for a moment?"

Jake smiled so broadly that his eyes nearly disappeared behind his ruddy cheeks. "Of course."

Ingrid winked at Annie and then disappeared down the hall.

Annie quickly began scrubbing the dishes so that Ingrid wouldn't have so much to do later. "Where shall we shop?" She glanced over her shoulder to see what Jake was doing.

He was staring at her with a confused expression. "What are you doing?"

"I'm washing the dishes."

"Isn't that Ingrid's job?"

Annie tossed a damp cloth to him. "Wipe down the table,

please. If we get them done now, she won't have to do them later."

"But..."

"It's the decent thing to do. Shopping with us *isn't* her job, and it will take away from the time she has for her own duties." She scrubbed the last cup and placed it carefully in the drain, then turned to watch him finish with the tabletop.

"Your mother raised you to look out for others." He handed her the cloth.

Annie nodded. "And my daddy, too. Treat others the same as you like to be treated. That's what he always said."

Jake's smile softened, and he took a couple steps toward her, dropping his jacket on the back of a chair. "Wise words, indeed." He placed his hand on the edge of the basin and leaned close to her face. "He sounds like a good man, Love."

Annie swallowed hard. She hated that he was just inches away from her, and somehow she liked it, too. She wanted to let everything she heard last night fade away, but she knew that she had to bring it out. Annie realized that he was looking at her lips, and for a second, she couldn't breathe. She forced herself to say something.

"You keep calling me Love. My name is Annie."

"What?" He blinked.

"My name is Annie, not Love." She took a step back and turned toward the hall.

He grabbed his coat again and followed. "It's a thing. A nickname. It's not an insult."

"You don't call Ingrid by anything but her name. Nor Cody or Dhabi. Not Bart, neither."

"Well, technically, Bart is a nickname for Bartholomew."

She spun in her tracks, and Jake nearly bumped into her. "You know what I mean." They were out in the hold now, with the rest of the crew.

"I do." He plastered a crooked grin onto his face as he noticed the others watching them. "It's just something I say."

Annie felt a swell of courage rise. "So, you don't always

mean what you say?" The volume of her voice rose with her emotion.

"No, well, yes. I don't know which is right." Jake's typically cool façade seemed to crumble around the edges.

Annie couldn't think straight. It was going to come out now, right here in front of everybody. She had intended to wait, but this was it. "Which is right? That's what you're wondering? Which is right?" Her face flushed. "Who were you talking to after you left here last night? I heard your call. I heard you tell them that if they wanted us, they had to get here right away. You're turning us in. Is that the right thing to do? Is that right?" she exploded.

Everyone stared at her with open mouths. Annie gasped once she finally said it.

Jake took a step back and shoved his hands in his pockets. He dropped his chin to his chest and began to shake his head.

Dhabi and Cody marched to either side of Annie, their faces solemn. Ingrid folded her arms and offered a proud nod in Annie's direction.

Annie was glad she had said it. With Jake's embarrassed reaction, it was apparent to her that she had been right. She didn't know what to do now, but she felt confident that Cody would. He could handle anything.

"What do you have to say for yourself?" Cody asked.

Dhabi clenched his fists, appearing ready to land one in Jake's mouth if necessary.

Jake lifted his head to face them, and his smile was back. He looked like he was on the verge of laughing.

"We're a joke to you?" Cody took another step in between Jake and Annie.

"No, man." Jake placed his right hand on Cody's left shoulder, and Cody pushed it off.

"My sister asked you a question. Did you turn us in?"

Jake held up both hands in surrender. "No. I didn't turn you in. She overheard me talking to a friend. He's the biggest ferry-guild producer there is." He finally laughed. "I told him to come and see you. This ferry has two stops before the show tonight. I told him to get here today if he wants to see your act because this will be your last show before you're famous. An act like yours will literally make a producer's career."

"You were talking to a producer and not Authority?" Annie let her arms fall limp at her sides.

"Yes."

Dhabi unclenched his fists. Cody relaxed his stance. Ingrid kept a steady gaze on Annie, who looked to her for direction.

"Well, then," Ingrid said, "this was just a misunderstanding. It's good to get the air clear after something like this."

Jake's laughter turned into a scoff. "But you don't trust me, Lov—Annie. You still think I'm willing to sell you out."

Annie swallowed hard. Her pride tasted bitter and scratchy as it inched down her throat. "I apologize." She wanted to say more. She felt that she had a good defense, with plenty of reason. She also remembered her momma's words. *I'm sorry* is all the explanation you need.

Jake turned and walked slowly toward the hatch door.

Annie had let her emotions get the better of her, and now they would all suffer because of her outburst.

Ingrid put her arm around Annie's shoulder. "You said what you needed to say. You did the right thing."

Jake stopped at the hatch and turned back to face them. "Are you birds coming?"

"What?" Cody knit his brows together and crossed his arms.

Jake shrugged. "I'm taking the ladies shopping."

"After all that?" Dhabi asked.

Jake sighed. "Listen, I understand that you all are wary of strangers. I don't blame Annie for thinking the worst. I'm not offended, and I don't see why anyone else would be."

Everyone stared in silence. Annie could hardly believe he wasn't mad.

Jake continued. "But we *are* on a schedule, so we need to go soon. Cody, can you and Dhabi handle getting the animals and such ready? I want Ingrid to join Annie and me."

The others exchanged glances and nodded. Soon the trio was out in the market square in the heart of the ferry.

Annie had never been in such a busy place. People barked from all around her, selling clothing, gadgets, cookware, food, and even antique books. She stopped and stared at a leather-bound book entitled Encyclopedia L-M, but Jake pulled her on.

"You can't afford books. Not yet. And we have to get you dressed for tonight."

Annie stared back over her shoulder at the bookshelves filled with volume after volume. "Maybe after we get paid from our show?"

Jake laughed. "You've obviously never shopped for books. You might be able to afford one after a dozen performances." He pointed toward a shop with every sort of dress in the display window. "This is our destination for now."

Annie's disappointment must have shown on her face because Jake added, "You know, I have an old com that's filled with stories, digitals from real books, and I hardly ever use it. I've read everything on it a dozen times, at least. It's yours if you'd like it."

Annie beamed with delight. "Are you serious?"

"Of course."

Ingrid smiled at their exchange and began searching the store's racks for something appropriate.

Jake held up a few blouses and a vest. "Something like this. And, Ingrid, I'd like you to wear a dress the same color as Annie's outfit." He handed Annie a long pair of wide-leg pants and a scarf. "These look right, and they will keep you covered when you do your flip."

"Too long." She wrinkled her nose. "They'll get caught in my stirrups, and they'll cover up my boots."

"She has a point." Ingrid nodded. "Her boots are her signature. You can't cover them up."

Jake's chin developed a crease, which made his thin beard

seem darker in the center. He examined the fabric of the pants and then smiled. "Not a problem. We'll cut them shorter, and then we can slice the bottom edge into a fringe. More authentic, and the crowd will love it. We can do the same with the vest."

Ingrid picked up a matching scarf. "This can work." She winked at Annie. "You'll look great."

Another hour of shopping and the trio had purchased four costumes for each woman, plus a few coordinating bandanas for Cody, Dhabi, and Jake.

"But if we're only doing one show with Bart, why would he pay for us to have several costumes?" Annie asked. Ingrid seemed pleased that Annie asked the question.

Jake did, too. "That's something I wanted to speak to your brother about, Love." He cocked his head to one side. "Annie." He paused and then started again, carrying all the shopping bags for the women. "I talked to Bart this morning, and he's agreed to let me travel with you and manage your act if you're amenable to it all."

Annie exchanged a confused glance with Ingrid. "I don't know. I guess you should talk to Cody and Dhabi. I don't rightly know what they'll say."

Jake shrugged as he nodded for the ladies to lead the way back to the ship. "The clothing is yours, whatever you decide. But if you, Annie, don't want me to work with you, I won't ask Cody, and that will be the end of it. I won't even mention the idea."

Annie wasn't used to being the decision-maker. Her heart pounded fast. She looked to Ingrid, who gave a slight shoulder shrug. She drew a deep breath and walked ahead. "I'll think about it for a little while. Can you wait until after our show tonight for my decision?"

Jake smiled. "I'll wait for you as long as I need to, Annie."

His words wrapped around her softly and pushed through her skin. She wanted to look into his eyes and see if he meant more than just waiting to talk to Cody. She didn't dare. Either way, she was swimming in deep water. Nobody had ever placed her wishes above Cody's before, and she wasn't sure how to process this feeling.

Back at the ship, Ingrid and Annie went to work adjusting the outfits for the show. Cody and Jake ironed out the details of moving the horses from their hold to the stage efficiently. Dhabi studied space maps while he tuned his sitar.

"I applied with the Ferry Master to be at the top of the list for fueling after the show. I explained that we'll have the expedition fee once the show was over, and he said that Bart had already advanced it to him." Dhabi smiled as Annie and Ingrid emerged from their cabins dressed for the performance. "Someone has certainly been promoting this show."

Annie tossed a bandana to her brother, and Ingrid brought one to Dhabi. She carefully tied it around his neck and arranged the ends to lay flat on his shoulder. Annie approached Jake, who made a twirling motion toward her with his finger. She spun in a circle, causing the fringe on her pants and vest to fly in every direction. As she finished her rotation, she threw his bandana into his still-clapping hands.

He caught the fabric square and then offered it back to her. "Could you please help with this? I don't usually wear this type of accessory."

Annie gulped a quick breath of oxygen and reached around Jake's shoulders to tie the ends of the bandana. "I'm leaving yours loose at your neck. I figure with your scruffy beard, you kinda look like a bad guy."

Jake's steely eyes smiled without disturbing the shape of his lips at all. "Do you think I'm a bad guy?"

Annie pulled her hands back from around his neck more quickly than she intended. "No. I don't think that."

"But I look like one?" His smile reached down to the corners of his mouth now.

Annie took a half step back. She was acutely aware that the others were watching. Her stomach fluttered, and she grasped for the right words to say. "Not in a bad way."

"I look bad, but in a good way? Maybe sometime you can

explain that one to me, Love."

Annie was almost glad to hear him call her Love again. "When will we leave?" She wanted to change the subject quickly.

Jake raised his arms and gestured to the whole room. "When you have everything gathered and ready, we can go."

Cody held up his scarf. "Sis, help me with this first. I don't know how to do it." While Annie knotted the bandana at her brother's throat, he whispered, "Watch out for Jake, Annie. I can see you like him, but he's just a one-time thing, you know?"

"What do you mean?"

"We're doing this show for him tonight. Afterward, we'll leave and never see him again. He'll have other stars. You'll meet other men." He stared for a few seconds as Annie waited. "Don't give him anything you can't get back. That's all I'm saying, okay?"

Annie nodded and swallowed hard. She couldn't decide whether to defend Jake, the man she had accused only hours earlier, or herself. She had the right to her feelings, didn't she? And she wasn't handing her heart over to anyone. Not yet, anyway.

"Don't worry about me." Annie patted his chest. "You're the one who ain't never been on stage before."

"That's not," he started, but Annie held up her hand to stop him as Jake approached.

"Let's get going," she said.

The troupe began the short trip from the Nightingale to Bart's theater without incident. Jake towed the handcart containing the sitar, Cody's vet bag, and a few other props for the horses. Behind him was Cody, leading Nero, followed by Ingrid and Jefferson. Dhabi led Liza Jane, and Annie brought up the rear with Stubbs.

Once out in the common areas, the crowds began to gather and follow them.

"What is it?"

"Are they real?"

"Bartholomew always brings in the best shows."

Annie heard the same things over and over. Jake had advised them not to say anything to anyone. Just smile and nod and keep walking. She had been worried that people might try to touch the horses and scare them, but everyone seemed to keep their distance.

Bart welcomed them at the door, and once they were inside, he went out to greet his guests. Annie could hear him announcing the showtimes and ticket prices to the crowds.

As they ran through their routine, Bart counted down the hours and then minutes until showtime. Five minutes to go, and Jake motioned for Annie to come and see.

Annie peered from behind a curtained wall onto the broad stage and beyond. She allowed her eyes to adjust to the bright lights and the darkness beyond, and then she saw the audience. Every seat was filled. People chattered and leaned forward. Jake smiled and kissed her cheek.

"For luck."

Annie could hardly think a single thought. One second before, she had been nervous and excited and anxious to take the stage. Now her brain felt empty. Erased with one gesture.

Bart took the stage and began welcoming his guests. Within seconds, he was saying her name and reaching toward her.

"Why did you do that?" she asked.

Jake shook his head. "Get going, Love. It's time." He nudged her out to the stage.

Dhabi followed and took his place with his instrument. Annie pasted a smile on her lips, and the audience burst into applause. As if on auto-pilot, she began her song.

Is a cowboy still a cowboy
When all the cattle's gone?
Does he wear his hat and spurs
When there's no horse to ride upon?

For dusty trails, his heart is longin',
He yearns to sleep under the stars.
For open skies his voice is songin',
With his lonesome guitar.

Is what makes a man a cowboy
His boots and hat and weathered hands?
Is it just his trusted horse
Or riding cattle 'cross the land?

When they take his horse away,
When they take his cows and land,
Is a cowboy still a cowboy?
Is he less of a man?

Is a cowboy still a cowboy
When all his cattle's gone?
Does he have a place in this world
When there's no horse to ride upon?

For crackling fires, his heart is longin',
He loved to hear the dogies bay.
But now the cattle have all been taken,
And his old life has passed away.
And his old life has passed away.

The crowd erupted with cheers before Dhabi could finish his last chord. Annie took a quick bow, and then, as they rehearsed, she welcomed the horses to the stage. Each animal was led out and took turns with a deep bow. Annie began with Nero's counting, moved on to Jefferson's march, Liza's prancing, and then to Stubbs's set of tricks. At one point, the whole audience was standing, cheering on the horses and singing *She'll Be Coming Around the Mountain* with Annie.

Cody, Ingrid, and Jake kept the horses moving and calm

while Dhabi played a background theme. For the finale, Annie kicked off her boots and climbed onto Stubbs's back. The crowd went wild as she began to sing while standing the saddle. Stubbs trotted the perimeter of the stage, bringing Annie closer to her fans. She sang *I'll Fly Away* with her arms outstretched. As Stubbs ended at center stage, Annie lowered herself to his back and rolled herself into a backflip over the saddle, landing on her feet beside the horse.

As the audience demanded an encore, Jake helped her back into her boots. She took a deep bow, and when she came up, Jake swept her into his arms and danced her around the stage—not as they rehearsed.

"What are you doing?" she asked as they danced.

"This is bigger than even I imagined, Love." He spun her once more and then released her for another bow.

The others brought the horses forward to bow as well, and the crowd began cheering and jumping in their seats. Bart came out to settle them all down but was interrupted when the stage lights flickered, and an alarm sounded.

Silence fell heavy. The audience knew what it meant, even if Annie didn't.

Jake turned to face them. "GO! Get the horses and get back to the ship. The ferry is being boarded."

The theater emptied quickly. Bart gestured to his house managers to clear everyone out. He nodded to Annie and the others. "Good show, now go!"

They all hurried as fast as they could go without panicking the horses. Back in the Nightingale, Dhabi raced to the bridge while the others secured the horses.

Jake was on his com with one person after another, trying to see what was happening. "Look, I don't know how to help. You should have your fuel soon." He shrugged.

"We have it now. The ferry is coming to a full stop in two minutes." Dhabi nodded to the others. He checked one control panel and then another. "Authority is docking on the other side of the ferry, and the Ferry Master will release our dock at the same time. He says we can disengage and clear before they can scan for us. We just gotta be ready right now. Everybody get braced."

He gestured to Ingrid. "Come to the bridge with me."

Jake looked at Annie. "Don't worry about me. I won't let them come after you." He kissed her and then ran to the hatch door. "Goodbye, and good luck."

"Wait!" she called after him.

Cody shook his head and then threw his hands up in surrender. "Come with us, Jake. There's no time."

Jake turned to face them both. "Are you sure?"

Annie yelled and motioned to the jump seat at the wall. "Get your butt strapped in now, or you'll be plastered to the floor."

"Locked and sealed." Dhabi's voice sounded from the com speakers. "Disengaging from the dock."

The ship lurched and then steadied, floating free from the ferry port. Annie heard Dhabi's voice reciting numbers as he communicated with the Ferry Master. In an instant, the numbers turned into curses, and Annie heard Ingrid scream. The ship lurched again, and the horses shifted quickly to avoid falling against each other. Annie's stomach jumped and pressed hard into her lungs. She could feel her heart pound as the engined surged, and a loud bang sounded against the hull, followed by an echo of thunder.

"Oh, no. Oh, no." Annie could hear Ingrid repeating behind Dhabi's swearing.

"What's happening?" Annie cried. Cody and Jake exchanged glances and shook their heads.

The ship rocked from side to side for another minute, and Annie knew something was pounding the outside of the Nightingale.

"Ho," Cody instructed the horses. "Shhh, now."

Annie tried to calm them, too, but her stomach was passed the point of no return. She knew that if she opened her mouth for anything, she was going to vomit. She tried dry-swallowing to help.

The ship stabilized, and Dhabi ordered Cody to the bridge. As soon as Annie unsnapped her harness, she grabbed one of the horse buckets and puked. When she looked up, she saw Jake doing the same.

The two of them checked the horses before joining the others. Liza seemed to have a tender leg, but the others looked fine. Their sedatives were kicking in, and Annie could finally let herself breathe.

They got to the cockpit and crowded in with the others. "What happened?" they asked simultaneously.

Annie saw that Ingrid had been crying. Dhabi's face looked permanently etched with anger.

"They were waiting for us. Authority had two ships standing by for us to detach," Dhabi growled. "They shot, and I still don't know how they missed us."

Jake frowned and searched the stars around them. "You outmaneuvered them."

Dhabi nodded. "They hit the fuel arm on the dock."

"The ferry?" Annie asked.

Ingrid sobbed.

"Gone. Exploded. Along with all the ships that were still docked." Dhabi punched a few buttons on his screen. "There were maybe a couple dozen ships that escaped. Maybe thirty."

Tears poured from Annie's eyes. "But, there were hundreds of ships on that ferry."

"Gone."

EPISODE 9

Won't Back Down

"We did that." Annie swallowed hard.

"No," Cody said, shaking his head.

They all stared at the debris collecting in the void where once the ferry and two-hundred-plus ships had been just moments before.

Dhabi checked and set the navigation data in the Nightingale's system. Her engine still ran hot from the sudden maneuvers. "We have to get a burn going right away. Authority ships seem to be disabled, but that won't last long. When they realize that we didn't go up with the others, they'll be on us like mustard on a carney."

Jake gestured to a few blips on the space chart in front of him. "Here. Get to Georgetown Colony. I know people there."

Annie still sobbed as Ingrid watched through the observation screen. "If not for us, Authority wouldn't have been here. All those people would still be alive."

"We can't take the blame for this." Dhabi nodded as he finished entering the sequence and putting the ship on course. "Ferry's aren't under their jurisdiction. The whole section is voluntary submission."

"Nobody volunteered for this." Annie crossed her arms and shivered. Space felt much colder than she expected, even in an over-heated ship.

"Authority isn't allowed to discharge anything stronger than a disruptor array this close to a ferry. This is their wrong, not ours." Cody's voice was hardly assuring.

"On Earth, Authority is bound by rules. Out here, those rules don't always apply." Jake pointed to movement on the fringe of the debris field. "Look there. A few other ships escaped the explosion."

Annie squinted to see the lights of other ships flickering through the scattered scrap metal floating in front of their spaceship. One blipped brightly and then shot off in the other direction. A couple others sputtered in place.

"They're trying to calculate how far they can get on what fuel they have." Dhabi punched a few more buttons. "Like us." He checked another read-out. "Engine at 78 percent. Time to go."

"Georgetown?" Jake asked.

"Not sure we can make it, but that's our heading." Dhabi turned to the others. "Authority will be on us the whole way. We need to get going before their ship is enabled. Get strapped in." He faced Ingrid. "Do you mind staying up here with me?"

She smiled. "I'll stay."

The others went back to the hold. Jake and Annie returned to their jump seats, and Cody made one more check on the horses before securing himself. "I'm worried for Nero. The others seem fine, but his legs have a tremor. It may be the sedatives."

Annie turned her red-rimmed eyes to face her brother. "Are we wrong to go against Authority? The Bible says to render to Caesar that which is Caesar's."

Cody shook his head. "And to God that which is God's. Those animals are God's creatures. The laws are wrong. Authority is wrong."

Jake turned from listening to Cody on his left to face Annie on his right. He seemed to be waiting for her sharp response. Instead, she burst into tears as the ship lunged into its trajectory.

"Annie, Love," Jake said once his body stabilized against the force. "It's okay to cry. Your brother is right. The laws are wrong, and we must fight Authority to get them changed. So cry now, and get it out of your system. Cry for your home. Cry for your family. Cry for every last soul that was wasted today. Cry for those of us who are going to die tomorrow fighting for change. Because once we start fighting, there won't be time to cry."

Annie's tears dried on her cheeks as she listened. This man whose loyalty she had questioned minute by minute now declared himself to be on her side. Not only that, but he had distilled in just a few words what she feared most. They were no longer just running. They were fighting. And they would not all survive the war.

Her stomach seemed to flip as the ship shifted, and warning lights flashed. Cody started to unbuckle his harness.

"Stay in place," Jake cautioned. "You don't want to be our first casualty for doing something stupid. The lights mean something or someone is too close to the ship. Nothing you can do from here to change that."

Cody scowled and dropped his chin to his chest, holding fast to his harness. Annie thought he might be praying.

Jake reached out for her hand. She took his and held tight. "This isn't your battle, you know? They aren't after you. It's us. It's our animals." She stared into his steady eyes. "You should go at your first opportunity."

Dhabi's voice rattled through the ship's com system. "Authority ship preparing to board. Nothing I can do to outmaneuver. Hold tight."

Jake grimaced and shrugged. "Oh, sure. I'll run at my very next chance, Love."

Cody looked up and stared at Jake. "Yes! Go and hide now. Authority doesn't know you're here. Get to Dhabi and tell him. Then hide. Maybe you can get away and find some help for the rest of us."

Jake shook his head, but Annie nodded in agreement with her brother. She squeezed Jake's hand. "Please. Please find help. At the very least, let others know what Authority is doing. Someone has to stop them."

Jake slipped free from his harness and knelt in front of

Annie. He placed his hands on her neck and caressed her cheeks with his thumbs. "I won't abandon you. I'll fight with every—"

Another voice crackled over the speaker. "Prepare to be boarded. All cargo and illegal animals or persons will be confiscated or detained. Anyone raising weapons will be disarmed or disabled. You are ordered to comply."

Jake kissed Annie and disappeared down the hall to the mess.

Dhabi and Ingrid joined Annie and Cody in the hold and helped them unstrap. Without a word, Cody gestured that Jake was hiding at his suggestion. Ingrid and Annie took defensive positions between the horses.

When the overhead hatch opened, a sharp pop stabbed at their ears, and Authority—the same officer Annie had shot—descended into the hold on a cable lift. He was followed by three more officers, all training weapons on Annie and the horses.

The officer's voice sounded like metal on gravel. "We don't want to make this more difficult than it has to be. Cody and Charlotte Birchfield are under arrest, and the horses are to be confiscated." Authority maintained a calm, even demeanor. "Ramal, you and your co-pilot are free to go once we have them in custody."

Dhabi took a step toward the officers. "You have no place on your ship to keep the animals. Let me follow you to your port office. I can keep them on my ship until then. We don't want any trouble, either."

Annie exchanged a relieved glance with Ingrid.

"You're correct about our ship not being able to transport animals of this size." Authority approached the horses. He leveled his weapon at Annie's forehead while another officer set his on Ingrid's brow. Cody and Dhabi both tensed and held their breaths. "We will have to destroy the contraband here and take their heads back to Earth for proof. I hope we don't have to do the same with our fugitives."

Annie stood tall and stared into the man's black eyes with every ounce of defiance she could manage. "I refuse to surrender my animals."

Cody and Dhabi both swore as they lept froward to disarm and fight the man guarding them. The women ducked and swung at the officers closest to them, each knocking the pulsers from their grasps. Ingrid kicked and punched at her man with sharp, controlled jabs, and he was soon face-down on the floor. Annie rammed her whole self into Authority's chest, knocking him back on his butt. She attacked like a whirlwind, with her knees and elbows flying, landing blows against his head, neck, and torso until he gasped for air.

The men fought for a few minutes with the other officer, and soon two more joined the scuffle from the ship above. Annie watched the fight, and then, from the corner of her eye, she saw Jake making his way up the cable lift toward the other ship. He was stopped and knocked off the cable by another officer at the hatch.

Two more lawmen came down the lift, and within a few minutes, had Annie, Cody, Dhabi, Ingrid, and Jake on their knees in a line in front of Authority. "Problem solved, I would say." Authority spat blood from a split lip. "Now, we have five fugitives in custody and a new ship with which to haul them away."

He stooped down to within inches of Dhabi's face. "Give me the control code for your ship."

"No!"

Authority smiled as if he had been hoping for that response. He pushed his pulser into Dhabi's shoulder socket and fired. Ingrid and Annie screamed, but Dhabi only gritted his teeth and buried a groan.

"I have plenty of pain for you all. That was just a low setting. Even that breaks bone and burns flesh. And depending on where I aim—and at what distance—it can kill." He moved his weapon to Ingrid's forehead, and Dhabi growled.

"I'll give you the code. Don't hurt her."

Authority raised his eyebrow, and the motion was even more pronounced because now the brow was swelling. "I knew you could be reasonable." He stared at Ingrid for a few seconds, and then Annie noticed a curl forming at the corner of his bleeding lip. "Do they know what you are?" he asked. "Have you told them your secret? You're worth almost more to me than these horses. Almost."

Annie and Dhabi shook their heads, but Cody spoke up. "We know *who* she is. And we see her as our equal. She's not property. She's not contraband. She's done nothing more than come to our aid when we needed her most."

Annie's stomach tightened. She didn't want her brother to say anything more. She didn't want him shot with a pulser.

"That in itself is punishable by death. I would be within the law if I carried out all four of your executions." Authority paced in front of all of them, as Dhabi struggled to remain upright on his knees. "Yes, four and not five." He looked straight at Jake, who didn't make eye contact with anyone.

Annie's heart sank as she turned her head to face Jake. She wanted to believe in him. He couldn't have betrayed them. *Please don't let it be true.*

"Yes, Mr. Stewart. You will be well compensated. Your message was very helpful to us."

EPISODE 10

Doin' What Comes Naturally

The whole ship lurched, knocking everyone to the floor. Ingrid crawled to Dhabi's side. Authority and his officers scrambled to recover their fumbled weapons. Warning lights flashed, and alarms sounded overhead.

Another impact. Annie stifled a scream as the horses shuffled to steady their footing. She squeezed her eyes shut and whispered a quick prayer for survival. "Lord, be with us. Protect us and keep us in Your will. And thanks for seeing us this far."

Authority appeared worried. "What is that?" he seemed to ask to no one and everyone at the same time.

A voice boomed from the coms above. "Authority Vessel 0765, you are to stand down immediately. This is Ferry Commander Rebecca Dale, acting under the MW Treaty Three. Your actions regarding Ferry 327, intentional or not, were outside your jurisdiction, reckless, and resulted in extensive loss of life and property. You are ordered back to your vessel to receive a reprimand."

"I am not taking orders from any Ferry Commander," Authority growled.

FC Dale was apparently listening. "If you do not comply with my instructions, my agents will systematically dismantle your ship. You are beyond your legal boundaries."

A warning siren blared from the Authority ship. "They're boarding our vessel." He gestured to his men to get back up the lift.

They started but were met with weapons in their faces at the hatch opening.

Rebecca Dale's voice grew sterner. "Authority, this is your last warning. Return to your vessel and stand down. Do not test me."

Authority sneered. He pushed his chin out and leaned close to Annie's face. "I will be back for you and your beasts." Spit and blood pushed out from the corner of his lip. Annie could feel her bones shaking, but fierce anger burned in her gut.

"I'll be ready for you." The words were out before her brain had given them release. Another challenge. Maybe she was ready for a fight, but what about the others? What about her horses? She wasn't even sure they had survived this one.

Authority turned to the lift slowly. Annie searched the man's expression for defeat but saw only defiance. There would be another fight, but not today.

Cody helped his sister check on the horses as the lawmen returned to their ship. The animals looked okay. Rattled, though uninjured.

Ingrid led Dhabi to a quiet place to sit and lean back. She examined the wound on his shoulder. Singed flesh, cauterized by the pulser, held fragments of shattered bone. She searched for bandages before she attempted to clean the site. This was going to be a messy process, and Dhabi would never heal completely from this injury.

Another man began his descent down the cable lift into their hold.

"I'm Corporal Philips. Commander Dale asks if you are in need." His tall, straight stance gave him a look of a man in control, Annie thought. He wasn't harsh like Authority. Instead, he seemed calm and capable. "We're here to pick up survivors and assist stranded ships." His starched uniform barely creased as he held out his hand in peace. "We scanned your systems, and this vessel appears fully operational, with only minor damage to your outer heat shields. Your headings are set for Georgetown Colony. Is that still your destination?"

Cody looked toward Dhabi. "No, we won't be going to Georgetown. Not sure where right now. Our captain has been severely hurt by that rogue officer. We'll need a little time to regroup."

Philips leaned into the com on his shoulder. "Medical assistance required for pulser wound." He glanced at the others. "Anyone else hurt?" He looked over Cody's shoulder to the horses and raised his eyebrows, apparently confused about what he should offer.

Cody shook his head. "I think everyone else is fine."

Jake approached the men. "There is no reason not to go to Georgetown."

Cody's eyes seemed to glow with anger. "Except that it was *your* suggestion." He started to charge, but Annie stepped between Cody and Jake.

"Don't, Cody! Stop!"

Cody paused and took a deep breath. Philips had his hands up, as if ready for anything.

Jake released a heavy sigh, obviously relieved that Cody's fury was under control. He smiled, even. "I'm glad you have a steady head on your shoulders, Love."

That did it. *Love*. Without a second thought, Annie made a fist and let it fly. Before anyone could blink, she had punched Jake squarely in the nose.

Jake stumbled backward, tumbled over a crate, and landed in Nero's stall area, in a mixture of hay and fresh manure. Annie smiled and turned her back on him. She could hear him struggle to stand up.

Philips raised his brow and offered him a hand. "I don't know what you did to upset her, mate, but I'd advise you not to do it again."

"I didn't do anything." Jake examined his filthy hands before reaching up to his swelling nose. "If anything, I saved the ship from being obliterated with all the others."

Annie whipped around and stomped toward him. Philips stepped aside for his own protection. "Saved us? Is that how you see it?"

"My connections got us permission to refuel and detach ahead of the explosion, so yeah. I'd say I saved us." Jake scrubbed his hands over his pants, wiping as much of the filth away as possible.

Annie scowled and thought about spitting in his face. Not very lady-like, but maybe more consistent with the behavior of punching him. "Authority told us you sent them a message. You betrayed us." She curled her hand into a fist again, and Jake prepared to evade another blow.

"Now you believe everything Authority tells you?" Jake took a step behind Philips.

By this time the medic had arrived, and Cody and Ingrid stood by to help assist him with Dhabi. Only the horses paid any attention to Annie, Philips, and Jake.

"I don't believe Authority anymore today than before. But why would he be offering you a reward for capturing us?" Annie glared at Jake, perturbed that he was using Philips as a shield. "You come out from behind him and look me in the eye."

"I don't want you to hit me again." Jake shrugged.

Annie almost smiled. Her daddy had taught her how to throw a mean punch, and she was pretty proud that it was good enough to scare a grown man. Daddy would sure be proud right now.

Philips tapped away on his data-com. "Ms. Birchfield," he said, hesitating to interrupt. "I'm searching the transmission log from this ship, as well as all devices aboard, and I find no message sent to Authority. Nothing direct. And nothing that could have been intercepted."

Annie shook her head. "He could have sent a call from his own personal device."

Jake pulled his data-com from his pocket and offered it to her. "Check it yourself. Have Philips here check it."

Philips shrugged. "I did already. I've scanned every device on this vessel. No transmissions at all."

"That doesn't mean he didn't send something from the

ferry. Yesterday, maybe? Before our show?" Annie chewed on her lip as her mind churned.

Philips scrolled through lists on his com. "I can do a deeper scan, of course, but right now, I don't see anything to Authority. Hold on a second; I have an idea." The uniformed man tapped in a few numbers. "We'll do this in reverse."

Jake and Annie stood close on either side of Philips, watching as he pulled up the transmission log of the Authority ship.

He shook his head. "The only messages I see between that vessel," he motioned to the hatch above, "and the ferry are warnings to halt travel and not to let any ship refuel and disembark. Not even any piggy-backs or encrypted messages."

Jake tugged on his shirt-tails and broadened his shoulders. His grin spread across his dirty face. Philips seemed satisfied that he'd salvaged the situation and turned to see where the medic was with Dhabi.

Jake took a step toward Annie. "You're still afraid to trust me, Love."

Annie boiled over. Her fist popped up automatically, hitting his nose and landing him back on his butt again. "I ain't afraid to trust you. I just ain't afraid to knock you down, either."

Cody approached his sister. "Stop hitting the man." His tone was matter-of-fact.

"Why?" she asked. "He deserved it."

"It was my turn." Cody sneered at Jake. "Listen, I asked one of the officers if he could take you into custody, and he says he has no cause. FC Dale says she can't spare the room if you're not hurt. She suggests we dock with the next ferry, which will be here shortly. If I had my way, you'd land with the other employables." Cody gestured to Dhabi and Ingrid. "*They* want you to stay on board the Nightingale."

Annie growled. "No. Absolutely not."

Cody held up his hand to silence her protests. He squared his shoulders and leaned in toward Jake. "The officer looked you up. He says you know how to pilot, licensed even, and Dhabi is out of commission for at least two weeks."

Jake nodded, this time keeping his grin subdued. "And without a licensed and able pilot at the helm, you can't legally dock on a ferry." He raked his fingers through his hair. "And so you're left with the options of heading to Georgetown Colony or keeping me with you."

"Or ejecting you right out the airlock." Annie perched her hands on her hips and shifted her weight to one side. "We can find another place besides Georgetown."

Jake brushed himself off again. He kept out of Annie's swing range. "I suspect that's already been discussed. I would also guess that this ship doesn't have the fuel to get anywhere but Georgetown. It appears you need me."

Annie felt helpless. This is not what she wanted. Philips said that Jake wasn't their betrayer, but that didn't mean he was innocent. She hated his stupid, charming smile. She despised his confidence and those ridiculous blue eyes. And the way her skin warmed and tingled when he touched her. This was not okay. She marched right up to his face and took a deep breath. Her nose twinged with the odor of manure, but she knew Jake's nose was throbbing. "You smell like horse crap."

Jake laughed. "I'll get a shower just for you."

Ignoring his last statement, she frowned at her brother. "Is Dhabi going to be alright?"

Cody nodded. "Yeah. The medic is almost done patching him up now."

Philips joined them. "FC Dale has the Authority ship ready to go. I will be going through their vessel on my way back to my own. The other ferry will arrive in fifteen minutes. Will you be docking?" He flashed a reassuring smile in Annie's direction.

Cody shifted his gaze from his sister to the Corporal. "Yessir, we'll dock."

Annie stormed away from the three men. *Let them sort it all out. She didn't have any say in the matter, anyway. Jake was staying. The horses were going to be stuck on a ferry instead of running free in a meadow.*

She retreated to her cabin and picked up Buffalo's tube. It felt lighter than the last time she held it. He was losing his battle. He needed real attention. He needed a new home.

She cradled him in her arms and started an old hymn. "On that great gettin' up mornin' fare you well." She hugged her dog, and though she wanted to, she couldn't cry. "Buffalo, what am I supposed to do? There's a man on this ship, and I hate him."

She stared at the dog's face, wishing his blue-white eyes would open. "I know I'm not supposed to hate people. Mom and Daddy would be ashamed to hear me say it. And the real problem is...that I don't...I don't hate him at all."

Annie felt the Nightingale shudder as the Authority ship unlocked and removed itself from the upper hatch. Her room fell still and silent for a few minutes. She looked around and held her breath. She wished. Wished herself back home. Wished herself running free with her horses. Flying down a dirt road on her bike. She wished Buffalo was well, licking her face and chewing on her hair. She wished and wished.

The ship clanged loudly when it docked with the new ferry. The sound of the Nightingale, while it startled her from her dreams, was becoming familiar to Annie. That thought weighed heavy on her heart.

"Is this our home, now, Buffalo?" The question seemed to hang in the empty space just inches from her lips. She could almost hear the darkness answer back.

Home.

EPISODE 11

Suspicious Minds

Morning came, at least what everyone recognized as the morning. Annie was still getting used to simulated day and night, as they were really nothing more than a display on a clock face in space. She hadn't realized how much she would miss the earth's sky with its constant sun and moon. Her body felt weary, and her mind could barely function.

She walked in on an argument over breakfast.

"Well, I have to report to the dockmaster. I'm the pilot on record, and our captain is still not ready to leave the ship." Jake nodded to her when she entered the mess, but didn't stop his debate. "I can take Ingrid with me, but I think it would be best if you came, too, Cody."

Annie's brother shook his head. "I don't know what difference I could make."

Jake shrugged. "I dunno, maybe since you don't trust me at all, just being there might ease your mind 'bout all this?"

"I trust Ingrid to see that you don't hand us over to Authority."

"And why is that?" Jake's tenor sounded strained. "What do you think you know about her that you don't know about me?" He regarded her with a wave of his hand. "No offense, dear, but you came on board as an employable. You didn't have any credentials or references."

Ingrid smiled. "None taken. But Cody does understand me in a way that most others cannot."

Her words seemed to pique everyone else's interest, especially Dhabi's.

"What exactly does *that* mean?' the injured captain asked.

Annie could see the jealousy in his eyes. Ingrid reached out and took Dhabi's hand. "It's nothing unseemly. He just knows a little about my background."

Dhabi took a deep breath and winced through obvious pain. "Maybe soon we will have more time to talk."

Ingrid smiled again, but the tender moment was interrupted by Jake's return to the heated conversation.

"Look, I can report to the dockmaster. I can even make a few inquiries about another show." Jake pulled out a chair for Annie to sit at the table. "I'd just like to have a Birchfield at my side to witness my trustworthiness."

Cody growled. "I just feel like there's too much to do on board. Dhabi's injured. The horses need someone to look after them."

Annie sighed. "For cryin' out loud, I'll go."

"No!" Cody shouted. The sound rang all the way down the hallway beside him.

All eyes faced Cody, demanding an explanation. Annie was the first to respond. "And why, in heavens, not? I'm perfectly capable of making sure Mr. Stewart behaves himself."

She had no idea why she called him *Mr. Stewart*. All she knew was that she wasn't sure she could say the name *Jake* without a flutter, and that's the last thing she wanted right now.

Cody crossed the room and stood behind Annie's chair. He rested his hands on her shoulders. "I don't think you should leave the ship right now."

Annie shifted away from his hold. "Are you afraid?" She met Cody's gaze and realized she was right. "You are afraid. Just what do you think Jake would do to me?" The question was out before she realized that Cody wasn't afraid of her being alone with Jake.

Cody wrinkled his brow. "I'm not afraid of you with Jake. You've already proven you know how to handle him."

Jake held up his hand to Cody, as if in an oath. "I personally guarantee her safety."

"You can't do that. You may have the best intentions, but you can't control what others do." Cody looked at Annie and shook his head. "You aren't leaving this ship."

Annie stood up and frowned at her brother. "You can't force me to stay here the whole time we're docked. You're my brother, not my parent. I'm an adult. You can't ground me."

"I'm not grounding you."

Annie took a step toward Jake. "Cody, you said yourself that what happened to the other ferry wasn't our fault. Were you just trying to make me feel better?"

"No, but." His words trailed off.

Jake reached for Annie's elbow. "Maybe Cody is right, Love." He paused, pressing his lips together. "Maybe it would be best if you stayed on the Nightingale until we check out the disposition of the other travelers on this ferry." He nodded in Cody's direction. "I'll take Ingrid, and we can speak with the dockmaster before anyone else gets out."

Cody offered his hand to Jake. "I just don't want anyone else to get hurt."

Annie watched as Jake and Cody made their peace, but she couldn't stay silent. "You're both cowards. Authority is out there making all kinds of laws to hold their thumb over people—shoot, over every living creature, and that's not right. I'm just fighting to take care of what God gave us, and at the first sign of trouble, you both wanna tuck tail and run."

Cody shook his head, and Annie thought he looked an awful lot like their dad when he'd had enough. "Annie, we are trying to take care of you. The blast that destroyed that ferry and killed all those people was meant for us. And right or wrong, the innocent folks on this ferry might not want to have anything to do with us. That's just the cold hard facts."

Ingrid spoke up. "That's true. They might not." She took Annie's hand. "But don't you think Annie's woman enough to face that fact with her own two eyes?" She cast a sweet smile toward Dhabi. "I know our captain shouldn't venture out to the ferry plaza, but I think it might be a nice gesture if we all went out to meet the dockmaster together. We can gauge his reaction before any of us go beyond that point."

Annie's heart swelled with appreciation. Just having Ingrid believe in her bolstered her courage. She wanted to throw her arms around Ingrid's neck and hug her but thought perhaps she should wait for the men's reaction.

Dhabi nodded. Jake and Cody exchanged an unsteady glance. Both men grimaced but didn't respond. If they said the wrong thing, she needed only to rebel to force their concessions, and Annie knew that neither man wanted that. Better they surrender right away.

Jake dipped his chin. "Then, as a united crew?" The others agreed.

Annie felt satisfied as she finished her breakfast. Half an hour later, they all left the ship and headed toward the dockmaster's station to check in. Annie walked at Jake's side, ahead of the others. "Why not an inspection like we had before?" she whispered.

Jake glanced over his shoulder and then back to her. "The dock master requested we appear before him personally. An inspection may follow later." He lowered his voice and forced a weak smile. "Or perhaps he'll ask us to leave altogether."

Annie nodded. "Thank you for not leaving me behind."

Jake gestured toward the official-looking doors ahead. "Ingrid is right. You are tough enough to face all of this. You're not a child, Love."

"Ugh! Why do you insist on calling me that?"

Jake laughed as he held open the door for everyone to pass. "I don't understand why it bothers you. I'm not calling you a beast or imbecile or anything like that."

Annie sighed. "But what's wrong with my name?"

Jake's lips widened into a broad smile. "Nothing at all wrong with your name. But, Love, everyone calls you Annie. I want something that's just between you and me. And it's what comes to my lips whenever I look at you."

She felt that warm flutter in her tummy again, but she tried to downplay it with a quick eye-roll.

They came around the corner to the dock master's station and found a dozen official-looking people waiting to greet them. A stout man with a data-com held up his left hand to stop them. "You are the crew from the CT04 Nightingale?"

Dhabi stepped forward. "Yes, sir. She's my ship."

The man studied Dhabi's injured shoulder. "And who is the Pilot of Record for docking with us?"

Jake took a deep breath and moved to Dhabi's side. "I am. Jacob Sterling Stewart, at your service."

Annie noticed everyone staring at both Ingrid and her. A woman wearing all black, with her dark hair pulled into a tight knot at her neck, moved away from the others and toward Ingrid. "Are you the young woman with the horses?"

Ingrid gestured to Annie. "This is the woman."

Annie swallowed hard. "Yes, ma'am?" She wasn't sure how she was supposed to respond. She assumed the woman was in mourning. She wondered if she blamed Annie.

The woman moved her lips without making a sound, as if she wasn't sure what to say, either. She suddenly reached out to Annie and pulled her into a tight hug. "You poor girl," was all that Annie heard.

The rest of the group moved quickly to envelop the others. The dockmaster shook hands with all three men and kissed Ingrid and Annie's hands and cheeks. "We're honored to have you traveling with us. We hope you will feel welcomed by everyone."

The small crowd seemed to all be of the same sentiment. A tall man in a medic's vest attended to Dhabi. "I want you to come to my station later. I can check your wound and get you fresh dressing. No charge."

The woman in black took Annie aside. "Dear girl, do your horses have the care they need?"

Annie nodded. "My brother is a vet. He takes good care of

the animals. He might like to have access to a proper facility, though. My dog is in a coma, on life support—in a tube."

"I had no idea you had a dog, too."

"Authority shot him before we jumped planet. He's in bad shape." Annie looked up and saw tears in the woman's eyes. She took the woman's hands in hers. "Why are you all being so kind to us? We were afraid you'd be mad and wouldn't let us stay aboard."

The woman shook her head. "Everyone, every soul docked to a ferry out here, and every member of every colony off-earth knows what you've done. You stood up to Authority. You fought back. Annie Birchfield, you're a hero."

Annie didn't understand. She hadn't fought back. She'd run. She was nobody's hero—at least she shouldn't be. She had to confess. "You're wrong."

The woman hugged her again. "I'm not wrong about you. You shot at Authority with a long gun, didn't you? That's what the reports say."

"Well, yes. I did shoot him. With rock salt, though."

"And you all rescued your animals by taking them out of the reach of the law, yes?"

"Yes, ma'am. But the lawmen attacked the other ship. All those people are lost because..."

"Because Authority is out of control. They want to dictate who and what survives their latest test epidemic. They have the whole earth in their grasp. They can't take space, too. People need you, Annie. They need a hero. Please be her." The woman clutched at Annie's hands and didn't let go until she nodded in agreement.

Jake joined their conversation. "Ma'am," he made a respectful bowing gesture to the woman. "Annie, Love, they would like to have a performance. Maybe several. If you agree."

Annie smiled, though her brain felt like it was spinning in her skull. "I think that would be okay, so long as the horses are up to it. What did Cody say?"

The woman's worried expression softened into relief.

"Thank you all. And will you bring out the long gun you used against Authority? Please? If you still have it."

Annie raised her brow. They weren't allowed to bear arms. Not on earth, and certainly not in space. Annie shrugged, but before she could speak, Jake answered for her.

"Of course, she will. And what a show she will give, too. Not tonight, of course. But perhaps tomorrow. This afternoon we'll need to see your arena and acclimate the horses." He took Annie's hand from the woman. "We'll let Cody know right now."

Jake and the others thanked the greeting party and moved away for a moment for privacy and to organize before Dhabi and Ingrid went back to the ship.

"What was that?" Annie asked, once out of earshot. "We can't just do another show like nothing happened. People died after the last one."

Jake raised his brows. "Don't you see? This is why they were all here. This is what they want. This is what they need."

Cody shook his head. "No. Absolutely not. Just because a handful of folks come out and ask for a show, doesn't mean that everyone else on this vessel feels the same. All it takes is one person who wants revenge."

Dhabi looked as though he wanted to shrug, but knew it would hurt. Ingrid patted his hand. "These people represent the crew and the leaders on board. I don't think they would ask you all to perform if they thought there would be any danger." She glanced from Cody to Jake and then finally to Annie. "I think you could give these people a real boost. You're new to space, but I've been out here for a long time. Morale gets low, even in the best of times."

Annie sighed and wrinkled her nose at Cody. "I think maybe we should. There's something about that woman who asked me specifically. She seemed to really need this."

Jake nodded. "Annie and I will go on to the arena." He flashed Annie a broad smile. "Ingrid can take Dhabi to the med center when he's ready, and Cody, you should see after the animals. That last ride was rough. Maybe see what you can find at the med center, too."

Cody appeared unconvinced. Annie took his arm and pulled him aside for privacy. "I can take care of myself. The horses need you. Buffalo needs you. Dhabi and Ingrid need you."

"But you don't. That's what you're telling me?"

"O'course I need you." She leaned in for a hug that would have made their mother proud. "I need you to trust that I can do this without you holdin' my hand, okay?"

"Do you trust Jake?" Cody stared over her shoulder at the others.

"I can take care of Jake."

He laughed and jabbed at her arm. "I know. But what does your gut tell you about him?"

Annie swallowed the idea and looked at her boots. She didn't want her brother to have any idea about what her gut said regarding Jake Stewart. She waited for a second before meeting his gaze again. "I'm not rightly sure yet, but I don't think he's all bad. And if he did try to signal Authority about us before, I doubt he'd try again. He knows for sure they aren't on his side, either." She flashed her *pretty-please* expression, and Cody relented.

"Y'all go on and see what we need to do before a show. I'll see what the animals need. And don't sign anything committing the horses. They don't perform if they're not up to it, understand?"

"Yessir." Annie kissed her brother on the cheek.

Cody, Ingrid, and Dhabi returned to the Nightingale while Jake and Annie rejoined the welcome crew. The woman in black gestured to the only man not wearing a uniform. She nodded at him. "Eldon, please take them to the Great Hall. Let the attendants there know that Ms. Birchfield and Mr. Stewart should be given whatever they request. And will you please take notes and run errands for them? If they need things moved or brought in, see that it's all done." She turned from Eldon to face Annie and Jake. "Eldon manages the facilities here on this ferry. He will take care of whatever you need."

Eldon bowed to the woman and then bowed to Annie and

Jake. "Follow me."

They exchanged a quick glance and kept pace just a few steps behind Eldon. This ferry was similar to the other in that there was a vast plaza punctuated with occasional lifts that moved people between levels. Near each lift were congregations of employables, trying to make eye contact with each passer-by. The shops and service centers were arranged differently, though. Annie noticed that this ferry seemed more organized. Medical facilities of all kinds were grouped together. Education areas, then security services. Clothing, housewares, ship maintenance. Every type of store for every need.

And then they came to the food. Sweet smells mingled with savory. The aroma of bacon hung in the air from a nearby vendor, though Annie dared not guess what animal provided the meat.

Beyond the food market, they found the Great Hall. Six sets of double doors lined up across the wall, waiting to be opened for the next event. Centered above the doors was a sign that read THE THING. Annie guessed that the sign would glow with bright colors when the time to gather the masses arrived. Eldon opened the door on the far right. "Come on in, you two. I'll get all the lights up for you. And meet with my people. If I'm not back before you need me, just call out. The acoustics in this place will carry anything above a normal speaking voice." Eldon bowed again and disappeared.

Annie and Jake explored the space for a few minutes. They looked through the backstage area and the dressing rooms. They inspected the room where the animals would be prepped before the show. Everything seemed good. They went through a large arch with curtains pulled open at each side and found the main hall. It was oblong, with the sunken rectangular stage running longwise in the center. Stadium seating rose from three sides, causing a bowl effect. There would be plenty of room for the horses to run, prance and do whatever tricks Annie wanted. Jake's attention seemed to be focused on the seating.

"This one room will hold thousands," he said. "You'll have

the biggest show yet."

Annie nodded. "I just hope the horses are all well enough. I won't sacrifice their health for entertainment."

"Of course not, Love."

Annie looked around the arena. "I wish the seating was a different color."

"Simple gray not your color?" Jake laughed. "I know the woman said they would take care of all our needs, but I don't think they're going to repaint the chairs for us."

She rolled her eyes. "I don't need them to paint the chairs. I just wish there was a way to see the edges of the stage more easily. I'll be running the horses very fast, and they will have lights shining in their eyes. Even a bright stripe to show the boundaries would keep them from bumping into the wall and hurting a leg or something."

"Anything else? Chocolate in your dressing room, maybe?" Jake teased her with a bow and flourish of his hand.

"We can do that as well," Eldon's voice said from somewhere behind them. "And would you prefer a particular color for the stripe on the wall?"

Annie's eyes widened when she realized that the man had been listening to everything they said. "Umm, the color doesn't matter, so long as it's bright and different than the rest of the room." Annie spun on her heels until she saw where Eldon was sitting. She smiled in his direction. "Thank you."

Eldon stood and approached them. He wore an amused expression. "I did tell you the acoustics were marvelous in here." He chuckled. "Good thing you didn't love-talk. Although I've heard it all, I suppose."

Annie felt the warm blush creep into her cheeks as she tried to meet Eldon's eyes. "I don't need any chocolate, either. He was just kidding."

"My dear lady, how long has it been since you tasted real chocolate?" Eldon had his tablet poised for notes.

"I don't know if I've ever had real chocolate."

Eldon glared at Jake. "Sir, you must learn to take better

care of your lady."

Now it was Jake's turn to blush. "Noted. But we're not..."

"I understand perfectly. You two don't know yet. It's fine. I won't breathe a word. Forget I said anything." Eldon flashed a knowing smile to both of them. "You shall have chocolate. Real chocolate." He made a circle and pointed to the half-wall that separated the floor from the seats. "Now I haven't seen your show, but I have read a few reviews."

"Reviews?" Annie asked. *Were people actually writing about me?* She wondered.

"Of course." Eldon exchanged a look with Jake as if to ask if anyone could be so innocent. "Now I know you said to paint a stripe, and we shall do whatever you prefer, but I just thought we could use bunting on this perimeter wall separating the stage from the audience. What do you think?"

Annie wanted to ask what bunting was but decided to wait for Jake's reaction. She was getting tired of sounding like the ignorant child. Jake only shrugged and faced Annie with a goofy grin. "Would you prefer bunting, Love?"

She narrowed her eyes for a second and then had a flash of inspiration. She inhaled and put her hands on her hips as she surveyed the wall. "Eldon, what color would the bunting be? And would it be on the whole wall or just at the top?"

Eldon didn't skip a beat. "We have blue and white or red and white. I suppose we could drape one for a while, and then the other. And if we do use both, we would have plenty to make the swags cover the whole wall."

Annie nodded. She realized that bunting was a material that draped on the walls. "Would it be secure? I wouldn't want it falling or confusing the horses."

She looked to Jake, who seemed genuinely impressed with her improvisation. "Right. It wouldn't do if the horses or my lovely rider-friend couldn't see a clear boundary."

Eldon smiled and nodded. "Absolutely secure. And the swags look magnificent in the lights." He tapped on his tablet for a moment and pulled up a photo of the room draped in bunting.

Annie looked at the picture and smiled. She had seen this type of fabric swagged on porch railings during the summer holidays when she was a child. Before the reunion of states.

She nodded. "I think I would like the bunting. Thank you, Eldon."

"Outstanding, Ms. Birchfield."

She placed her hand on his shoulder. "Please call me Annie."

Eldon nodded and made a note about the bunting. "Annie." He pointed around the arena. "Now all of these seats will be full, right down to the wall. What type of ammunition will you be using?"

"Ammunition?" Annie and Jake said together.

Eldon raised his brow. "Yes. For the shooting exhibition. You told Madame Dale you would show your long gun."

"Oh, yes. That." Annie hadn't quite decided how to bring her gun into the show. "I have all the ammunition I will need right now."

Eldon nodded again. "Then I will leave you two to discuss whatever else you like. If you need me again, just call. Otherwise, you can just pull the door around behind you when you leave." He gestured to the main door behind them. "One more thing. What time would you like the show to begin tomorrow?"

Jake shrugged and gestured to Annie. She shrugged back to Eldon. "Whenever you think will bring the biggest crowd."

"Excellent. I'll make it for eight in the evening. You may come anytime before seven to set up. And just let me know if you think of anything else you'd like." Eldon bowed once more and disappeared beyond the spotlights.

Jake walked over to the edge of the arena and leaned against the wall. "Annie, Love, I believe our troubles may be over." He crossed his arms over his chest and grinned.

"Are you an idiot?" Annie shook her head and sighed. "We have trouble following us. We've already brought disaster on one ferry full of people. It's not out of the realm of possibility it could happen again. No, our troubles are not over."

Before Jake could respond, the door slammed behind them, and they both jumped and turned to find the source of the noise.

"Your troubles aren't over yet. Not by a long shot." The voice came from the woman in black, who was now running toward them, holding a long gun in her hands, aiming directly at Annie.

EPISODE 12

Pistol Packin' Mama

Annie raised her hands in surrender as the woman in black charged toward her. Jake was less compliant. He threw himself in front of Annie, pushing her to the ground and landing on top of her.

The woman dropped her gun and held her hands to her face. "Oh, no! What have I done? I didn't mean to hurt or scare anyone."

Annie pushed Jake off her. "I'm not hurt, but what the fire are you thinking, running in here shouting threats and waving a gun like that?"

Jake stood up next to Annie and mumbled. "You're welcome."

The woman appeared crestfallen. "I just got worked up. Eldon said you might still be in here."

Annie swatted at the dust on her jeans. "No excuse for being reckless. Ain't you never been told to treat every weapon like it's loaded? You're gonna get folks killed. Probably yourself."

The woman shook her head. "No. That's why I'm here. Nobody's taught me anything. I want to learn, though. From you." She handed her gun to Annie. "I don't have any ammunition, but I can get some."

Annie looked over the aged stock. She tucked the butt into her armpit and looked down the barrel, carefully aligning the sights. "No sense in fooling around with live ammo 'til you know what you're doing. Salt is good enough for the time being."

"Jake was still on guard, shaking his head. "How do we know this isn't a trap? Guns and ammunition are both outlawed. You could just turn us all over to Authority."

"I didn't have to rescue your ship before. I could have ignored the whole situation and just let the lawmen take you. You were all dead to rights until my men stepped in. And like I was saying, your troubles aren't nearly over yet."

Annie's jaw dropped. "You're Ferry Commander Dale. Forgive us. We didn't realize."

"It's Rebecca—and there's nothing to forgive. Just please teach me. Authority is out of control." She drew a deep breath. "I can pull rank and jurisdiction for now, but laws change. Usually to favor the powerful. Folks out here don't have any way to fight back."

Jake nudged Annie. "You can do this, Love. Make it part of your act. Show these people how to stand up to Authority. Make them want to."

"Yes," Rebecca agreed. "Authority's grip is tighter every day. Even the independent colonies are starting to feel it. Please?"

Annie sighed. "Let me figure this all out." She looked at Rebecca and smiled. "I'll teach you. I just need to work at how. Ain't never taught nobody before."

Jake took the weapon and handed it back to Rebecca. "Come early to the show. We'll do it."

Jake and Annie left Rebecca in the arena and went back to the Nightingale for the animals.

"How can I put gun lessons for one person into a show for thousands? I ride my horses. I sing." Annie rolled her eyes. "I'm not some hero."

Jake scoffed. "Maybe not yet, Love." He took her hand. "Did I hurt you back there? You know, when I saved your life?"

Annie bumped into his side to make him stumble. "You didn't save my life." As she said it, though, she thought that he had been quick and selfless in reacting to a potentially deadly situation. She felt her heart pound harder, the more she considered it. She wanted to linger a little longer in his hand. She wanted to feel his smothering protection over her for a minute more. She wanted to change the subject.

"I used to shoot targets while riding Jefferson. For fun. I'd set old cans on fence posts and then run the horse around the yard and shoot from the saddle. You think anybody would want to watch something like that?" Annie considered if it was feasible for the arena.

Jake laughed as the two of them reached the ship. "Can you sing at the same time?"

Annie almost began to explain how difficult that would be before realizing Jake was teasing. She punched at his arm.

Jake held up his hands in self-defense. "I think it would be incredible. Now let's get this show figured out."

The whole crew worked together through the night and into the next morning to get the animals prepared. Dhabi and Ingrid strategized for the perfect program. Introduction, two songs, two or three horse tricks, another song to allow time for the target set up, and then the gun exhibition. It was almost time for the show.

Jake and Annie discussed the best way to engage an audience while teaching Rebecca how to safely operate her weapon. In another hour, they had the horses and all their gear packed and ready for the short parade to the stage.

Once in the theater, Cody again pulled out his equipment to check the horses. He brushed their coats and hummed to keep them calm.

"Beautiful animals," a young woman in a trim brown tee shirt and jeans said as she leaned against the gate to the stalls. She flipped her long dark curls over her shoulder and flashed her baby-blue eyes in Cody's direction. She reached out and scratched Nero's nose. "Is he yours?"

Cody looked around for his sister, or for whoever allowed this woman access backstage. "Umm, yeah. But you shouldn't be back here. You could get hurt." He gestured to the door leading to the stands. "Best if you find a safe place to sit."

"You're Cody, right?" She didn't move from her place near the big black horse. "You're an animal doc. Do you ever work on people?" Her full pink lips curved into a knowing smile.

"Not often." Cody's frustration infused his voice with a quiver. "Look, I don't think…"

Annie bounced passed. "Hi, Rebecca. I see you've met my brother." Annie gestured for her to follow. "I almost didn't recognize you with your hair down. Are you ready for your first lesson?"

"Before the show?"

"Just a few basics so no one gets hurt. Rule number one: always treat every gun as if it's loaded all the time. Get it?" Annie picked up her own rifle, careful to point the barrel to the floor.

"Yes, ma'am."

As Annie and Rebecca went to the other side of the room, Jake approached Cody. "I think she likes you."

"Who is she?"

"That, Mate, is Ferry Commander Rebecca Dale. The same Commander Dale who saved our ship from Authority. Your sister has agreed to teach her how to shoot a gun. Right here in front of the whole audience." Jake gestured for Cody to look at the women, who were both smiling back at the two men.

"I suppose we can trust her?"

"If not, she's taking her sweet time to bait the trap." Jake nodded to Annie.

Cody dropped the brush into the basket and checked Nero's bridle. "Why would you say something like that?"

"What? I can't sneeze without you all questioning my motives. I make one joke." Jake shook his head. "This show is going to be one for the books. Your sister is something else."

Annie joined the men as Rebecca left for the stage door. "Whoo, Cody, she sure likes you."

"If I had known who she was, I would have thanked her for her intervention." Cody helped Annie up onto the saddle on Liza Jane's back.

Annie raised her brow. "I think she'll give you a chance

to thank her." She listened for Rebecca's voice introducing the show. "Y'all get ready. This is gonna be a big one."

Commander Dale addressed the crowd over the loudspeaker. "My fellow travelers, as you all know, we lost a ferry full of good souls to the oppressive hand of Authority acting far beyond what the law allows. Tonight we celebrate the lives of our friends by saluting a brave company of refugees. This young woman, Annie Birchfield, along with her brother and friends, have stood face to face with Authority and didn't back down. Please welcome Miss Birchfield, riding one of her prize horses, Liza Jane."

Annie rode out to the center of the ring amid deafening cheers and flashing lights. She began by singing "Amazing Grace" and had everyone on their feet. Annie couldn't see an empty seat in the house. She sang about her horse, Ranger, and then led the horses through the routines of counting, prancing, bowing, and jumping. Annie finished her cowboy song and brought Rebecca back out as Cody and Jake placed poles topped with green balloons around the floor.

"Ladies and gentlemen, I want to talk to you about why we are really here." Annie took her horse's reins from Jake's hand. "This is Jefferson. He is a registered Quarter Horse, and that registration marked him for death. Following our registered arms and our registered cattle, all our registered horses were to be confiscated by Authority and destroyed. My brother and I left earth to save these amazing animals' lives. We had watched everything we held dear destroyed by the heavy, greedy hands of our government for decades. My parents lost nearly everything they loved until they were lost themselves."

She pulled the rifle from Jefferson's saddle strap. The crowd gasped. Rebecca held up her hands, asking for calm.

"Years ago, these weapons were every person's right. That was a long time ago. Now they are banned. Of course, not in the independent territory, but out here, finding one is a challenge. And I think that's a shame." She pulled up the shotgun and demonstrated the proper stance and grip for the safety of the shooter and anyone in the vicinity. "This is the gun I used to defend myself and my property against Authority. Tonight I intend to show Commander Dale how to use one properly, for self-defense and for the defense of others."

As the audience watched, Annie and Rebecca went through a few pre-planned moves. The crowd went wild when Dale finally discharged the sawed-off shotgun. Annie patted Jefferson's neck, thanking him for remaining quiet.

Annie raised her hand again when the cheering stopped. "Some of you may wonder why any woman, anyone at all, would need to know how to fire a gun." She paused for dramatic effect. "I'm here to tell you that *I* needed to know. And if things don't change, you may need to know, too. I believe that bearing a gun should be as natural to any woman as bearing a child. Too often, we have to be the ones to defend our homes. Our families. Our own children. And friends, it doesn't matter from what or whom we have to defend ourselves. What matters is if we can."

Annie nodded to Rebecca and took the shotgun from her and replaced it in the saddle strap. Rebecca bowed slightly and waved to the audience as she trotted out of the lights.

Annie mounted Jefferson and began a slow run around the ring, turning right and then left around the balloon-topped poles. The people cheered and pumped their fists in the air. "An-nie! An-nie! An-nie!" they chanted as she picked up speed.

When Jefferson was taking each turn with pounding force, Annie tightened her grip with her legs and pulled out a pair of pistols from her hip holsters. She found her first target. Pow! The green balloon popped. Another turn, another shot, another balloon disappeared. Another. Another.

With each popped balloon, the audience roared louder. Three more. Four. Five. The people were jumping in their seats. Annie found the last green target in her sight, but instead of racing past with a final shot, she pulled Jefferson to a halt and dismounted. She slipped the pistols back into her holsters and pulled the shotgun back out from beneath the saddle. The screams and cheers faded. Cody came out to see what she needed. After a word with Annie, he took Jefferson back to his stall.

"There's one left, y'all." Annie tucked the gun under her arm and sauntered a full ten paces away from the last balloon. She waved as Jake offered her the hand mirror that Cody gave him.

He placed it in her hand, but before he released it, he pulled her close and kissed her. A loud whoop rose from all around.

Annie blinked back her surprise.

"You're fantastic, Love." Jake left her standing in the spotlight, holding a shotgun and a mirror, and licking the taste of his kiss on her lips.

A few seconds passed before she could collect her thoughts. "Do you think I can hit it from here?"

Sounds of confidence and doubt mingled.

She took three more paces away. "From here, then?"

More cheers.

She carefully balanced the shotgun on her right shoulder and turned her back to the balloon. "Backward?"

Howls.

She held up the mirror in her left hand and slipped her right thumb gently against the trigger. She knew the shot would make her deaf for a moment. The audience was almost that loud already. Her heart slammed against her ribs. She had done this trick dozens of times back home, but never with more than her family watching. She didn't dare miss. She held her breath, and the sounds around her faded.

She only heard Jake's whisper in her ear. *You're fantastic, Love.*

She pulled the trigger. Pow! And then nothing else. No cheering. No pop. She couldn't hear anything at all. She stared into the mirror, but couldn't find the balloon in it. She looked up to the crowd. Everyone was jumping and waving their arms and yelling. Annie heard nothing but a distant ringing. Jake and Cody were on either side of her, both of them smiling and congratulating her. She thought they looked like mimes at the circus. She laughed, but couldn't even hear herself.

Annie had done it. With one shot, she was a star.

EPISODE 13

I Wanna Be a Cowboy's Sweetheart

Annie sat on her bed, tapping her stylus against the tablet edge in rhythm. She couldn't decide if *more* rhymed enough with *go* for her second verse. She figured to write it out anyway, and change it later if she thought of anything better.

A rap at her door mixed with the beat of her song, and she almost forgot to respond. "Uhh, come in."

Ingrid poked her head in and smiled. "Hey, Annie. There are a lot of people out there who'd like to see you."

"What do you mean?"

The slim blonde stepped into the small cabin and took a seat beside Annie on the berth. "It's a lot to take in, isn't it?"

"It sure ain't what I expected. I thought when a person was on the run, you were supposed to hide out."

Ingrid nodded and sighed. "Usually, that's how it works. But every once in a while, it's a good idea to hide out in the open. If everyone is looking at you, nobody dares touch you." She turned to look at the LS pod. "How is your dog?"

Annie set the tablet and stylus aside. "Ingrid, how old are you?" Ingrid's face went pale, and Annie shook her head. "I'm sorry. I know my manners are bad. I guess I didn't have my mother with me long enough. But that's why I ask. You always seem to know just what to say and do in every situation. You're not really like a mother, but a big sister."

The color returned to Ingrid's cheeks. "What's troubling you, Annie?"

"Everything, I suppose. It don't really feel right for me to be making money and getting heaped up with praise for going against the law." Annie fidgeted with her hands in her lap. "Even if the law is wrong."

Ingrid reached out and took the girl's hands in her own. "A wise man once said that when injustice becomes law, resistance becomes duty."

Annie raised her brows. "Who said that?"

"The third president of the United States, Thomas Jefferson. I believe one of your horses is named after him." She squeezed Annie's hands. "That's all you're doing. Resisting injustice."

Annie sighed. "But Authority—they are the law. I don't want to be a criminal."

"Authority has put themselves above the law for decades." Ingrid rocked her head back as if recalling an ancient memory. "Maybe even centuries." She lowered her chin and met Annie's gaze. "One man or woman gets a taste of power and wants more. Authority wiped out half of North America's population once, just to see if they could."

"What?"

Ingrid folded her hands in her lap, like an old woman telling a story. "They had vaccines. Good and helpful medicines. Many diseases had been completely irradicated because of them. But then Authority approved a new vaccine—some say they had it specially developed. It caused breathing problems with children. Babies were dying before they learned to walk."

"That's awful." Annie realized what she was talking about. "The cough?"

Ingrid nodded. "It was awful. Because of that, people stopped getting their children vaccinated at all. Some states required it. Some outlawed it."

"The great divide?" Annie asked.

"Exactly. And with so many people unprotected, Authority only had to introduce one little virus strain into the world. Within a year, the nation's population was cut in half. The desperate states begged for reunification. It was terrible. The cost in human life was unbearable. The cost in human dignity was worse." Ingrid's voice trailed off in a rattle.

"All because of a few people's greed?"

Taking Annie's hand, Ingrid continued. "The thirst for power is insatiable and always leads to injustice. Always."

"It's just not right that they kill an innocent animal. They aren't going to use the horses for food. It's not to help the starving. It's just to kill them."

Ingrid nodded. "You're right about that. And that's why you have to keep your chin up and keep going. The money is temporary. Just use it while you have it, and do the very best you can with it. The praise is temporary, too. So while people are watching you, it's your obligation to be the very best person you can be. Give them the very best message you have. And ask them to do the same."

"None of it seems temporary." Annie scowled and twisted her lips from side to side. She wanted to be back home where nobody knew her name. "I have people asking me to write songs and do special tricks for them. People want to take snaps with my horses and me. Isn't that weird?"

Ingrid sighed. "It's all weird, and it's all normal. And right now there are half a dozen people on board who want to meet you, and another fifty waiting in the docking bay. Dhabi has been playing his sitar one-handed for half an hour. And that's not easy, even when one has both hands healthy. Your brother and Rebecca are grooming the horses, and Jake..."

"Uggh!" Annie interrupted. "I can't think about Jake right now."

Ingrid blinked several times and leaned close. "I was just going to say that he is doing his best to answer questions for you." She reached up and raised Annie's face to mirror hers. "I thought you and Jake were getting along. What's happened?"

"Oh, he just irritates the fire outta me." She clenched her hands into fists. "Did you see him kiss me at the end of the show last night?"

"He likes you. And, he knows how to put on a show for the crowd."

"Well, I don't need him slobberin' all over me in front of God's whole creation." The longer Annie thought about it, the madder she became. "I'm not some...some..."

"I believe he knows that," Ingrid said in a calming voice, "but you can always tell him if you don't wish to be kissed. He might not understand how you feel. Men often have trouble understanding women."

"Are you taking his side?" Annie hopped to her feet and planted her hands on her hips.

"I'm not taking sides at all, Annie." Ingrid stood and faced her, matching her stance. "I came in here to see if I could help and to let you know that everybody else is taking care of your admirers. I understand that none of this is what you expected or wanted. But this is what you've got. Like it or not, you have to be an adult and deal with it the best you can." Ingrid's voice grew louder as she spoke, but her emotion never seemed beyond her control. "You have a lot of people here to help you. Maybe you should show a little gratitude and join us."

Ingrid didn't wait for Annie to reply. She just left.

Annie's heart felt as though it dropped into her stomach like a cold hard stone. She took a moment to let the flush of indignation settle out from her cheeks. She carefully placed Buffalo on her bed and blew him a kiss as she closed the door behind her.

The hold of the Nightingale was filled with people. As Ingrid had said, Cody, Dhabi, and Jake all entertained small groups of people wanting to listen to music and see the horses. She glanced over to see if Ingrid was watching her, but the woman was already talking to the small crowd around Dhabi.

Jake noticed her and waved for Annie to join the small group of fans with him. "Ladies and gentlemen, here she is now. Miss Birchfield, these lovely people would like to get to know you a little better."

Annie wanted to say a hundred rude things to Jake, but she

wasn't sure why. Probably because Ingrid had just smacked her with an ugly truth that she was selfish and ungrateful. Maybe because Jake had kissed her in front of the whole ferry. She'd like to see him try to do that again. *Please.* "Hi, folks. How are y'all today?" she asked instead.

Thirty minutes later, she had made the rounds inside their ship and had gone outside to wave at the crowds. People asked her to take pictures with them or sign her name on their hands. Jake helped her answer questions about what she liked and how she felt about Authority.

"I was reminded today that laws are not always right." She glanced over her shoulder toward Ingrid. "When we're faced with obeying an evil law, the only right thing to do is resist. That's all we're doing here. We're resisting. But we can't do it all by ourselves. I mean, we will if we have to, but wouldn't it be better if we could count on all y'all to resist, too?"

The crowd went wild with cheers. Annie looked back at Jake, who stared at her as though she was glowing.

Annie faced the crowd again and waved. A young boy in the front row waved for her to sing a song for them all. Within seconds the whole crowd chanted for a song.

She shrugged as she looked back at Jake. "What do I sing?"

He shook his head. "You've been in your room all morning working on one. Just sing that."

"It's not finished."

"Sing what you have, Love. It will be enough." Jake raised his hands to quiet the congregation. "Miss Birchfield wants to sing a brand new song for you. In fact, she's still writing it, so you will hear it before anyone else."

The cheers swelled and then softened as she cleared her throat and began.

"Ridin' down the dirt road kickin' up dust,
Wonderin' what happened to the two of us.
You and me, darling, made a pretty pair,
But scratch that surface, and there's nothing there.

So I've packed my bags and cut those strings.
Climbing on my wheels, and they will be my wings.

Revvin' up my engine, this bird has flown,
And these wheels will be my wings.
Yeah, these wheels will be my wings."

Annie sang two more verses as Jake watched the fans dance and clap along to her honied voice. When she was finished, he raised his arms overhead again.

"Thank you all for coming out here to visit. Miss Birchfield needs to go back in and finish her writing. She'll have another show in two days, and we hope to see you all out again."

Annie watched as the people nodded, waved, and blew kisses in her direction. They all took their cues from Jake, though, and soon everyone was walking away, many still singing her chorus.

"That was incredible, Love. You gave them just what they wanted."

Annie strolled back to the mess area and plopped into her chair at the table. The others were already seated and eating.

Cody poked his fork in her direction. "Sorry we didn't wait, but we didn't know how long you'd be out there."

Ingrid handed Jake a plate of food. He slid it in front of Annie and took another for himself. "You should have seen her. She's a natural." He took a bite and swallowed. "Sang a new song for them. It's good, too."

Annie pushed her dinner around for a second. She stared at Ingrid for a moment and then at the others. "It's a lot of work for all of us. Thank you for being patient with me while I'm tryin' to figure it all out." Once she had said the words, she felt better. After a few more seconds she could smell the food on her plate, and her appetite started to return. "I'll just be glad when it's all over, and we can settle someplace where the horses can run."

Cody glanced toward Rebecca. "Funny that you should say that. We were just talking about getting to Georgetown."

Annie had barely finished her first bite, and already her brother was encroaching on her peaceful meal. "I thought we weren't going to Georgetown."

Cody laughed. "I know that's what we'd decided, but after talking to Rebecca, we think it might be a good idea. We've missed the first window of course, but the next one is in a week when the ferry drops from warp again."

Annie drew a deep breath and then exhaled slowly. "I thought you said we couldn't go there because we couldn't trust the residents, that they might alert Authority. You said we couldn't go because it was Jake's suggestion. What if Authority is already there?"

Dhabi sat up straight in his seat at the head of the table and repositioned his shoulder. He grimaced for a moment. "I am still the captain of this vessel, even if I'm not able to fly her yet. I have made the decision that it is safe to go to Georgetown."

Annie plastered a fake smile on her face. "And what changed *your* mind?"

"We have all discussed the matter." Dhabi nodded toward Ingrid, who returned the gesture.

"Well, obviously not all of us." Annie turned to face Jake, but he was keeping his head down. "Oh, I see."

Cody gritted his teeth. "Listen, Ann, you are not in charge of this ship and everyone else on it, no matter what you think."

Annie grimaced. He only called her Ann when he was really upset or very serious. "But those are my horses out there."

Rebecca Dale inserted herself into the debate, using her most official tone. "They are your horses. And everyone on this ship wants them to be safe and healthy. Being inactive in confined spaces isn't healthy for anyone, including horses. Getting them into a meadow with green grass and fresh air will be best for them."

"Excuse me for doubting, but how do you know that's available in Georgetown?" Annie dropped her fork and crossed her arms.

"I'm from Georgetown, actually. My grandfather was one

of the first settlers there sixty years ago." Rebecca wiped her face with her napkin. "I have a family home there."

"Sixty years?" Jake gasped. "That's not possible. That would make it the first colony. Those people died in that meteor field accident. Everyone knows."

Ingrid and Rebecca exchanged a glance. "People know what Authority has told them," Ingrid said. "And that's never the whole truth. It's whatever serves their purpose."

Rebecca shrugged. "I wouldn't be here if my grandfather hadn't made it to Georgetown. The news that the first colonists all perished was to discourage interest in leaving earth."

Dhabi furrowed his brow. "But why? Overpopulation was causing starvation and disease. They needed people willing to go off-planet."

Rebecca shook her head. "That wasn't what caused the starvation and disease. The first colonists were causing dissent. Stirring up trouble. My grandfather always told us stories about their escape. Authority tried to kill them all, but they made it. My family is tough."

Annie listened, but couldn't understand. A few days ago, Georgetown colony was a danger to her animals, but today it was a safe haven. Before they couldn't go because Jake had suggested it. Now that it was Rebecca's idea, the decision was made. Annie liked Rebecca, but this was too much for her.

"I'm sorry, but how do we know we can trust her any more than Jake? I know she saved us from Authority, but there are other bad things in this universe." Annie leaned back in her chair and surveyed the others' faces.

Jake nodded. "I understand why you didn't trust me." He glanced at Cody. "And I understand why you *still* might not trust me. But her," Jake nodded to Rebecca. "No offense. Can we trust her? I mean, what do you really know about her, except what she tells us? Well, we do know she's the commander over the fleet of independent star ferries. Okay, so we probably should trust her." He turned to face Annie. "Why *don't* you trust her, Love?"

Ingrid shook her head. "Annie's upset with me already, so

I'm going to speak up. What Commander Dale says is true. Her grandfather was one of the first colonists. I knew him."

Everyone stopped and stared at her. Annie scoffed. "Not possible. Rebecca, how old is your grandfather?"

Rebecca shook her head. "He passed away ten years before I was born. He was fifty-eight years old. You couldn't."

Ingrid looked up to the ceiling and then to Cody.

He shook his head. "You don't have to."

"Yes, I do."

Dhabi leaned toward Ingrid. He reached out and took her hand in his. "What is it?"

Ingrid cast a sad look toward Dhabi and then turned to Rebecca. "Your grandfather was a good man. I was in the second group of colonists at Georgetown. We landed two years after the first group."

Dhabi laughed. "This is a joke."

"No, it's not. Dhabi, I was genetically altered as a child. I am one hundred twenty-six years old. I will be one hundred twenty-seven next week."

"What?!" Annie and Jake gasped.

Cody nodded. "It's true. I read the studies in med school. There was an experiment. It worked but was considered a failure. The subjects were all terminated. Well, not all of them, obviously."

Dhabi pulled his hand away from Ingrid's and walked out of the room. Ingrid watched him leave and then turned back to the others. "All I'm saying is that you can trust this woman. Georgetown has people who will help you. There is plenty of space for your horses, and they will be safe. Nobody in the colony has any love for Authority. You'll be safe, and so will your animals." She got up and took a step toward the door. "I'm sorry."

As Ingrid hurried out of the mess hall, Rebecca turned to Cody. "We should go too. He isn't going to listen, and she shouldn't be alone."

Annie sat in her chair, staring at Jake. Jake stared back.

"What was that?" she asked.

"I have no idea." Jake laughed. "I suppose we're going to Georgetown. Your horses will get their meadow. You'll get your ammunition." He leaned back in his chair and laced his fingers behind his head. "You were mad at Ingrid? Why?"

"I wasn't really mad."

"Listen, Love. She's a hundred twenty-six years old. She would know if someone's mad."

Annie rolled her eyes. "I was mad because she sorta yelled at me. I'm not angry now."

Jake got up and took Annie's hand. "Come on. You're going to tell me all about it."

Annie stood and walked with him back to the horse stalls. "I don't want to talk about our disagreement. I need to go back to my room and work on something."

She rubbed Nero's nose and noticed that Jake was patting Jefferson's neck and scratching Stubb's ears. He smiled at her. "Yeah, we're all friends now."

Annie laughed. "You're not scared of them anymore?"

Jake took a step toward Annie and reached for her hand. "I'm still a little afraid of you, though." He leaned forward to kiss her but got a mouthful of Liza's nose. The little mare pushed her long face between the two of them and whinnied.

"Hah! Liza's always looking out for me." Annie flipped her hair as she turned and walked away.

Jake followed on Annie's heels. "Oh no, you don't. We need to talk about a few things."

"Everybody wants to talk to me. I'm tired of talking."

Jake hurried ahead and positioned himself between Annie and her cabin door. "Then, just tell me about the song."

"What song?"

"The song you sang today. You wrote it. Who is it about?" Jake looked her over from boots to brow.

Annie cocked her head to one side. "It's about me and my motorcycle. I was thinking about riding my bike in a show."

Jake shook his head and let a slow smile curl into the corners of his mouth. "Yeah, actually, that would be great, but that's not what I'm talking about. The song is about leaving someone. Who did you leave behind?"

Annie detected a trace of doubt in his voice. "Do you think I'm making it up, or are you jealous?"

"Jealous?" Jake laughed. "Did he kiss you like this?" He slipped his right hand around her waist and planted it firmly in the center of her back, pulling her against his body. Before their lips met, Annie pushed her fingers between them.

"Nope. I don't wanna be kissed right now." She pushed Jake a step back.

He looked surprised. "What are you doing, Love? What's wrong?"

"Nothing's wrong. What are you doing?"

He raised his right eyebrow. "I'm trying to kiss you. That's what I do."

"You never ask if I want to be kissed. Sometimes I don't. Sometimes I don't even like you, Jake Sterling Stewart. You can't just kiss me whenever you get the urge." Annie wasn't sure how he would respond. She wasn't even sure she meant it, but she felt empowered just saying the words.

Jake blinked. He apparently hadn't expected this. Annie watched as his expression changed from shock to indignance, and then again to mischief.

She was a little scared by his confident attitude. "What's going on in that mind of yours?"

"Oh, Annie Birchfield, if I told you what I was thinking, you would blush. Oh yes, Love, soon you will beg me to kiss you." Jake dropped his arms to his side and stepped aside to allow Annie to enter her cabin.

She instead moved back. "Why is everybody so eager to tell me what I want, what I need to do, and what I need to think?"

Jake laughed again. "You aren't happy unless you're complaining, are you? You don't want to be kissed. You don't want to be a hero. You don't want to be the reason other people are being hurt or killed."

Annie felt as though Jake had slapped her.

"Annie, you are a hero. And you are going to be the reason some people will die."

She couldn't listen to another word. She pushed through her door, but before she could close it after herself, Jake was there. Annie pointed back toward the hold. "Get out! I don't want you here."

"You don't want. You don't want." He took her arms in his hands and held her close. His grip was firm, but not tight. "All of this that you don't want, but you have."

"I don't want...I can't be the reason." Tears spilled from her eyes no matter how she fought them.

"Shh, it's okay." He pulled her closer until her forehead rested against his chin. "I know that you feel helpless out here. Everyone else is making decisions for you. And you don't want to be the leader of this resistance. But like it or not, you are the face of this battle. And what a beautiful face it is."

Annie sobbed in Jake's arms. "Ingrid said that I was selfish and ungrateful to all of you. You all are making sacrifices and taking care of me, and I'm behaving like a child."

"Ingrid is right."

"I know."

Annie looked up into his steely blue eyes. She looked down at his lips and turned her face to his, pursing her lips toward his. "Please, Jake. Will you kiss me now?"

Jake's hands dropped from her arms, and he stepped back. "No. I won't."

"No, it's okay. I want you to." She took a step forward, but he held up his hands.

"I won't kiss you. I took a vow—just now when you were talking before. I vowed not to kiss you again until after I can shoot a bullseye in a show." Jake walked to the door and stood on the threshold, smiling back at her.

"You barely even know how to shoot a gun." Annie's lips pushed in and out. Her hands clenched again into fists.

"Well, Love, you will just have to teach me, won't you?" He stepped out into the hold.

"Teaching someone to shoot a gun is a little different than turning them into a marksman, you idiot." Annie marched right up to face him, only inches away from his mouth, hoping he would change his mind and kiss her anyway.

He seemed to let the *idiot* comment pass without reacting. "Marksman, huh? I like that." He leaned a fraction of an inch closer to her ready and willing lips. "I guess we'll find out how badly you want to be kissed."

EPISODE 14

I Go to the Rock

Annie spent her mornings fitting salt slugs into the casings for her pistol and rifle ammunition and packing the shotgun shells with extra loose salt. Early afternoons she went to the arena, teaching Jake and Rebecca to shoot, spending most of the morning's production of ammo on practice. She reserved only what she needed for her shows, which were scheduled for every other night on the ferry.

Dhabi's shoulder healed slowly, but he insisted on practicing with his sitar whenever he could. Annie noticed that he had barely spoken to Ingrid since their argument. Dhabi explained that it was a good thing for them to have a break from each other. He said that he needed more time to focus on his music and getting back to helping with their circus.

Cody didn't talk much about anything these days. He listened to the news articles whenever he could, and Annie caught him speaking in low, serious tones to Rebecca when either could spare a minute.

"Attendance at each show grew as Annie's tricks and musical numbers became more elaborate. She observed that the horses were slowing. Her concern increased with each performance. After the final curtain call, Annie would finish up her evenings brushing down the horses with Jake.

"Do they seem slower to you?" Annie worked a tangle out of Liza's mane. "Especially my girl, here. She isn't even holding up her head as high as she used to. I'm a little worried."

Jake scratched at Stubbs's ears. "Maybe they're a little slower, but they've worked hard for us, haven't they? Three and four shows a week is tough on any performer. And remember, they have twice as many steps to take as you."

"I suppose. I'll talk to Rebecca and Eldon. We're supposed to do two more shows on the ferry. Maybe we could cut it back to just one." She dragged a blanket over Liza's back and turned her attention to Jefferson.

Cody joined them and picked up Nero's brush. "They don't need an easier schedule. They need fresh grass."

Annie and Jake both stopped their work and waited for Cody to continue.

"We're going to Georgetown. We have to get these animals on solid ground and fed something green. Hay and pellets are only good for so long, and we've been asking a lot from these beauties. Space travel still affects them, even with artificial gravity. They need space to run. They need work to do. They need to be doing the things God made them to do." Cody ran his rough hands over Nero's flanks and down to his ankles. "I have to say, in light of the confining quarters, I'm surprised we haven't had a broken bone already."

"Don't say that!" Annie's voice sounded hoarse and gravelly.

Jake wagged his finger in her direction. "The horses aren't the only ones needing a rest."

Annie rolled her eyes. "I'm just fine. And I want the horses to get whatever they need, but is Georgetown the best answer? You were against going there before."

Jake didn't utter a sound, and Annie realized that she might have just unwittingly started another argument.

Cody shook his head. "I was wrong before."

Jake raised his head and faced Cody with wide eyes, but before he could respond, Cody stopped him.

"I have reconsidered my objections. Georgetown is our best option." Cody nodded toward Jake. Jake nodded back. Annie figured that was probably the last time she would hear Cody admit he was wrong.

Jake raised his hands, with a brush strapped over each palm. "Please don't think I'm arguing with you, but if there is another, safer place…"

Cody's mouth formed a crooked smile. "I've weighed our choices. The thing is, Rebecca has family there. Ingrid knows people, too. They both feel the climate in that colony, politically speaking, is suited to our present situation. We could go to other places, but the unknowns are risky. Better to take the path where we know what we're facing, and have allies for protection."

"Georgetown, then." Jake slipped his right-hand free of its brush and extended it for Cody to shake.

Annie watched them agree, finally. "Georgetown." She could barely remember what it felt like to stand on solid ground. The aroma of dirt and grass swirled in her mind. She noticed her legs feeling unstable as if her knees would buckle beneath her fatigued body. Voices boomed in her ears and then seemed to fade. Everything seemed to fade.

***

"Annie, can you hear me?" Ingrid's voice. Annie couldn't open her eyes. The blackness all around began to pale. Still, her eyelids didn't budge. They felt as though they had been sealed with wax or even glue. She could feel the softness of her bed. She could smell the rosy scent of her soap on her pillow. Ingrid's hand was on her forehead. "I think she's waking up."

Annie tried to speak, but as with her eyes, her tongue wouldn't work. There was another hand—this one against her cheek.

"You need to wake up, Love." It was Jake.

Annie tried to move, but her muscles felt strapped in place as if mummified. She struggled. Nothing. The voices were close. Her friends were right there with her. She strained to open her eyes. A tiny slice of light pushed between her lashes, and her right eye opened. Jake's face was there, smiling through worried tears.

"Cody, she's back." Ingrid stood and backed away as Cody

came into Annie's view.

Annie had her brother on one side, listening to her heartbeat through his stethoscope, and Jake on her other side, clinging to her hand as if she held his future.

With both eyes open, the room seemed more brightly lit than usual. Annie pushed her lips out, willing them to part. "I didn't mean to faint." There. She had spoken, though, by the expressions on the men's faces; she doubted the words came out right.

Cody shook his head and grinned. "She'll be okay. Just needs a little more rest. What's our ETA?"

Annie could see Ingrid moving toward the door. "Dhabi says we should be able to touch down within the hour. Rebecca's uncle will meet us at the docking center before sunset."

Cody nodded and squeezed Annie's left hand. "No more scares like this one. Take your time waking up." He didn't wait for his sister to respond. He got up and followed Ingrid out of the room.

Annie tried to sit upright to face Jake, but he shook his head. "Stay still. It will take a little time to fully wake up. We'll be in Georgetown soon, and you'll have plenty of play-time then."

"What happened?" Annie struggled to piece together what had happened. "Did I faint after last night's show?"

Jake laughed. "Something like that. One minute you were with us, grooming the horses, the next you were in a heap on the floor. Apparently, the sight of your brother and I agreeing on something was just too shocking for you."

Annie couldn't help but smile.

"That's what I like to see." Jake squeezed her hand. "You really scared us, though. From here on out, I'm in charge of making sure you don't get over exhausted."

"I'll be careful. You don't have to worry. I didn't realize I was so tired. But I guess a good night's sleep was all I needed. I think I'm feeling better now." She tried to inch up in her bed again.

Jake put his hands on her shoulders, gently holding her in

place. "Please, don't sit up yet. You should stay still for a while, yet. You needed a bit more than a night's sleep. You've been in and out for three days. Ingrid has been right here at your side the whole time, making sure you have everything you need."

"Three days?" Annie bolted up, but the sudden movement caused her to feel as though she slammed into a brick wall. Every cell in her body seemed to scream out in pain.

Jake grimaced. "Please, Love. Cody calls it Space Fatigue. He says you'll need a few more days to recover. When we get to Georgetown, we'll offload everything to the Dale compound. Rebecca has arranged for us a place to stay in the guesthouse. You will have your own room, as well as your own personal servant to see to your every wish and whim."

As the all-over-ache subsided, Annie relaxed into the pillows. "I don't need a servant. I need some strength to get my horses well."

"Cody and Rebecca will care for all the animals and get them ready for another show. That's right; the show will go on. And Dhabi and Ingrid will make sure we're safe. They're scanning the waves and checking in with their contacts for news that could affect us."

"Are Dhabi and Ingrid…?"

Jake shook his head and shrugged. "Not really. I don't know if they ever will be again, but listen to me, Annie Birchfield, everyone on this ship, everyone who knows you, everyone, is working together to get you well and safe. The least you can do is behave and get better."

Annie scowled. "You know I don't like to behave."

"I know. That's why I'm asking as a personal favor."

"I still don't need a servant to take care of me."

"What if that servant is a devilishly handsome Irishman?"

She smiled. "Only on one condition."

"Anything."

"Call me Love, not Annie."

Jake laughed and nodded. He leaned over her for a kiss, but before their lips met, the ship's alarm began to wail. Jake jumped to the door and leaned on the button for the comlink. "What's happening?"

Cody's voice buzzed through the speaker. "Proximity alerts. We have escorts to the dock. Get strapped in."

Jake pulled the safety cover over Annie's berth and secured the snaps down the side. One big bump knocked Jake on his butt. He grabbed Buffalo's pod in one arm and looped the other through the strap on the jump seat in the corner.

Annie locked her gaze on Jake, trying to ignore the rumbling of the ship as it pushed through the atmosphere toward Georgetown Colony. His expression was stoic. He stared straight ahead at nothing for several seconds. He clutched the tube with both arms, not relaxing his muscles an inch. With another big bump, he shifted his attention to her.

"It's going to be okay." His expression told Annie that he was trying to convince himself as much as her.

She nodded. "For someone who has spent a lot of time traveling the stars, you aren't real comfortable with it, are you?"

"Not really, no. I don't mind once I'm out there, but the take-offs and landings get me nervous." He winced through another jolt. "A little."

Suddenly the turbulence stopped, and Annie felt as if she was floating just above the mattress, pressed against the safety cover. Another second more, and she felt heavy and pushed down into the springs. The ship had landed.

Jake stayed in place until the alarms fell silent. Cody's voice crackled from above. "We're gonna have inspectors on board shortly. Everybody get yourself pretty."

Jake stood, placed Buffalo onto the jumpseat, and scanned the cabin. "Let's get you ready for sunshine—assuming it's daytime in Georgetown." He unsnapped her covering and kissed her forehead.

"Can't you please help me sit up?" Annie tried to prop herself up on her elbows.

Jake sighed and tugged at her pillow. "I'll do what I can, but you have to be patient. We can't do a thing until the dock inspectors approve us all."

"How long before they board us?" she asked.

Before Jake could answer, Annie felt a sudden pop in her ears, and her stomach flipped.

"I would guess that's happening right about now." Jake pulled at his earlobe. "I hate this part," he muttered.

An hour later, the passengers of the Nightingale received permission to disembark, along with their animals and cargo.

Rebecca's uncle, Bull, met them at the end of the dock with a truck from his compound. Ingrid rode with Bull after helping load up with all the perishables from the kitchen. Cody and Annie drove their truck, horse trailer in tow, and Jake took Annie's bike. Dhabi remained behind to shut down the ship and finish reports for the technical log. Bull would come back for him later.

Annie stared out the truck window, noticing a breeze rustling tree branches. She smiled. The trees looked wider than back home, with lower branches, fatter leaves, and thick, tall brush growing along the side of the road. The grass covering the meadows appeared a darker green than she had ever seen before. It looked thick and lush. She longed to stretch out in it like a child playing in her mother's yard back home.

Her fingers began to tingle, and then her toes, her ears. She didn't know if it was her body adjusting to the planet, or if it was the excitement of being somewhere that wasn't shooting through space.

She glanced down at Buffalo's tube. The status indicator light was no longer yellow, or even orange. It was now blinking red. Even with the help from the ferry medics, Buffalo was dying. Annie hugged it as tightly as her weak arms would allow.

Cody didn't look down or seem to notice at all. Annie watched as he stared straight ahead, following Bull's vehicle turn for turn, through a gate marked Dale. She jumped when he finally spoke.

"I don't know if I can do anything for him, but at least Buffalo won't die out in space. Maybe I can get him one last breath of real air."

Annie wanted to cry. She wanted to scream and hit and stomp her feet. Mostly she just wanted to hug her puppy again and feel his slobbery kisses on her face. But sitting in the old pickup, bouncing toward a gray farmhouse at the end of a dirt road, Annie could barely feel anything at all.

As the truck slowed in front of the house, a stream of family members poured from the front door. A few young men and women around her age ran out first to help unload the horses. An older woman, probably in her forties, led out a man who appeared ancient to Annie. His hair was white and seemed to spring from everywhere but the top of his head.

Behind him were a half dozen children and two young women carrying babies on their hips. Annie watched them form a line on the edge of the porch, smiling at their visitors.

Jake opened her door for her and took the LS pod from her lap. "I've got you. Just lean on me, and we'll get you to your own room."

Annie nodded and stretched her right arm over Jake's shoulders. She slid out of the truck's cab, and Jake slipped his left arm around her waist. The small crowd on the porch began to cheer.

"What is this?" she asked.

Bull laughed and gestured toward a smaller house just beyond the end of the main home. "Young lady, you're famous here in Georgetown. A hero to these kids." He turned to face Cody. "Doctor Birchfield, let us get you unpacked. We'll have introductions around the supper table later. Daisy will settle you in the north quarters, and my hands will take your animals out to the meadow."

Cody nodded and took the tube from Jake. "Thank you, sir. Is there somewhere I might attend to my sister's dog. He's not well."

Bull pointed to a barn on the opposite side of the big house. "We have a little room at the end of the stable for the animals. It's not a full-fledged clinic, but we have all the basics.

Anything you need that's not there, you let me know, and I'll have someone run into town for it in the morning."

Annie waved at the children, and leaned against Jake, willing her legs to walk normally. The older woman opened the door for them and stood back as they passed. She twisted her lips to one side and looked from the parlor to the staircase. "Well, Miss Birchfield, we might have a little problem. All the bedrooms are upstairs."

"No problem at all." Jake swept Annie into his arms and headed for the staircase. "Just direct me to which room is hers, and I'll deposit her there."

Daisy shook her head and planted her hands on her hips. "Absolutely not! No men in the women's' rooms and no women in the men's. You're not on Earth anymore, you know."

Jake almost laughed and then realized that Daisy was definitely not kidding. He exchanged a glance with Annie.

"Mr. Stewart, why don't you just deposit me on the couch here in the parlor? I'm sure I'll be able to get the rest I need down here." Annie motioned to the sofa against the back wall. Jake set her down carefully and fluffed a cushion for her back.

"Anything else, Miss Birchfield?" Jake took a step back and dipped forward in a quick bow.

"I'd sure appreciate a drink of water, but I don't want you to be trouble for Miss Daisy." Annie took a deep breath and then settled back into the couch.

"Yes, ma'am." Jake bowed again and turned to Daisy. "If you'll point me toward a sink, please, I would be obliged."

Daisy raised her eyebrows high and held out her hand to the doorway at the other end of the parlor. "I'll be happy to, Mr. Stewart."

Annie could hear them chatting in the next room.

"Are you two not courting? You look to me like lovebirds."

Jake's voice lowered, but Annie could still make out his words. "Miss Birchfield and me? Hah! My dear, I'm her servant since she's taken ill with fatigue. Just trying to keep her happy. And she can be a bit demanding."

Annie stretched out her arms and legs and smiled. She was finally starting to feel normal. She could hear the faucet running and then their quiet voices again.

"I just thought, you know, the way you looked at each other?" Daisy's tone was suggestive.

"I can't speak to her feelings for me, of course, but I can assure you that I have made my opinion of her very clear."

They returned to the parlor, and Jake handed the glass to Annie. "Will there be anything more you require, Miss Birchfield?"

Annie kept her face as expressionless as she could manage. She cast a blank stare toward the front door. "That will be all for now, Mr. Stewart." Annie smiled at Daisy. "Thank you for your gracious hospitality, Mrs. Dale. Rebecca told me how lovely you are."

Daisy tipped her chin and smiled. "I must get to my own kitchen now. Rebecca will be along soon. We'll have dinner in an hour or so." She went to the door and then turned back for one more thing. "Mr. Stewart, I wouldn't object to you taking Miss Birchfield's belongings up to her room and unpacking them for her. So long as she's down here."

"Yes, ma'am." Jake stood and offered bows to both women as Daisy left the guest house. He stood for another minute, waiting for her to go inside to the other house.

Annie didn't waste the opportunity. "I'm demanding?"

"Well, Miss Birchfield, you have very high standards." He bowed again. "And I..." He bowed again. "I do hope that I've made clear my feelings for you...Love."

"Hmmm." Annie sighed again, trying to sound bored. "I'm aware of your fondness for me. I'd prefer to see it in action, though."

Jake flexed one eyebrow and knelt beside her. "Whatever you want. You need only ask."

Annie stroked his jaw. She leaned close to his face. "Fetch my things and put them up in my room, please."

Jake laughed and hopped to his feet. "At your wish and

whim." And he left her alone in the parlor.

Annie rocked her head back to stretch her neck. They were back on solid ground. The horses needed it. She needed it. For the first time in, what was it now? A month? Two? Annie felt safe. Her body ached, but she could work that out soon. Buffalo was in rough shape, but Cody had the means here to offer help. Dhabi and Ingrid were still not patched up, but maybe they just needed a little rest, too.

And Jake. He walked through the front door with a bundle of her things under each arm. He stopped for a second and winked at her, then bounded up the stairs. Jake loved her.

EPISODE 15

Dog Days are Over

Annie and the rest of the crew sat at the supper table with Bull and Daisy and the other ranch hands, as well as Rebecca and a few other members of the Dale family. Ingrid had only just arrived at the house when Daisy called everyone to the dining room.

Bull asked Cody to bless the meal, and everyone reached for the dish nearest to them after the final *Amen*.

"Your horses look good and healthy, Doc." Bull addressed Cody from the opposite end of the long wooden table. "You and your sister did a fine job maintaining their strength and muscle tone on a ship."

Annie smiled at her brother, who hadn't realized he was Doc. She poked him in the arm until he replied.

"Thank you, sir. Adding the horses to Annie's show gave them a chance to exercise, and it certainly helped bring attention to the cause." Cody shot a grateful glance toward Rebecca. "But we owe the world to your niece. If not for her quick action and compassion, we'd be headed back to Earth in chains, and the horses would be lost."

Annie couldn't tell for sure, but she thought that she saw Rebecca's left arm shift forward under the table, and Annie imagined that she was reaching her hand for Cody's. She sighed. This is what she wanted for her brother. Family, a woman who respected him as an equal, and a place to call home. This is what she wanted for all of them.

"Well, I'm afraid we won't be able to stay long," Ingrid said as if she'd been reading Annie's mind. "My contacts here warned that there is talk of an Authority squad headed for Georgetown."

Daisy scowled, and Annie thought she might even spit. "Let them come." Daisy waved her fork over her plate. "I'd be glad to finally face those tyrants. Bull and I have been collecting and making weapons and ammo for years. And we're not the only ones."

Rebecca's brow raised. "You have? I had no idea."

Daisy shrugged. "We kept our secrets from you. You're a ferry commander. Didn't want you put in a position to have to lie for us."

Annie's heart sputtered and dropped into her stomach. "This is not what we intended. I don't want to start a war."

Bull snorted. "Dear girl, you didn't start anything. But you might just give us all the courage we need to finish it."

Annie stared at the food on her plate. She shook her head. "I'm not your hero. I'm not anybody." She jumped up and ran from the table and out the front door into the yard.

She rocked her head back and stared up at the darkening turquoise sky. A chilled breeze rushed through her hair and raised goosebumps on her arms. Jake joined her, wrapping his arms around her.

"You don't have to run, Love. This is what they're trying to say. This fight isn't just yours. Your fight may have started with your horses. Your dog, maybe even your parents. I think you've been fighting a war for a long time. Before you were aware. But all the battles that come together and make a war—they aren't only yours. We're all fighting unjust Authority." Jake snuggled her closer. "Bull and Daisy have been fighting for a whole generation, so you can't take credit for everything."

"What about you?" Annie rested her head on Jake's shoulder.

"I've had my share of battles with Authority. Lost most everything I thought was important. I'd given up until I met you. Now I have my fight back. And that's what we all need."

Ingrid stood in the doorway and called to them. "Please come back inside. The nights here get cold quickly, and we still have much to discuss."

Annie sniffed and rubbed her hand over her eyes and nose as Jake walked her back to her place at the table. Her dinner plate had been replaced with a bowl of sliced fruit.

"I'd like to apologize for my behavior." Annie straightened herself in her chair and was careful to make honest eye contact with each person as she spoke. "Y'all have been nothing but gracious to us—to me, and I've been rude, selfish, and demanding. I don't deserve the measure of kindness you've offered, but I'm surely grateful for it."

Daisy scoffed. "Don't give it another thought, Annie." She brushed her fingers over some invisible crumbs on the table in front of her. "I get a little heated when I think about protecting my corner of the colony. I didn't mean to add burden to you."

Bull seemed to think it was time to change the subject. "Did you get the chance to see our horses, Annie?"

She took a bite from a raspberry and swallowed. Sweet, tart, full of juice. She couldn't remember the last fresh berry she'd eaten. She shook her head. "I haven't yet, but I hope to see them tomorrow. Did I hear someone say that you had a pair of Welsh ponies?"

Bull sat up straight and puffed up his chest. "That I do. Both silvery gray. Bonnie is dappled, and Beau is solid with a nearly black mane. But I thought you might be more interested in my other horse. She's a lovely roan called Charlotte."

Annie shot a glance at her brother. He was the only one here who knew her first name was Charlotte. Cody just shrugged and shook his head.

"I'd love to see her, of course. Why do you think I would be more interested in her?" Annie scooped up another bite.

Bull picked up the napkin from his lap and reached around to a small data-com on the table behind him. "She's a quarter horse. Fifth-generation from a cloned quarter horse called Jolly Roger."

Annie's jaw dropped so swiftly, she thought it might have made a noise. "My first horse was the fifth generation from Jolly Roger. We called him Ranger. I have a picture of him in a locket. And Jefferson is the sixth generation."

Bull nodded. "I know. When Rebecca sent your manifest for me to approve, I saw the registration number on Jefferson. I saw how close it was to Charlotte's, and I knew. You need to come out early and take a ride on her. She won't do tricks, but she's a gem for a trot."

Annie nodded. "I would love to see her."

Annie realized that she'd become so focused on her conversation with Bull that she hadn't heard what any of the others were saying. She saw that Dhabi and Ingrid were talking to Daisy and one ranch hand. Rebecca, Cody, and Jake spoke quietly with two others. They all seemed to be making plans without her. Oh, she'd be involved. She'd be required. But she would not be consulted.

She scanned the table again, trying to decide on the most appropriate outburst, and then recalled her own words just minutes before. Her temper simmered. *I will not behave like a child. I will not throw a tantrum or demand to be coddled. I will be an adult.* She took a deep breath to settle her ire.

Bull tapped on the table in front of her. "Once you're up and about, I'll escort you on a grand tour of the place. Even if you must leave us again, I want you to see it all, so that you'll know you have a home here whenever you wish."

Annie rested her hand on his. "Thank you, Bull. Cody told me that he was going to let me hold Buffalo in the morning. It may be my last time."

Bull's expression wilted from a high-cheeked smile to a drooping-jowled frown. He turned to Cody. "Even with all our supplies and equipment, Doc? There's nothing you can do to save the pup?"

Cody turned his attention to Bull and Annie. "I don't hold out much hope for him. He's worked hard to hang on this long in the life support pod. But from the readings I got this afternoon, his prognosis isn't good. His wounds were deep, but they're cauterized. The outer tissue has somewhat healed and stabilized through the purified air and the nutria-tabs. There's no indication of significant infection, but the dog is weak. Once he's out of the tube, which has to happen soon, I just don't think he has the strength or immunities to survive very long."

Dhabi leaned forward in his seat. "What about a blood transfusion? Would something like that help? I heard one of the medics who treated my injury say something about that."

"It might help." Cody shrugged. "There's no way to be sure. But I wouldn't want to risk the life of a ranch dog here, and there are no animal blood reserves anywhere in the colony. I checked."

Daisy stood and collected a couple of plates from the table. "Can humans donate blood to dogs? I'd be happy to offer an arm to tap."

Cody dipped his chin toward the woman. "Thank you. That's generous. But we'd need to do a lot of testing, and I'm still not sure it would work. Human to canine transfusions have been done before, but they don't have a high success rate." He offered a compassionate hand toward his sister. "I don't want to get Annie's hopes up."

Jake reached out for Annie's hand, and Daisy shot him a knowing glance. "Servant, my eye."

"Until my dying breath," he whispered into Annie's ear.

Ingrid and Dhabi went back to talking as Daisy finished cleaning the table. Annie started to help, but Rebecca shook her head. "You need more rest. I'll be the one to help my aunt, not my guest."

Annie thought about Buffalo. She wanted to play fetch and teach him a few more tricks. She wanted to nap in the grass with him stretched out across her legs. She wanted to hold him in her arms again. But not for the last time. She didn't want there to be a last time.

From the other end of the table, Ingrid laughed, and it shook Annie from her thoughts.

"Why do you always laugh when I say that?" Dhabi held

his hand out to Ingrid as though he was pleading.

Ingrid covered her laugh with her slim fingers. "I laugh because it doesn't make sense."

"It does make sense."

"It doesn't."

"My father used to say it all the time." Dhabi turned to the others for support. "You all have heard the expression 'like mustard on a carney,' right?"

Everyone else at the table returned a blank stare. "I've never heard it before," Bull said. "What does it mean?"

Dhabi took a deep breath and released it slowly. "A *carney* is like a mild sausage on a stick. People used to dip it in a sweet batter and fry it until it became a bread shell over the sausage. Then they would dip it in mustard. I've heard they were delicious. To say, 'like mustard on a carney' simply means that it's all over it, in a good way."

At the explanation, Ingrid laughed even harder. "Darling, that's not a carney, that's a corned dog. They didn't use dog meat or anything, that was just a weird name for the sausage. But the batter was made of cornmeal."

Dhabi looked like an embarrassed child. "I guess you know everything then."

Ingrid contained her laughter and put her palm to Dhabi's cheek. "I'm sorry. But I just couldn't help myself."

Annie laughed, too. She was glad to see Dhabi and Ingrid back on friendly terms. "Isn't there such a thing as a carney, then? What is that?"

Ingrid blinked several times, trying to maintain a more serious expression. "A carney is someone who works at a carnival or circus. They're not usually the main act or star of the show, but they set up the show, keep it running, and then tear it all down when it's over." She looked around the table and grinned. "It's us. We're all carnies. Maybe not Annie, but the rest of us."

Bull started with a slow, deep laugh that grew into rolling guffaws. "Daisy, get the mustard."

Soon everyone at the table was laughing, even Dhabi. He reached out to touch Ingrid's face, and she quieted her giggles. He looked into her eyes. "You are beautiful. That's undeniable."

Annie stared down at her hands, suddenly uncomfortable at the intimacy being shared in front of everyone.

Dhabi shook his head. "I want to ask you something, Ingrid. I don't want to fight. I want to understand. I want to know what I'm facing."

"I'll answer any question you ask."

"If you are one hundred and twenty-six years old, how old will you—what is your...?"

"When I was twelve, the doctors said that I had a life expectancy of two hundred years. But when I escaped the hospital, along with a few other test subjects, the estimate had increased to about three hundred fifty years. By my approximations, that's pretty close." Ingrid's lips twitched as if she couldn't find the right position. "The current life expectancy on Earth is about fifty-two years, and mine is nearly seven times that."

"Like human-to-dog years," Annie said.

Ingrid nodded. "Yes, about that." Her face suddenly changed, and she turned toward Cody.

Cody looked up at Ingrid and their gazes locked together like lasers. They jumped up from the table and ran out the door, leaving Annie and Dhabi dumbfounded.

Dhabi glanced at the others. "What was that? Did I miss something?"

Jake and Bull both grimaced, and then a look of realization overtook them, too. Jake stood swiftly, nearly up turning his chair. "That's how they're going to do it!" He took Annie in his arms and lifted her to her feet. "Come on, both of you. Let's go."

Dhabi stood, and Bull motioned for them all to head out.

Annie followed Jake. "What are you talking about?"

"They're going to save your dog, Love."

EPISODE 16

They Call It Puppy Love

Annie watched Cody prepare Ingrid for the blood draw. The blonde leaned back in a chair and began pumping her fist to raise a vein. Cody nodded and after another minute, pushed a needle into the bend of Ingrid's elbow, and the scarlet flow began. Dhabi had been sitting at her side to comfort her, but when his face started to lose color, Ingrid told him to go outside for a breath of air.

Annie turned her attention to Buffalo. He was still in the tube, and now all the lights on the control panel were blinking red. He had to come out right away.

"I have everything ready for him, Annie." Cody motioned to another chair. "I want you to sit here beside the table so he can feel your touch and hear your voice."

Annie took a seat but resisted. "I want to hold him."

Cody leaned close to her. "It may be hard to watch. He may try to bite if he has the strength."

"I'm holding him."

Cody stretched his shoulders, and Annie guessed that she was causing him more tension than she should, but she couldn't help it.

"Okay, you can hold him. But you have to commit to it. You can't say you're going to hold him and then change your mind if it becomes too much for you." Cody raised his brow as he held a full syringe between them.

"I can do it. What is that?" Annie sat back in the chair,

making as much room in her lap as she could. "That's not gonna hurt him, is it?"

Cody shook his head. "No. This is just to help with his immune system. I can't give him much. He's still a small pup."

Jake, Dhabi, and Bull stood at the counter near the doorway. They wanted to help at Cody's behest, but they didn't want to be in the way. One of Bull's ranch hands was overseeing Ingrid's withdrawal. "Smooth as silk," the young man said with a whistle.

Cody nodded to Ingrid. "You feeling okay?"

Ingrid smiled back. "It's been a long time, but I've always been good at giving blood."

Annie turned to her friend. "Thank you, Ingrid. I'm sorry I've been such a bellyacher. I sincerely wish I was more like you."

Ingrid shook her head. "Please don't pin all your hopes on me. I do have some pretty great sauce in me, but I'll be praying right beside you that it makes a difference."

Yes, prayer. Annie took a deep breath and calmed her thoughts. "Lord, thank you for your mercy and your protection. Thank you for my skilled brother and for the dear folks you've knit all around us. You are mighty, and you are sovereign. Lord, I ask an extra measure of mercy on Cody, Ingrid, and on Buffalo. May we always walk in your Way. Amen."

"Amen," said Ingrid and the others in a single voice.

It was time.

Cody put the syringe in its place on the tray, and moved the pod to the side of the exam table, closest to Annie. He punched at the buttons on the end until the lights turned solid red. The end made a popping sound, like when a vacuum-sealed bottle is opened. Cody moved his stethoscope over the dog's barrel chest and nodded.

Annie looked for the rise and fall of his tiny body as he took his first breath outside the tube, but she couldn't see anything moving at all. Cody picked up the pup and placed him gently into Annie's arms.

"Is he alive?"

"He is." Cody moved his front paws to position them for easier access. "He's barely hanging on. You should talk to him. Sing to him or something."

Tears dimmed Annie's vision as she held her little love. "You are my sunshine, my only sunshine." She choked out the words as Cody poked a tiny needle into the top of his leg, just above his paw.

He got the first pint of Ingrid's blood flowing from the IV stand and then secured the port with medical tape.

"Please don't take my sunshine away." Annie's voice trailed away as she licked salty tears from her lips.

Cody looked up at Ingrid, who was just finishing her second pint. "Do you think I can get one more from you?"

She nodded. "When I was a young girl, they had me giving four pints a day. I'll be fine."

Annie turned her face to Cody. "Is it working?"

"We won't know for sure for a little while."

Dhabi seemed to gather the courage to go back to Ingrid's side. "Why exactly might this work? What makes her blood so different than anyone else's?"

Cody didn't look up from his work as he took the second unit and placed it carefully on the stand next to the first, half-drained pint. "First, Ingrid's blood was engineered to be universally accepted by any recipient. That's why we didn't have to do any of the basic preliminary tests. Also, it was designed, on the molecular level, to resist oxidation. Oxidation is the process that causes humans to age. It affects our whole body, inside and out. She will still age, but because her blood—which carries the oxygen to every system—is so resistant, she ages at a much slower pace than the rest of us."

"And this helps the dog how?" Dhabi squinted his eyes and crossed his arms over his chest.

"It's difficult to explain, but in simple terms, the blood should work like a booster for his whole system. I'll alternate saline and blood until he responds. He hasn't shown any adverse effects yet, so I'm feeling hopeful."

Annie shifted her arms slightly to keep her fingers from falling asleep. "When will we know?"

Cody laughed. "We have to be patient, and you need to be still."

"He hasn't moved at all." Annie leaned over the dog to see his eyes. "Shouldn't he be waking up soon?"

Cody shook his head. "I gave him a mild sedative with the antibiotics as I was putting in his IV. I want him to wake up slowly so that he doesn't pull or chew at his line."

Annie sat back and sighed. "I'm sure glad you know what you're doing."

Dhabi, Ingrid, and Bull went back to the main house for the night, wishing the others luck. Cody monitored Buffalo's slow progress. He placed a lead on the dog's chest that sent a signal back to a heart monitor. Soon it was beeping at a strong and steady pace. Jake moved a chair next to Annie's and put his arm around her shoulder as she held the pup.

"You should go on to bed," she whispered as she let her head rest against his arm. She didn't want him to leave, but she didn't want to be selfish, either.

"I'll go when you do." Jake combed his fingers through her hair. "Not until then."

Cody yawned and stretched. "You should probably both go get some rest." He thumped his finger on the second bag of saline. "I'm going to start the last pint. I believe he'll make it, but I don't think he's going to wake anytime soon."

Annie shook her head. "I don't want to leave him until he wakes up."

The door opened, and Rebecca entered the room with a tray of juice and coffee. "Daisy wanted me to bring these over." She handed Cody a mug of steaming black liquid. "What can I do to help?"

Cody took the mug, and Annie noticed that her brother laced his fingers with Rebecca's for several seconds in the exchange. He smiled and thanked her. "I could use a hand getting a kennel ready for him."

"Sure thing." Rebecca went to the raised wire crate against the wall and opened the latched door. "Looks like they've had rabbits in here. I'll get it cleaned out."

Annie watched Cody and Rebecca work together to get the small crate prepared for her dog. "How long will he have to stay in there?"

Cody shrugged. "Won't know until he wakes up. Maybe a day or even a week."

Annie shook her head. "Well, I ain't leaving Georgetown without my dog."

Jake shifted in his chair without removing his arm from Annie's shoulder. "We have to consider all our options, Love. We want to keep your animals in the safest place for them. If that's with us on the ship, or if it's here with the Dales, we'll do whatever is best for them."

Annie stared Jake down. "I ain't leaving my dog. Period."

Jake raised his brows and deferred to Cody.

Cody blinked slowly, and Annie knew he was exhausted. She felt the tug of sleep in her eyes, too, but she didn't want to give in at a moment of weakness.

Cody just shook his head. "I won't make you leave Buffalo. No matter what."

"Good."

"But I will make you go on to bed." Cody checked the monitor again before switching to the last unit of blood. "I think he's going to be fine. I won't leave him tonight. I promise."

"I'm not tired." Annie shifted in her chair. "And Jake's here to keep me company."

Cody held out a blanket toward the dog. "Nope. We're going to wrap him up in this for now. Rebecca and I will hold him until after he's done with his IV, and I'll keep the monitor on him until he wakes. You're still recovering, and I won't let you spend the whole night in a chair."

Rebecca handed Annie a glass of juice. "Drink this. It will help. And I'll come to get you in the morning. Daisy has your room all ready for you."

Annie tried to resist, but when she drank the juice, she could feel a tingling sensation in her fingers and toes, and she felt a terrible urge to stretch out and sleep. "If *anything* bad happens..."

"It won't." Cody furrowed his brow in the stern expression of their father.

"But if it does?"

Rebecca reached out for her hand. "Then, I'll be pounding at your door and dragging you down the stairs."

Annie wrapped the warm blanket around her beloved dog. Cody scooped him up with a firm but gentle motion, placing him on the examination table. Jake helped her to her feet and to the door.

"Wait," Rebecca said, slipping out of her coat. "It's turned much colder, and the wind has picked up. Take my jacket."

Jake held the jacket while Annie slipped his arms into the sleeves. "I'll get her to her room."

Cody placed a firm hand on Jake's shoulder. "And then you'll get to your own room."

"Yes, sir." Jake smiled at Annie.

Rebecca laughed. "And don't tarry, either. Daisy will be after you both before you can see her coming."

Annie looped her arm around Jake's and shrugged. "Y'all haven't heard, I guess. Jake won't even kiss me again 'til I make him a marksman. I'm afraid I'll be older than Ingrid before that happens."

Jake saluted Cody, and then took Annie through the black night wind to the guest house.

Once inside, Annie shivered and then shook herself out of Rebecca's coat. "It's freezing out there." She hung the jacket on the hook behind the door. "I'm leaving this here so that I don't forget to get it back to her."

Jake took her hand. "Then shall I carry you up to your bed, fair lass?"

"No, you shall not!" Daisy's voice boomed behind them, and they both jumped.

Annie's hand slapped over her mouth to stifle the ready scream. Jake released a shaky gasp and gripped the back of a nearby chair to steady himself.

Daisy continued with a trace of a smile curling her lips. "I will take Annie up to her room. You, sir, will remain down here until I return and release you to your quarters. Is that clear?"

"Absolutely clear, Mrs. Dale." Jake bowed slightly forward. "And thank you for doing this for me. She can be terribly demanding."

Daisy shook her head and ignored him as he rambled a few more silly offerings. She took Annie's arm and helped her up the stairs to her room.

Annie looked around and sighed. The bedroom was simple but elegant. Everything was white or coral pink. The high window over the bed was draped with white lace curtains tied back with pink ribbons. The space was easily twice as big as the bedroom where she grew up.

"You have your own bath right through this door, and your clothes are hanging in the closet in there." Daisy gestured from one door to another. "There's some milk in the cooler in this cabinet and some chocolate on the nightstand. Don't eat too much chocolate right before bed, though. It'll make you sick."

Annie felt like a princess. Never before had she seen such accommodations, let alone stayed in them. "Thank you, Daisy. This is beautiful. I'm sure I'll sleep well."

"Sleep is what you need, dear. Don't wander through the house and get yourself in trouble. Understand?" Daisy stood at the door, wringing her hands and scanning the room for anything she might have forgotten.

"Yes, ma'am."

As soon as Daisy left her, Annie went right to the bath to prepare for bed. Her thoughts jumped from Jake to Buffalo to Cody to Daisy and back to Jake. She was too tired to focus on anyone or anything for very long. As soon as her head hit her pillow, she was dreaming.

Singing to Buffalo, dancing with Jake, riding Ranger

through the field behind her home in Texas, and finally flying through the night on her motorcycle. Someone was chasing her. Authority. His flashing lights grew closer. She could hear Buffalo whimpering. The sound turned into sirens. Authority was right there, inches from the back wheel of her bike.

BUMP!

Annie woke up on the floor. This bed was twice the size of her bed back home, and four times as big as the one she'd slept in for the last month, and she still fell out.

On the bright side, the thorough jostle woke her completely. Annie jumped to her feet and dressed as though her Prince Charming waited for her downstairs. It was almost true. Annie's strength was nearly back, and despite the sudden tumble, she felt balanced and determined.

She hurried down the stairs and out the front door of the guest house, not stopping to rouse Jake or anyone else. The morning sky in Georgetown glowed like the golden flesh of a peach, and to Annie, it smelled just as sweet. She bounded through the doors of the barn, bumping into Cody and Rebecca, who were engaged in a kiss.

"Whoa, girl." Cody spun around to face his sister as a bright pink flushed through his cheeks. "Slow up. You're going to hurt someone."

Annie's brows raised high on her forehead as she regarded them, but she soon turned her attention to the metal crate against the wall. "How is he this morning?"

"Still asleep." Cody gestured to the pup. "But, you're welcome to peek in."

Annie skipped to the crate and pulled back the blanket covering the box. At first, all she could see was another blanket. After a little more light had crept into the bed, Buffalo raised his head and whined.

"My precious Buff!" Annie didn't wait for permission to open the door. She released the latch and scooped up the dog with one quick motion. "Can I take him for a walk?"

Cody nodded and gestured to the door. "Don't take him

far. And gather up his business when he's done. I need to run a couple of tests."

Annie scrunched her nose. "That's nasty."

"That's medicine."

Grabbing a plastic bag from her brother's hand and winking at Rebecca on the way out the door, Annie carried the dog to the little stretch of grass at the side of the barn.

She scratched Buffalo's ears and set him on the soft grass. "I missed you, puppy." She sat against the barn wall and waited for the dog to relieve himself. She gathered up his droppings into the bag and sealed the closure carefully.

"May I help?" Jake asked, coming around the side of the building.

Annie handed Jake the baggie. "You can take this inside to my brother."

Jake scowled when he realized what he was holding. "Yeah, I'll do that." Jake left with the bag and returned a minute later. "I didn't hear you leave the house this morning."

"I was too excited to wait. I had to come out and see my little man." She plopped down on the grass where the pup was playing.

Jake joined her. "Maybe I'm a little jealous."

Annie patted her chest until Buffalo climbed up to lick her chin. "You wish you could be shot by Authority and spend a month in a coma in a pod?"

Jake shook his head and scratched at Buffalo's belly. "I think you know what I mean, Love."

Annie sniffed and held her dog close. "You're the one who wanted to wait until you were a marksman. It wasn't me."

"Maybe I've changed my mind?" Jake tugged at her hair and leaned closer.

Annie shook her head. "No, you were right. We shouldn't be rushing things." She picked up Buffalo and stood, barely waiting for Jake to get up, too. "I should take him back inside."

Annie waited as Jake held open the door. She carried the dog to where Cody was tapping at a data screen. "How is he doing?"

Cody shrugged. "Everything looks good. He needs to rest, though. Put him back in the kennel for now, and we'll get him out again this afternoon."

"Can't he just stay with me?" Annie snuggled Buffalo under her chin. "I promise to take perfect care of him."

"Nope. He needs rest. You do, too."

Rebecca entered from a storage closet near the back door, carrying a basket of linens. "I just checked on Ingrid. She's well this morning."

Annie smiled and tilted her head as she addressed her brother. "Please?"

Cody shook his head. "Let Buffalo recuperate for a while. You can play with him more this afternoon."

Annie was reluctant but finally put the pup back into his bed and closed the door. Buffalo didn't whimper. He nosed at the blanket, and then after turning three circles, he plopped down and closed his eyes. Annie felt better about leaving him.

She turned back to Cody. "Then am I clear to ride and shoot?"

Cody frowned. "You shouldn't overdo."

"And I won't."

Rebecca finished putting away the linens and stood at Annie's side. "I can make sure she doesn't do too much."

Cody shot a glance toward Jake. "They're ganging up on me."

Jake shrugged. "Not the worst problem to have."

Cody laughed. "What about you?"

Jake glanced at Annie and back to Cody. "If Annie starts to look tired at all, I'll take her back to her room." He stopped short. "I mean, I'll have Rebecca take her to her...to the house."

Cody laughed again. "You know, Jake, you've got it easy. You just have to go through me. If our father were still alive, he'd make you dance."

Annie nodded. "It's true. Daddy was protective of me. He'd usually give in after a while. But only if it was something I really wanted."

Jake and Cody both looked uncomfortable, and when Annie noticed, she redirected the conversation.

"And I really want to teach them both how to shoot." Annie batted her lashes against Cody's frown.

He furrowed his brow. "Get something to eat first." He looked up at Rebecca. "And not more than an hour or two at most."

Rebecca nodded.

Cody continued. "And only a gentle ride. Nothing extreme. No tricks and no racing."

Annie saluted. "Yessir." She kissed her brother on the cheek. "I'll be good. Promise." She linked elbows with Rebecca and headed to the door. "Should we bring you some breakfast?"

"I ate. But thanks."

Annie and Jake sat at the small table in the guest house as Rebecca brought out a plate of eggs. "The protein should help," she said with a nod to each of them. "I'll get the range set up with targets and ammo. You two come out when you're finished eating."

Annie and Jake cleaned their plates and washed up the dishes in a matter of minutes.

Jake grabbed her hand as she placed the last cup on the shelf. "All games aside, I'm glad you're well, and I'm glad you have your dog back." He leaned his lips close to her ear. "I can't wait until after my gun lesson."

Annie took a step away and turned to face him with an amused grin. "How many lessons have you had so far?"

Jake puffed a breath through his nose. "A few, but you said that I had natural talent."

"You do." She put her hands on her hips, requiring another step away to keep from poking Jake with an elbow. "But natural talent is raw. My daddy always said that talent is refined with practice. Someone with good aim can become a marksman with practice. You can probably hit the target six or seven times in ten shots. With practice, you'll be able to hit the bullseye every time."

"How much practice will that take? For me to hit the bullseye every time?"

Annie sighed and turned away from Jake and toward the door. "I guess that depends on how bad you wanna be kissed."

EPISODE 17

Time to Get a Gun

At the far end of the property, Annie and Jake found Rebecca lining up ammo boxes and long guns on a table under an awning. Just beyond was a berm of soil with straw bales fixed with paper targets. Annie blinked, astonished by the volume of munitions.

"Where did all of this come from?" Annie asked.

"I suppose I'll get my practice today." Jake's broad smile and sideways glance sent a warm rush through Annie's belly.

"This isn't all for you and me." Rebecca regarded the table and then nodded to a small storage building to the side of the awning. "Those folks would like a lesson, too."

Annie looked over to see more than a dozen people lined up along the side of the building. "I can't. How could I?"

Rebecca shook her head as if she was only asking a small favor. "Most of them know how to shoot. They just need a refresher to help with accuracy. They just want to know that they can do what needs to be done if a bad situation arises."

Annie swallowed hard. The air weighed heavy on her shoulders. "They wouldn't even need this if not for me."

Jake patted her shoulder. "Don't think like that. Authority takes everything it can. Chews it up and spits it out. Georgetown has long been a target. This isn't because of you, Love. But you can give these people a fighting chance."

Rebecca agreed. "He's right. The Essex and Lisbon colonies are already under Authority control. They have been for nearly a year. Those people banned all weapons and didn't have the confidence or the means to stand up for their independence. We do—with your help."

Annie drew a deep breath. "Well, come on then."

In a matter of 90 minutes, Annie had everyone in the group hitting the target and reloading in quick succession. Rebecca and Jake both improved their aim as well, but as the temperature rose with the sun, Annie's stamina wore thin. She sat on the grass and watched for a few minutes.

Jake approached her after taking his last shot—a bullseye. "Did you see that one?"

Annie looked up and nodded. Jake placed his gun back on the table and hurried to her side. "Are you okay? You look exhausted."

"I'm alright. It's a little warmer than I expected." Annie smiled, but her bottom lip quivered.

Jake waved to Rebecca. "I'm taking her back for a rest. Do you think you can manage without us?"

"Sure." Rebecca helped Annie to her feet. "Are you sick?"

Annie shook her head. "I'm fine. I don't have to go back."

Rebecca waggled her finger at Annie. "Yes, you do. I don't want your brother scolding me for letting you get worn."

Jake cinched his arm around Annie's waist. "I should have been keeping a closer watch. I'll get her back to the house."

Rebecca pulled out her personal com. "I'll let Daisy know you're on your way." She nodded and went back to take care of the others at the table.

Jake walked with slow and steady paces, leading Annie down the dirt road that tied each piece of the Dale property together. "Let me know if I'm going too fast."

Annie liked being in his arms but didn't want to feel babied. "I can walk on my own, Jake."

He loosened his hold. Annie took a step out of his arm but reached out for his hand. He gave her hand a squeeze. "We should be more careful. While Georgetown is a great deal like Earth, these temperature variations can wear on your system when you're not used to them."

"I'll be fine."

"And the stress isn't just physical, is it? You've had an ocean of people putting all their weight on you. For all sorts of reasons. You've hardly had a chance to catch your breath." Jake walked her up the steps to the porch.

"Can we sit out here for a bit?" Annie didn't wait for Jake's answer. She dropped herself on the top step. "It's cool in the shade."

Jake poked his head into the house and exchanged a word with Daisy before taking a seat beside Annie. "She's making you something to drink. She'll be out in a moment."

Annie nodded without thinking. "I'm not the only one, you know?"

Jake looked confused. "The only one what?"

Annie wrapped her arms around her knees and bent her face down for a second before looking up at him again. "You baby me because of all the stress and pressure of all this. But we're all in the same situation. Cody and I wanted to save my horses, so we ran. Took all our stuff and bought passage off-planet. Dhabi is a victim, too. As much from us as from Authority."

"You didn't shoot him in the shoulder."

"No, but that was because he agreed to carry us. He'd never had faced a pulser if not for us." She sighed. "And poor Ingrid. Dhabi wouldn't have even met her if not for us. She's been trying to stay under the radar for a century, and we come along and drag her into a spotlight." Annie shook her head and slowly lifted her gaze to meet Jake's. "And you."

"Shut up." Jake drew a sharp breath.

"Because of me, you lost everything but the clothes on your back." She took his hands in hers. "I'm sorry, Jake."

"Just shut up about that. I didn't lose anything."

Annie started again. "But you lost your work, your friends. Because of me, you lost your home."

Jake pulled her close and kissed her. When he finally let her go, he said, "I haven't lost anything. I found you."

Annie blinked and swallowed hard. "But I'm…"

"Do I have to shut you up again?"

"Yes, please."

He started to pull her body close again, but Daisy interrupted. "I have drinks for you both." She set two glasses of pale pink liquid on the railing beside Jake. "That is—if your lips are available." She laughed and went back inside.

Jake handed Annie a glass and took one for himself. "Listen to me, Love. Yes, you and your situation may be the catalyst for the chain of events in which we find ourselves. But that doesn't mean you are to blame."

Annie sipped a long slow draught of the sweet juice. "I'm not sure everyone is as forgiving as you."

Jake leaned back against the porch post. "Don't be such a martyr. What do you think we've been talking about ever since you passed out on the ship? We understand how life works. It's about time you did, too."

Annie stiffened. "You all have been talking about me?"

Jake scoffed and looked at the porch ceiling. "My mother used to tell a story about a young woman who'd been chosen from all the peasants in a vast kingdom to become the queen. The king was mighty and had a terrible temper, but he loved the queen with all his heart and would do anything for her. One day the queen overheard a plot to kill all of her peasant family. She was afraid to confront the king about it because of his temper. She went to her advisor and asked what she should do."

Annie laughed. "I know this story. She was reminded that she did not become queen because of anything she had done, but that her position had been given to her. She was told that maybe she'd been given her place for the purpose of saving her family. And if she ignored that responsibility, well then, she would be ignoring her opportunity to save others."

"Mum told me that she'd made the story up from her imagination. How do you know it?" Jake leaned forward, almost studying her.

Annie felt her lips curve into a smile. "My mother told me

the same story. It's from the Bible. Queen Esther. She went to the king and exposed the plot and saved her people."

Jake nodded. "Yes, Annie. And these are your people." He gestured to the make-shift shooting range, but Annie understood who he meant.

"I'm certainly no queen." She took another drink, hiding behind her glass.

"You are to them. They will follow your lead." He waited for a minute and then took her drink from her hand, setting it back on the railing. "I will follow you. Anywhere."

Annie was about to protest when Ingrid rushed toward them from the main house. Cody and Dhabi followed close behind. A bell began to ring from somewhere in the distance.

"We just got news from the dock station. Authority ships, at least three of them, landing immediately. They'll be here directly." Ingrid reported as if she was ready to take orders.

Annie looked to Jake, but he seemed to be waiting for her to give direction. Even Cody and Dhabi were focused on her. Panic rushed through her bones and muscles. She didn't want to be anyone's leader. She didn't want to let anyone down. She didn't want to get anyone hurt. These were her friends. Her family. All the people she loved.

Rebecca now joined them, leading the small crowd from the gun range. She stopped just short of the porch steps. "I've explained what's happening to our group, and they've all called their families and staff. Everyone is ready for a fight."

Annie took a deep breath. She realized this was hers to do, whether she liked it or not. But she'd never had to face anything like this alone before. She looked to her brother, to Dhabi, to Ingrid, to Jake, and finally to Rebecca. Another realization swelled in her heart and in her mind.

She stood to face the growing crowd. "We are not alone in this. We have each other." She more quietly addressed Cody. "Remember how Daddy used to tell us about the Battle of New Orleans?"

Cody nodded. "That's it. Good girl."

She raised her voice. "Back on Earth, several hundred years ago, there was a fierce battle that took place in a swamp area called New Orleans. A few hundred men faced thousands and defeated them because they knew the land, they had the right skills and weapons for the fight, and they had the courage and patience to wait until the enemy was close enough to spit on. They were a bunch of pirates and sharpshooters—much like us. The enemy was a great army, wanting to conquer and control. Sound familiar?"

A few laughs drifted up from the crowd. Annie glanced at Jake, who nodded and smiled.

"You all are our core. Assemble in the barn in five minutes, and we'll launch our plan." Annie nodded to the others around her. "Let's take a moment to organize. We're about to go to war."

EPISODE 18

Running Battle

Rebecca and Ingrid both juggled calls on their coms and messages from new arrivals. Cody and Annie explained the strategy to a few dozen squad leaders, sending them out as soon as they understood their objectives. Dhabi and Jake organized the weaponry.

"Stay where you are and be ready. We can't be sure Authority will only attack in one area. Best if we're prepared everywhere." Rebecca clicked off one call to answer another.

Ingrid put her com away and gestured to one of the hands at the door. "We need to secure the animals. Bring everything in, and lock the doors. We should post guards on every side of the barn."

Annie listened and then interrupted. "Wait. We should use the animals. The horses, anyway. They can be significant assets in a fight. The rider stays above the chaos and has a better vantage point. They can outrun a man in a sprint; they're more stealthy than a vehicle."

Everyone turned to focus on Annie. Dhabi asked, "I thought that's what this was all about. Protecting the horses. And now you want to put them in danger?"

"It's not just about my horses. It's about everything you hold dear. Authority takes and destroys at whim. Look at Ingrid. They'll have her dissected tonight if they win." Annie grimaced in Ingrid's direction, hoping she hadn't offended her friend.

Ingrid shook it off with a nod and then added to Annie's

suggestion. "Look in the mirror, Dhabi. They hurt you. They nearly took your ship."

"We're outlaws." Dhabi shrugged, and Annie could see the guilt in his tired eyes.

She couldn't let him take any more blame. "You took pity on my family and agreed to carry us off-planet. You didn't do it to snub Authority. You didn't do it to break the law. You did it because you have a compassionate heart. You had plenty of opportunities to turn us in and collect reward money. Instead, you protected us. You didn't do that because you're an outlaw. You did it because it was the right thing to do."

Ingrid shook her head. "We don't have time to discuss right or wrong. Authority is on the road now. Dhabi, are you willing to fight at my side?"

"Yes, of course."

Annie watched as Ingrid marched toward the door. "May I have Liza Jane?" the blonde asked.

Annie nodded. "She'll take good care of you." She watched as Ingrid saddled the buckskin and led her to the sliding doors.

Ingrid grabbed Dhabi's hand. "Let's go."

Rebecca picked up her weapons and motioned to the others. "Mount up quickly, and let's get out there. We have folks all over the hillside ready to fight. And take a wrap with you. It will get cold quickly."

Cody and Annie helped saddle the other horses. Rebecca took Charlotte, and Cody climbed on Nero. A couple of ranch hands took the remaining ponies, and Jake pulled himself up on Stubbs. Annie led Jefferson to the edge of the room and knelt down to kiss Buffalo in his kennel. "I love you, boy. You wait for me here, eh. I'll be back soon."

She spoke to the other men about defending the barn and the main house as she closed and bolted the door behind her. "Hold your positions as long as you can. Don't fire until you can see their faces, then let them have it."

"Yes, ma'am," they answered together and then disappeared into their posts.

Cody and Rebecca moved to the south side of the property, and Jake and Annie rode to the north. Annie heard a little crackle at her shoulder. "Coms open." Jake's voice, nearly in a whisper.

A dozen responses answered with, "Open."

Annie and Jake found a tall, thick hedge along the road for their station and positioned their mounts side by side, facing opposite directions. Annie could watch the road leading to the main house. Jake could see as far as the stream. Everyone was in place.

"Lord, give us strength and courage to protect your creation. Let us always champion for right and keep ourselves clear of evil. Hide us under your wing." She prayed for another minute, and Jake listened, keeping a sharp eye on the road.

"Four squads coming to you," hummed Bull's voice through the com. "I'll close it up."

Annie and Jake watched four platoons of Authority soldiers march down the road. Annie tried to count the men, but gave it up after a few minutes, guessing there were more than two hundred, all armed with pulsers.

Jake nodded toward the back of the line of soldiers, where Annie's man marched. Annie searched until she found him. He was the devil that shot her dog. He was the one who shot Dhabi. He was hers alone.

Her heart pounded in her chest, and she was sure that Jake could hear it. Sweat formed on her brow, and her ears burned. She dared not move a muscle as the troops passed by. She was afraid to look directly at her man for fear that he would feel the glare from her eyes.

"Right here." Bull's voice buzzed again softly, and Annie caught a glimpse of him moving in the brush behind the last soldier. It was their cue. Jake and Annie followed the soldiers from a camouflaged position in the woods.

Though she couldn't see him, Annie knew Bull was mirroring their position from the other side of the road. They waited and followed.

Annie's stomach ached with anticipation. She knew that

once the first shot sounded, there would be no going back. Authority troops were known for keeping formation for as long as possible. The Georgetown fighters would have to wait until the enemy broke up to search. They would have to get close. Annie couldn't fire until she was nearly face to face with her target.

The colonists hid silently in the woods, patiently allowing the troops to pass. They were ready to close the gap at the signal.

Authority forces marched closer toward the big house. Annie knew it was a risk to let them so near, but the houses gave the colonists higher ground. Just another minute.

A pop sounded in the distance, followed by a long, low whistle. Annie watched as the small ball of light and smoke raced out of the sky and into the center of the troops' formation. The men scrambled in every direction as the small firebomb exploded and shot tiny pieces of rocks and shrapnel on impact.

The ranks were broken, and the soldiers scurried for cover. Annie could hear the Authority officers yelling into their coms. Several orders were cut short as soon as the gunfire began.

Loud pops and bangs erupted all around. Pulsers shrieked as Authority returned fire. Smoke rose from the brush, and a few small blazes began in the dry grass on the fringes of the road.

Annie kept watch on her man. She was able to pick off a few others as they fired blindly in her direction, but she was determined not to lose sight of him.

Suddenly the hum of light transports approached. The back-ups had arrived. The colonists had the advantage of the trees. The small hoverbikes couldn't maneuver through the dense brush.

What the colonists didn't have were heat-sensitive scopes. The Authority troops on the bikes dropped scopes to the ground soldiers and took a few soldiers on board with them. One could drive, and the other could find targets and fire. Pulsers were accurate up to sixty feet, with a sharp drop beyond that. The colonist's long guns had much better range and accuracy.

Gunfire sounded in every direction. As the soldiers

scattered, the colonists engaged. From the corner of her eye, she saw Jake ride Stubbs into the road and chase two troops into the brush on the other side.

Over her com, Annie heard moans and yells. Some sounded triumphant. Others rattled into nothingness.

She couldn't let fear control her. Instead, she listened to her daddy's voice echo in her mind. *Keep steady. Stand your ground. Let the enemy come to you.*

All around her was chaos. Screaming, smoke, dirt, fire, moans. Gunfire rattled, and pulsers shrieked. Annie heard none of it, now. Only Daddy's voice.

Annie chose a target. Followed with her sights. Fired. She watched them fall, then turned to the next target.

Her man was on the move now. She stayed in the shadow of the trees, gripping Jefferson's lean body between her knees. The horse moved smoothly, not affected by the noise, obeying Annie's silent commands.

Back-ups had stopped coming. Several of the hoverbikes were scattered in pieces on the road. The ones that still worked had retreated out of sight, probably to the main ship.

The main ship. It was a problem. Who knew how many more troops were on board? Had they already called for reinforcements? There were less than 25,000 colonists in Georgetown. Authority could match that number if the battle went on for a week or two. If it dragged out longer than that— if Authority decided to make an example of their little rebellion, they could double the number of troops. Or more.

No. Annie couldn't let that happen. This had to end today.

"Do we have eyes on the primary vessel?" Annie asked into her com, risking her position.

"Affirmative." Ingrid's voice crackled. "Dhabi and I are within striking distance. What is the status on the road?"

"Authority troops down and in retreat at my position." Annie watched her man scramble over his fallen comrades, picking weapons and gear from their bodies. He ignored the cries of the injured and stole whatever he thought might be useful. "Can you access enemy communication?"

"They have issued official retreat. There have been no transmissions beyond—hold. I'm getting something." Ingrid's tone was low and cautious.

Annie watched her man as he scanned the road for friends or foe. She wanted him to run back to his ship like the coward he was, but she also hoped he would come to her.

"Annie, the primary vessel has been ordered to leave Georgetown. I can't tell you more yet."

"Is there an opportunity to disable the vessel? Keep it grounded?" Annie asked.

"Possibly. Dhabi and I will try. Keep the fight." Ingrid's voice faded to static.

"Under heavy fire at my position. Help is appreciated." Bull's voice sounded frantic.

"Coming to you." Annie didn't recognize that voice.

In the distance, she could hear another burst of pulser blasts, followed by a barrage of gunfire. The two distinct sounds volleyed back and forth, growing louder as Annie followed her man. He stayed in the road, keeping his body close to the ground, making his way toward the main ship. She couldn't let him leave.

A pulser burst shot past her, splintering a tree branch behind her. She spun in her saddle to return fire. She only dared fire one shot. As another burst flashed at her side, and she squeezed her trigger. One bang. The soldier fell with a yelp.

It was enough. Her man ran to the other side of the road and took cover in the brush.

"Jake, what is your position?" Annie scanned the greenery for any sign of Stubbs. She couldn't find her horse. No response from Jake.

Moving a little closer to the road, Annie was careful to stay behind the first row of trees. She could see movement on the other side of the path, but couldn't make out if it was friendly or if it was her man. Crossing the open thoroughfare wasn't an option here. She needed to go a little farther, to the bend, where there would be more cover. She needed to get back into it. She needed to do her share.

Annie looked deep into the woods behind her and then back toward the house. She saw a line of colonists, shoulder to shoulder, guns raised, crossing from one side of the drive to the other, melting into the forest. Their determination fortified her resolve. It was time to join them.

Digging her heels into Jefferson's sides, she held her rifle at the ready. She enjoyed a moment of sunlight on her face and then narrowed her gaze once back in the shadows. Pops and whistles in the distance became thunder and lightning as she approached the last of the fighting.

"Jake, can you hear me?" she whispered into her com.

A soldier jumped into view with his pulser leveled at her head. He didn't have a chance to discharge before she dropped him in where he stood.

Two more charged her. Her rifle clicked empty. No time to reload. She let the gun fall on its strap and pulled her pistols from her sides. One shot, then another. Just like the green balloons.

But there was still no word from Jake. She pushed forward. As the gunfire grew louder, the smell of smoke saturated the trees. Closer to the last skirmish, she could hear a soldier yell, "Retreat! Back to the ship!" More gunfire and his voice fell silent.

She saw a handful of soldiers running through the trees. No need to shoot. No need to chase.

"Jake, can you hear me? What is your position?" She was pleading now.

"Ten meters in front of you," said the voice in her com. It wasn't Jake's voice.

Annie's heart slammed against her ribcage. Fear and fury competed for control of her body. Her pistols shook in her hands.

Holding her breath, Annie approached cautiously, unsure what she would find. A fog of smoke slithered around Jefferson's legs as he treaded over the uneven ground. Coming around another stand of thick-trunked trees, Annie saw him. She saw them both.

Authority held Jake by a shock of his dark hair. He had a pulser tucked under Jake's jaw. Annie saw at least two charred wounds on Jake's body. One on his upper left shoulder, the other on his leg, just above his right knee. Stubbs was on his side on the ground.

"You need to stop where you are and drop your pistols, Miss Birchfield." He pulled up on Jake's hair, forcing his head back. "Drop them, or I will drop him."

"Shoot him, Annie. Don't worry about me." Jake's voice was hoarse.

"I'm not playing games." Authority glared at Annie. "I have nothing left to lose. What about you?"

"Don't hurt him." Annie slid down from her saddle and tossed her pistols at the man's feet. "This isn't about him. It's about me. You want revenge on me."

The man scoffed. "You think this is about revenge? How selfish you are." He twisted Jake's hair tighter, turning his head to face Annie squarely. "How can you care for a girl like this? Selfish and manipulating. She prefers her animals to people."

"I am selfish," Annie said, holding up her palms in surrender. "I have blood on my hands that will never wash off. Please don't add his." She reached out toward Jake. "Please don't add his."

"His blood is already on your hands, little girl. I don't have to waste another shot on him. He's dead now. He just doesn't know it yet."

Annie took another step toward the men. She didn't know if what Authority said was true or just to torture her. She couldn't take the chance. "Then please, let him go. You have what you want. I won't fight you anymore."

"Don't, Annie." Jake's rasp struggled to escape his throat.

That was enough. Too much for her heart to endure. Annie dropped to her knees within arm's reach of Authority.

"I'd have liked to have had one more kiss, Jake." Annie held her hands up, palms open to the lawman. "Please, sir, let him go."

Authority laughed and released his grip from Jake's hair.

Jake crumpled to a ball at the man's feet. In the same split second, Annie and Jake both reached down for her discarded pistols, drew them on Authority, and fired two shots as one. Jake's shot went precisely between the man's eyes, while Annie's flew through his stony heart.

The man in black fell like a tree into the narrow gap between them. Their war was over.

Annie scrambled on her hands and knees around the body to get to Jake. "Are you okay?"

He didn't answer. Instead, he took Annie's face in his hands and pulled her to him. His lips pressed against hers for several seconds. His mouth suddenly relaxed, and his arms fell limp at his side as he collapsed beside her.

EPISODE 19

Flesh Wound

"Annie, are you there?" Ingrid's voice crackled through her com.

"Yes. I'm still here." Annie was in the process of evaluating Jake's condition. His breathing seemed weak. She pressed her trembling fingers against his neck, but she could hold steady long enough to get a sure read on his pulse. "What is the situation at the primary ship?"

"Under colony control now. We have 284 prisoners in custody, with 112 of those needing medical attention. A few may not make it." Ingrid paused for a moment. "I called for Bull a minute ago but got no response. Have you seen him?"

Annie tried to concentrate on her question while studying Jake's wounds. She wrapped the strap from her rifle around his leg and cinched it tightly. "I haven't seen him. Open all coms."

In a few seconds, Annie's com squealed with feedback from Jake's receiver. Annie reached over and snapped his device off. The squeal stopped, and she could hear Ingrid again. "All coms are now open. Bull, if you are able, please make your way to the primary ship. The commanding officer wishes to negotiate Authority surrender."

"On my way," Bull answered.

Cheers echoed through the communicators. Annie released a sigh of relief, though she still had one more battle to fight through. "Cody, are you there?"

"Annie, are you safe?" Her brother sounded exhausted.

"I'm all right, but I need you if you can come. Jake is hurt. Bad." She glanced around her. "Can you find me?"

"I have your location on my digital. I'm coming."

Annie clung to Jake's still body, holding his face against her shoulder. She hummed and rocked back and forth, praying for a miracle.

After several minutes, Cody appeared through a gap in the brush, throwing his medical bag at Annie's side. "Let me examine him."

"He was shot in his shoulder and his leg," Annie said, showing her brother the injuries. "I need you to get him healed up quick. He saved my life."

Cody glanced down at the body of the lawman. "He did this?"

Nodding, Annie made room for Cody to work by rolling Authority's corpse out of the way. "How is he?"

"Give me a second. He's banged up pretty badly. If these had been rifle shots instead of pulsers," he said, pointing to Jake's wounds, "he'd have bled out in minutes." He pulled the leather strap from Jake's leg and handed it to Annie. "Tourniquets are to staunch the bleeding. His leg wound was cauterized instantly."

"I'm not a doctor. What do I know?" She watched as Cody furrowed his brows and prepared a syringe. "What is that?"

Cody injected the clear fluid into Jake's arm. "We need to get him back to the house. He needs more help than I can give him here."

"But he's gonna be okay, right?"

Gesturing to the guns still lying on the ground, Cody sighed. "Gather everything up and help me get him up on Jefferson. We need to move him now."

Annie picked up her rifle, the pistols, and Jake's gun from the ground. She crawled over to Stubbs to say good-bye. She bent down over his face, crying. "My dearest friend."

The pony raised his head and snorted.

"He's not gone! Cody, Stubbs is alive." Annie holstered her pistols and strapped the rifles under Jefferson's saddle. She limped back to Stubbs to study the wound he had on his shoulder. "He's just grazed." She turned back to the horse. "Can you stand, boy?"

The horse rocked to the side and then raised his head straight up, lifting himself to standing, though he took a moment to regain steady footing. He favored his left leg and whinnied in pain. "It's okay, boy. Cody'll fix you right up."

As Annie comforted her pony, Cody lifted Jake on his shoulders. "Help me get him over to Jeff," her brother said.

She hobbled to the opposite side of Jefferson, noticing that her foot felt as though it were on fire. She ignored the pain for a second and pulled Jake's limp body across the saddle. Once he was up, she stumbled back and landed on her butt.

"What's wrong with you?" Cody asked.

Annie looked down at the black scorching on her jeans just above her right ankle. She didn't know what to think. "I don't know."

Before Cody had a chance to ask another question, Annie threw her right leg over Jefferson and made herself as comfortable as she could behind the saddle. "I'll take Jake back. Can you lead Stubbs?"

"Wait." Cody grabbed the reins and stopped the horse. "Annie, you've been shot."

"I don't think so."

He took hold of her boot. "I'm looking at it!

"I'm fine." Annie cinched up on the reins. "I'll meet you back at the barn." With a firm grip on Jake's back, she started off toward the house.

"If you don't let me fix you, you could end up with permanent damage to your leg." Cody's voice snapped over her com.

"I will let you work on my leg. Just as soon as you take care of Jake." She led the horse out to the road.

A few bodies were still moving. A group of colonists worked their way toward the house, loading survivors into the backs of trucks and covering the dead with sheets. Annie kept her eyes up, focusing on the house ahead of her.

"How's Rebecca?" she asked her brother. He and Stubbs had caught up and were walking just behind her on the road.

"She has a dislocated shoulder, but she'll be fine. I think it's from the kick of the rifle, but she's not admitting to that." Cody laughed. His voice suddenly turned solemn. "Daisy didn't make it."

"What?" Annie turned back to look at Cody. "What happened?"

"She was defending the barn with a few of the ranch hands. Authority got Daisy and two others before being stopped at the threshold." Cody shook his head. "She wasn't gonna let them near any of those animals. God rest her soul."

Annie felt herself crumbling. Her stomach was full of rocks, her leg was throbbing, and her heart was barely pumping anymore. Everything inside her went cold.

The barn had been turned into a hospital. Rebecca waved them inside with her left hand. Her right arm was in a sling. Annie slid off Jefferson and hopped around the horse as Cody pulled Jake down and lowered him onto a table.

"Oh, no." Rebecca shook her head at the sight of Jake's injuries. She looked at Cody. "Will he make it?"

Cody's face was stone. "I think so."

Annie pushed a chair to Jake's side. "He'll make it." She looked around the room. A dozen other tables were set up for injuries. Out of the back doors, she could see a row of covered bodies. Her shattered heart began to crumble. She felt something cold and wet on her cheeks as the first gust of frigid night air pushed through. Two ranch hands slid the back doors closed.

"She was shot!" a young woman cried as they came around the table next to Annie.

"I'm jus' fine." Annie held out her hand to the girl. "Come talk with me for a minute. You'll see."

The girl looked to be about the same age as Annie. She wrung her hands together as she pulled a chair over. "Your leg is hurt pretty bad. The blast went through your pant leg and your boot too. Doesn't it hurt?"

"I can barely feel it." Annie glanced down at her injury. "At least these boots weren't my favorite." She took the girl's hand. "Were you hurt?"

"No. I saw some bad...I saw plenty. But I wasn't hurt. I came inside to see if I could help the Doctor." She glanced around. "Your brother."

Looking toward Cody, Annie nodded. "What's your name?"

"Phoebe Elizabeth Dale. Bull is my uncle."

Annie watched the tears streaming over Phoebe's face. She squeezed the girl's hands in her own. "We have too much to do right now. Plenty of time later for crying."

Cody hurried to Jake's side after checking on another severely injured patient. "Let's see what we can do for your man here." He injected another syringe of clear liquid into Jake's arm. "Has he stirred any at all since we got him back?"

Annie shook her head. "Not any. But his arm is warm. Nearly hot. That's good, right?"

"Better than cold." Cody pulled Jake's shirt back from his shoulder wound as Rebecca joined them.

"Phoebe, can you help me cut his pant leg back. We need to see how bad his injury is." Rebecca glanced at Annie. "You met my sister?"

"I did. She's tough, like you."

Rebecca scoffed. "Tougher than me. Nearly as tough as you. Did she tell you that she's the one who defended the barn? She took five soldiers down without reloading."

Annie smiled at her new friend. "Then you're tougher than me." She glanced at the kennel where Buffalo slept. "You saved my dog. And all these people in here have medicine and the gear they need to recover. You saved much more than the barn."

Phoebe shivered. "I couldn't save everyone."

Rebecca shook her head. "Nobody can save everyone."

Cody cleaned up Jake's shoulder, then used his portable

anatoscanner to check for broken bones or dysfunctioning organs. "The shot has missed the heart, though it looks like his left lung may have been slightly scorched. I've given him something to help strengthen the muscles around the area. The clavicle looks okay, but the top two ribs may have slight fractures. I'll check them tomorrow to see if I need to go inside, but for now, he'll be fine."

He moved the scanner screen over Jake's leg. "His knee is fine. The blast seems to have ripped through the flesh, though. Muscle injuries take time to heal. Especially in the leg."

"Why isn't he waking up?" Annie asked.

Cody laughed. "There could be several reasons. Exhaustion, shock, but probably because I sedated him. He'll wake up soon enough."

Rebecca and Phoebe moved to the next patient, leaving Cody with Annie.

"Now that I've taken care of Jake, I need to examine your leg." Cody knelt beside Annie and carefully removed her boot. He slowly shifted the scanner from her knee to her foot. "You, my dear sister, have three broken bones in your ankle. I'm not sure how you were walking." He picked up another syringe from his tray.

"I don't need to sleep." She moved her foot away from Cody.

"Not a sedative. This is a local anesthetic. It will numb your injury, then I can make a cast for you. It's old-fashioned, but it works." Cody didn't wait for her to agree. He gave her the shot before he finished his sentence.

Annie winced at the pinch from the needle. "But I can stay here for now? I don't want to leave Jake."

Cody was about to answer when a quick pop snapped over the coms. "All coms open." Ingrid sounded official. "Stand by."

Everyone in the barn fell silent. "People of Georgetown Colony." Bull's voice was clear but heavy in tone. "While we mourn the loss of our loved ones today, we honor them by declaring victory in this battle. As magistrate of the colony,

I have signed a treaty with Authority that establishes full independence for this state. I have also negotiated independence for our sister colonies, Essex and Lisbon. Authority troops are in the process of withdrawing from this sector as we speak."

A loud cheer echoed from every direction.

Bull continued. "As soon as the dead and wounded soldiers have been gathered from our lands, Authority will withdraw completely from our colony planet, as well. I also have in my hand, issued this hour, official pardons for all crew and passengers from the CT04 Nightingale. May God in the Heavens save us all."

More cheering. Annie glanced up in time to see Cody kissing Rebecca. She smiled for a moment, then turned her attention to Jake. "We did it, Jake. We sent 'em packing."

Annie felt a slight squeeze on her hand.

She jumped up, balancing on one foot. He still wasn't moving, but his hand twitched within her grasp. "Come on. You need to wake up. We have some celebrating to do."

The front passage door on the barn whipped open with the wind, and Annie nearly lost her balance. Phoebe ran to the door and latched it closed. The air carried a sparkle of frost.

Annie clutched Jake's left arm to keep from dropping back into the chair.

"Blanket."

Annie looked around to see who spoke.

"Blanket, Love?" Jake whispered. His eyes were still closed, and his lips barely moved. "I feel cold."

"Cody, he's awake," Annie called out.

"Keep him still." Cody patted the hand of another patient as he walked back. "Is he talking?"

Annie nodded. "He said he was cold. He asked for a blanket."

Cody grabbed a cover from the shelf behind them. "It's not much, but it should help a little." He helped Annie spread the wrap over Jake. "It's important that he stay still and stay down for a while."

"Yessir." Annie nodded. "Can you wait for a few minutes before you work on my leg?"

Cody nodded. "I'll make rounds with the horses. Stubb's is fine, but a couple of the locals got over-worked. I want to make sure they aren't hurt."

Annie watched her brother walk to the stable side of the barn. "Jake, can you hear me?"

This time he opened his eyes. "I can hear you just fine, Love. I wasn't shot in the ears."

Laughing through tears, Annie leaned over him. "Jake Stewart, you have to get well fast. There's gonna be a big party around here soon, and I need you to be my beau."

"I can't really move. How badly am I hurt?" Jake managed to squeeze her hand again.

Annie leaned close to his face, trying hard to keep her balance on one foot. "Your left arm is going to be tied down for a bit while your shoulder heals, and your right leg, too. Cody says you gotta be still for a while, but that you'll recover good enough."

A wicked smile spread over Jake's chapped lips. "Good enough for what?"

"For this." Annie bent down and kissed him.

EPISODE 20

Let the Healing Begin

Two days stretched by slowly. Authority soldiers took their dead and injured back to their vessel and left Georgetown without fanfare. Bull and the other colony leaders made sure the troops cleared the atmosphere and then the sector. Bull wasn't taking chances. He asked Ingrid and Dhabi to monitor transmissions around Georgetown and the sister colonies.

Annie and the other injured colonists received treatments, medications, and surgeries to speed recovery. Everyone moved slower. Bodies ached. Hearts broke a little more every hour. Though the battle had been short, and the losses few, every family mourned for those who had died defending freedom from Authority.

Only eleven colonists died, but all were loved and admired, and their courage had been noted long before the war began. Daisy was one of two women who died and the oldest casualty of them all. Two dozen severe injuries and another fifty minor cuts and scrapes were counted and entered into the colony archives.

One home destroyed, four more damaged. Sixteen animals injured, but none fatally. The buildings could be replaced in a few months, and the animals healed with time, but for some, the loss and pain were deep and lasting. The colony would long remember what Authority had done.

On the third day, Bull called a meeting in the community building. The propped-open front doors showed scorch marks from pulser strikes. Everyone who was able packed into the auditorium.

At Bull's request, Annie, Cody, Dhabi, Ingrid, and Jake took seats on the front row. The whole room buzzed with stories from those who fought and those who watched, but when Bull took his place on the stage, the room fell silent.

The broad-shouldered, white-haired man crossed his arms over his chest and bowed his head. Everyone in the room followed.

Annie closed her eyes in silent prayer, remembering Daisy and the others who sacrificed their lives for the colony.

"Sisters and brothers of Georgetown," Bull addressed them solemnly. "I first want to assure you that we are keeping a close watch on every frequency, every transmission that we can, for any hint of retaliation or any threat from Authority. While we were victorious in our efforts, I am hesitant to drop our defenses. Our treaty with Authority is binding for now, but I do not trust them to keep their distance forever. They will squander their resources and surely come after ours, and we will be forced again to defend our homes."

Cheers erupted from the audience, punctuated with shouts of *Amen*. Annie felt like she was back at her home church in Texas. She glanced sideways at Jake, who nodded in respect.

Bull continued. "That being said, I am declaring tomorrow a colony day of mourning. We will officially bury our fallen family members at a sunrise ceremony. We will spend the rest of the day in quiet remembrance and healing."

Cheering again. Bull drew a deep breath as he prepared for the next part of his speech. He nodded to Rebecca and Phoebe, who stood at the side of the stage near him. He turned and gestured toward Cody and Annie, waving them up to the stage. Cody helped Annie up the three steps, and the two of them stood at Bull's right hand. The audience hushed quickly.

"After our day of sorrow, I would like to host a celebration of our victory. As part of that, and with the colony's approval, I wish to ask Cody and Annie Birchfield to help us celebrate with an exhibition—a performance with their heroic animals, with music, and tricks—something to lift our spirits and rekindle the fire we need to carry on. What say you?"

Annie's cheeks flushed red and hot. She looked up to see her brother's expression shift from his aw-shucks humility to his what-did-he-say dismay. She almost laughed. The colonists cheered. Annie glanced over at Jake, who simply blew her a kiss and nodded. Ingrid and Dhabi held up their hands, clasped together as one.

Bull turned to face them. "And what say you?"

Cody shook his head slowly. Annie knew that he wasn't sure about putting on a show so soon after the battle. He was just about to say *no* when Annie interrupted.

"We are both indebted to Georgetown, and to *your* family especially, for taking us into your homes, and giving us shelter and protection." Annie didn't dare to make eye-contact with Cody while she spoke. "And we are grateful beyond words for the kindness and hospitality that you and Daisy offered. It would be downright rude for us to refuse any request you make of us. We would be happy to put on a show for you all."

As the crowd applauded, Bull grabbed Cody's hand and began pumping it vigorously. Rebecca and Phoebe ran to hug Annie and her brother, and then to help them back to their seats.

"Marvelous!" Bull shouted, his fist raised over his head. "Then I shall conclude this meeting with simple instructions. We shall meet at the churchyard at sunrise. Plan tonight how best to remember and honor your loved ones. Make whatever preparations are appropriate. Tomorrow we heal. The next day we revel in our victory."

The final round of cheering seemed to last for several minutes. Rebecca took Annie aside for a moment. "Thank you for agreeing to do this for our family. I was afraid Cody wouldn't do it. This means the world to me."

Annie looked at her friend and smiled. "You like Cody very much, don't you?" She glanced over Rebecca's shoulder to see her brother speaking with Jake.

"Yes, but I'm such a mess right now. I don't know what to do. I have to get back to my ferry next week." Rebecca sighed. "And I don't want to leave him. What if he loves me? Oh!" She seemed to stumble over her words. "What if he doesn't?"

Annie almost laughed. "Don't worry, okay? Cody is head-over-heels. No doubt in my mind." She took Rebecca's hand in hers. "You have my word that by the time you have to leave, you'll know exactly what to do."

Rebecca shook her head. "I wish I was as confident as you."

Jake approached the women, hobbling on his casted leg. Before he reached them, Annie leaned forward to whisper in Rebecca's ear. "You don't have to wish. You're smart, beautiful, and capable in every way. Don't wish, just be."

Rebecca stepped back and blinked. "Really?"

Annie nodded as Jake slipped his right arm around her waist. She winked at Rebecca. "Just be."

Rebecca sighed and turned to find Cody and hurried away to his side. Jake raised his brow. "Just be what?" he asked.

Annie smiled. "Confident."

Jake chuffed through a grin. "Confident? Like agreeing to something before your brother can decline? That kind of confident?"

"Something like that." Annie shrugged. "Can we possibly get a show together in two days? With tired animals and injured performers? Is it even possible?"

"And just like that," Jake snapped his fingers, "your confidence has vanished?"

Annie shook her head. "Not vanished. But I should have asked you all first, maybe? We're all beat down so badly. Will we even be worth watching?"

"Have you lost your voice, Love?" Jake furrowed his brow as he asked.

"No."

"The horses? 'Ave they run off? Or have they forgotten what you taught them?"

"Of course, not."

"Then don't worry. Maybe the two of us can't waltz around the arena this time, but I have a feeling it will still be a show to remember. Do you trust me?"

A flutter filled her stomach. She flashed back to the first time Jake had asked her that question. It seemed like ages ago. She had doubts, then. Not now. "I do."

Jake's smile took on a devilish curve. "I like when you say that. *I do.* Yes, I do."

Annie placed her hand on the side of Jake's bruised jaw. "And will you help me plan out the show?"

The man lowered his gaze from her eyes to her lips. "No, Annie. I have other things I must attend to tonight." He seemed to avoid eye-contact for a split second and then looked up again. "I have quite a lot to do before tomorrow, actually. But I will look over the arena and make sure you have everything you need for the show." He leaned forward for a quick kiss on her forehead. "And save me a few minutes at the end of the show. I have a little trick I'm working on."

Annie raised a brow and laughed. "You're going to leave me to do it all by myself, but you want me to save you a place in the show?"

"I'm serious, Love. You said you trusted me." He released his grip on her waist. "I trust you to plan an amazing performance. And you trust me to get everything ready behind the scenes."

"What kind of trick are you planning? Do you need any help with it? Do you need a horse or a gun or anything else?"

Jake took a step back from her and looked her over from head to toe. "I will need you to assist me with my trick. But it's nothing you can't handle, Love. Trust me." He reached out and squeezed her hand. "I will see you at sunrise. Sleep well, Love. Dream sweet."

Annie held fast to his hand, not wanting to let go. "You're really leaving me?"

"For a few hours. You should spend the evening planning and tending to the horses. Oh, and see if you can add Buffalo to your act if he's healthy enough. I think everyone will love that."

As Jake hobbled away, Phoebe raced to Annie's side. "I just heard something about you," she said, bouncing on her heels. Annie watched Jake disappear into the crowd again, barely hearing Phoebe's bubbling voice.

"What? About me?" Annie turned to her friend to focus on her words. "What did you hear about me?"

Phoebe shook her head and rolled her eyes. "I heard Cody tell my sister that your birthday is in two days. How exciting for you! You'll turn eighteen on the day of the celebration. You have even more to celebrate than the rest of us."

Annie scowled for a second as she thought through the calendar. "Are you sure? My birthday is on July first."

Phoebe nodded. "Then, yes. Tomorrow is the last day of June." She squinted and glared at Annie. "Aren't you excited?"

"Yes, I s'pose I am. I haven't thought too much about it. Too much goin' on. How do you do birthdays here? Momma used to make corn cakes for us with honey syrup on top. Is it the same in Georgetown?" Annie felt a rise of anticipation. Eighteen.

Phoebe grabbed Annie's wrist and pulled her down to the steps on the side of the stage. "Corn cakes? No. Out here we have real sugar and real chocolate. My sister will bake you a cake and top it with chocolate icing."

Annie shook her head. "She doesn't need to do that. I don't want anyone fussin' over me. And with the show, I'll be too busy to think about it, anyway."

Phoebe leaned closer. "You don't understand. It's a surprise. They're planning to surprise you with the cake. I'll get in terrible trouble if Becca finds out I told you about it."

Annie laughed. "Then why did you tell me? If you hadn't mentioned it, I wouldn't have even remembered it was my birthday!"

Phoebe looked around them as if others were listening. "I don't like to be surprised, especially with a bunch of people watching. I just thought maybe you were the same." A look of disappointment fell over the girl's face. "I didn't mean to spoil everything for you."

Annie shook her head. She knew that Phoebe looked up to her and didn't want her to feel bad for telling. "No, you're right. But the hard part now is gonna be pretending that I don't know it's coming." Annie scanned from side to side. "Can you help me out, Phoebe? I need to plan the show, and I probably will have to do most of it myself. I could surely use another hand." She suddenly realized what she was requesting. "But maybe I'm asking too much. You'll be spending tomorrow honoring your Aunt Daisy."

Phoebe blinked and tilted her head. "How better to honor Daisy than to help you plan the celebration? She sacrificed her life for this victory. And she thought the world of you."

Annie's heart swelled with emotion. "I'm humbled, truly. Daisy showed me such kindness."

Phoebe hopped to her feet and offered her hand to Annie. "Let's get our jackets and head out to the barn. We can work on the plan out there until they call us for dinner. I'll bet we can get most of it done tonight. And tomorrow morning, Becca and I will take you and Cody to the churchyard."

Annie pulled herself up with Phoebe's help. "You're a good friend, you know?"

Phoebe smiled. "If you stay here in Georgetown, I hope we can become best friends." She leaned closer again. "My eighteenth birthday is in seven months. And it would surely be helpful if you could let me in on any surprises."

Annie laughed again. "You can count on me."

As they walked to the barn, Annie's heart felt full. She had a friend. She had a place where she belonged. It was almost like being home.

EPISODE 21

Cowboy Camp Meeting

A soft tap at the bedroom door pulled Annie awake. Phoebe's excited voice followed. "Hey, girl, are you up? We're fixing a little breakfast downstairs before we leave."

Stretching through a yawn, she responded. "I'll be down in five minutes."

"Take ten if you need it."

Annie hurried through her routine and made her way down the stairs, careful not to put too much pressure on her injured ankle. The smell of sizzling meat and butter triggered a growl from her stomach. Phoebe and Rebecca were setting the table and gesturing for her to take a seat.

"Perfect timing," Rebeca chirped.

"You shoulda got me up earlier. I'd have helped." Annie sat down as Phoebe took the chair next to her.

"Don't be silly." Phoebe tossed a napkin toward Annie. "You're still a guest, for now."

Annie noticed the sisters exchanging a quick smile, and wondered what it was about. She bowed her head once Rebecca was seated too. "Lord, bless this food and the hands which prepared it. Bless this day and keep us in your Way."

When she looked up, the others were smiling again.

"Thank y'all both for takin' such good care of my brother and me." Annie scooped her fork through the crispy bits of meat mixed with eggs. "This smells delicious." It tasted like the breakfasts her mother made for her as a child. Maybe better.

Certainly better than the fried protein bites that Cody cooked for her.

Rebecca nodded. "It's our pleasure. We'll head out to the churchyard as soon as we're done. It's still dark out, so you'll want a coat until sunrise. The service may take a few hours; I'm not sure how Bull will handle it all. There will probably be several speakers."

"And will the church hold everyone?" Annie wiped the corner of her mouth as she spoke.

Phoebe shook her head. "We don't actually have a church building. It never seemed to get built. We still use the community center for worship. We just call the cemetery the churchyard."

"It's a pretty place. You'll like it." Phoebe waited until they all were finished, and then put the dirty dishes into the sink. "We can take care of these later. We should get going."

Annie and the others grabbed coats and went to the front porch. Seconds later, Cody pulled up in his pick-up, and Rebecca joined him in the cab. Phoebe and Annie climbed into the bed with four of the ranch hands.

The black sky had turned to purple by the time they reached the churchyard. When the truck stopped, one of the ranch hands reached down for Annie's hand. "You want to see this," he said.

Annie shot a quick look to Phoebe, who nodded. "It's okay. This is Glen, my boyfriend." As Annie stood to look over the top of the cab, Phoebe stood behind her and rested her chin on Annie's shoulder. "Just watch for a minute."

A glow just beyond the horizon intensified, and Annie could see the silhouette of a man on a horse, then another. The riders appeared to be wading through a black, moving landscape. The land all around them tossed and shimmered like waves on water. But a cloud of dust assured Annie they were on solid ground.

"What is it?" she asked.

"Have a little patience," a familiar voice advised. Jake now stood beside her. "The sun will show you in a few seconds more."

Annie relaxed into the warmth of his presence. The orange glow pushed through the purple and bounced off the high clouds in a white lace above. The shapes on the horizon took form. It was a herd. Annie's heart pumped loudly in her ears.

"Those are the biggest sheep I've ever seen," she whispered.

Jake laughed. "Yes, I suppose they would be."

Phoebe giggled. "They're not sheep, Annie."

"Look a little closer, Love."

Annie squinted to make out the shapes. Huge animals, broader than the horses. At least a hundred. But what were they?

Cody reached up and patted her hand. "You're too young to remember them, aren't you?"

Annie blinked and held her breath for a second, leaning forward a few more inches. The glow of the rising sun seemed to cast a golden light onto her earliest memories. She was in her momma's lap, looking at pictures in a book. The animals in the photos were reddish-brown with white faces and pink noses and big furry ears sticking straight out on either side of their heads.

"Cows?" she dared to whisper.

Jake snugged his right arm around her waist. "Yes, Love, cows. It's nice to witness a moment when you don't know all the answers."

The others were climbing out of the truck and heading to where the crowds were gathering. Annie felt frozen in place. Tears rolled over her cheeks, and all she could hear was her heart beating. She couldn't remember seeing anything more lovely.

"We have to go." Jake lifted a tear still clinging to her jaw, and then offered her a handkerchief from his jacket pocket. "And if you're crying already, I suppose you'd better keep that. I doubt the day will get easier for you."

It didn't. The service began with Bull reciting Daisy's favorite poem about moondust and shadows and a flower that blooms only once. For the next two hours, family members of each fallen colonist spoke. Poems, memories, courage, even a little stubbornness. Brothers, fathers, mothers, children. Each memory pressed a little heavier on Annie's heart. Her tears had almost run out.

Now for eleven minutes of silence. One for each colonist who'd died in battle.

Jake sat on her left, and Cody sat on her right. She felt safe for the first time in months. She thought about her horses, her dog, her friends. They were all safe now. Georgetown gave them shelter. Made them welcome. It was like home. Everything was going to be okay now.

The silence was broken when Bull rang the bell that hung from the entry gate on the yard. Eleven times it pealed through the quiet. As the last chime faded, Annie looked up to the bright morning sky. The sun had warmed the crowd, and most of the gathered had already removed their jackets. Annie wriggled loose of her coat and folded it in her lap.

Before she had a chance to wonder what came next, Bull nodded and called Cody up to speak. *What?*

"I want to express my sincere sadness at the loss you all are bearing. The weight of this suffering my sister and I feel cannot begin to compare with your grief. The sacrifices made here this week will never be forgotten, and indeed, they represent a debt that I will spend the rest of my life endeavoring to repay." Cody's words sounded eloquent and mature. Daddy and Momma would be proud of him. Annie certainly was.

"And in that light, I want to thank you all for giving Annie and me a home here and assure you that I will forever be your servant. I'll be leaving Georgetown soon to work with Rebecca Dale on her ferry, doing my best to preserve the lives of animals, and keeping a close watch on Authority. I want to help prevent the overreach that led to the kind of tragedy we witnessed here. To make sure it doesn't happen anywhere else. That is my vow to you. It is the best way I know to honor your loved ones and their sacrifice. God bless this colony."

Every word bore into Annie like a bee sting. She knew it

was too good to be true. They couldn't really stay. It was too dangerous for the colony. For everyone. She was a silly girl to imagine that she would have a home again. Not after all she had done. After all the trouble she'd caused.

She heard Bull again reminding the colonists about the show tomorrow. Annie fixed a smile to her face, pretending. Pretending what, she wasn't sure. But she knew that her heart felt anything but joy. She wanted to cry again, but her tears were all spent.

Maybe Cody should have asked her before announcing this to everyone. Maybe it was better that he didn't. All she knew for sure was that she needed time alone to process. There would be a show tomorrow. She had to work out a few things with her horses. She needed to snuggle with Buffalo.

As soon as the memorial service was over, people crowded around Cody to thank him for his sentiments. Annie limped back to the pick-up truck, with Jake limping along beside her.

"I know you're upset," he said as Annie climbed into the truck bed.

"I'm not upset." She spat the words over her shoulder like bile and then threw herself down in the corner of the truck bed.

"Oh, but it looks like you are." Jake pulled himself carefully over the tailgate and crawled up beside her. Annie could see the achiness in his expression as he struggled to get comfortable. "You know this is why he didn't mention any of this to you before now. Cody knew you'd act like this. I told him you were a grown woman and could handle it, but he said you would throw a childish fit." He reached for her hand. "You still have a little time to calm down before he comes out."

Annie pulled her hand away from Jake's. "Don't tell me to calm down. I'm fine. Just leave me alone." She didn't want him to go, but she hated that everyone seemed to be treating her like a child.

Jake looked as though Annie had punched him again. He straightened up and scooted back to the tailgate. "I'll leave you alone for now. But you're not alone, Love. Remember that." His face seemed to twist in pain, and Annie wondered if it was from his injuries or from her words. As he dropped to his feet, Jake added. "I'm here for you, Annie Birchfield. I always will be."

He walked back to the yard and melted into the crowd. Annie tried not to watch him leave. She clenched her fist around the damp handkerchief he'd given her. Exhausted. That's how she felt. Tired of being the center of attention when it suited everyone else and then being ordered around when it came time for decisions to be made. She wanted to have the same consideration as all the others.

The others didn't throw fits when things didn't go their way. All the others behaved like adults. They took responsibility for their situations. They wanted to do their fair share. *They* didn't expect the universe to stop for them. Annie's heart broke a little more when she realized how truly selfish she was. It was time to change.

Half an hour later, Annie was back at the barn to pick up Buffalo. The pup was still stiff and slower than he had been on Earth, but Annie could tell he was growing stronger every day. The pint-sized sheepdog fell in step behind Annie as she marched to the corral where the horses rested.

As soon as Annie was at the gate, the horses ambled her direction. Her four, joined by Charlotte, were ready to play. Before she began, she looked them all over from head to hoof. They'd been through plenty, but Annie figured they'd enjoy a little attention.

She spent two hours working with them, jumping, counting, prancing. While Charlotte didn't know any tricks, she was more than happy to join the others in trotting around the corral. Annie had a few ideas about working her into the show. The afternoon passed quickly, and soon a couple ranch hands were bringing out feed for the horses.

Ingrid followed the young men and motioned for Annie to come inside. "Lunch is almost ready." Instead of herding Annie back to the house, Ingrid stood for a moment to watch as Annie gathered her training gear. She waited for Annie to secure the gate closed. "How are you all doing?"

Annie smiled at her friend. "The horses are well. And my leg is healin' good. I won't be able to ride my bike in the show tomorrow, but I can do nearly everything else." She looked toward the barn. "Have you seen my bike?"

Ingrid grimaced. "Well, during the battle, Dhabi may have borrowed your bike."

Shrugging, Annie smiled. "That's great." She laughed as a thought struck her. "Ha, he was an Indian riding an Indian."

A smile spread over Ingrid's face. "Yes, I may have pointed out that irony to him. He made a highly inappropriate comment, and—oh, Annie—I think I'm in love."

Annie nodded. "Me, too." She sighed.

Ingrid turned to face the house but didn't move from the fence. "That makes things even more complicated. How are you doing?"

Annie knew what she was asking. She resisted the urge to complain. Ingrid had always treated her as an equal. She set high standards, and Annie wanted to meet them. "I was a little surprised by Cody's announcement, but I'm handling things for now. I took it badly at first and was rude to Jake earlier. I will apologize to him—he didn't do anything wrong."

The blonde still didn't move from where she leaned on the corral. "You know, Annie, even though I'm a lot older than you, if you think about where I am in my life, compared to where you are in yours, we're not so different."

"How'd you figure that?"

"I mean, if I live to be three hundred and fifty years old, even at one hundred twenty-seven, I'm still not quite middle-aged. If you live to be fifty-eight, you aren't either." Ingrid winked at her.

"I understand what you're saying." Annie sighed. "But there are so many things that you have seen and experienced that I will never have a chance to know. You're an adult and can make decisions without having a committee meeting every time. You can do whatever you like, whenever you like."

Ingrid laughed and took a step toward the barn. "Let me help you with your gear." She took the whip and reins so that Annie could prop her saddle on the rack beside the gate. Ingrid followed Annie to the barn. "You're an adult, too, Annie. You just haven't had much experience being on your own," Ingrid started.

"I have *no* experience on my own."

"Maybe, but that's not what being an adult is about." She stopped while Annie put the gear in its place. "It's about controlling yourself—your words, your actions, your attitude. But it's also about being part of a world that's bigger than yourself."

Something in the corner of the barn caught Annie's eye. It was her motorcycle, but the front wheel was bent at a severe angle. "Oh gracious! How did...Dhabi not get hurt?"

"He jumped before the impact. He's scared to tell you." Ingrid laughed.

"I'm not angry. I'm glad he's not injured." Annie glanced at her bike again with pity. "That bike is old and can be really dangerous."

Ingrid leveled her gaze at Annie. "That's a very adult attitude. That's what I mean by being part of a world bigger than yourself."

Annie took a deep breath and released it slowly. How did Ingrid always seem to know everything about her? "I'm just starting to understand that idea. How are you so good at it?"

Ingrid stopped in her tracks and guffawed. "I'm not good at it. I've spent the biggest portion of the last century hiding. I've kept my eyes down and my head low. I've been so afraid of losing my life, that I've barely lived it. I mean, I've known love and family. I've been to lots of different places. But I haven't really enjoyed life like I should. You have. You're incredible at living. And you're not afraid of anything."

Annie swallowed hard as she pulled the heavy barn door closed. "I am afraid, though." She wrinkled her nose to keep her eyes from tearing up. "I'm afraid of losing everything I have."

Ingrid walked closer to Annie and linked elbows with her as they walked toward the house. "Annie, what do you think you'll lose?"

Annie motioned to everything around them. "All of this. My friends, my family, and my horses."

"You know as well as I do that none of this is forever. Time takes everything from us, sooner or later. The only way to genuinely have anything is to enjoy it while you can. Be grateful. Be present. You have been a savior, literally, for your animals. You have been supportive of your brother in everything he's done. Your rebellion, whether you meant it or not, has breathed life into hundreds of weary souls, including Dhabi and me."

"Dhabi?" Annie swallowed a refreshing gulp of air. "And you?"

"Yes. Dhabi told me that the first time he heard you sing, it changed him. Your willingness to openly rebel—he said you sang as if you were merely breathing. Like it was nothing. Daring Authority to arrest you. And then you performed in front of thousands. He told me that he thought you were possibly the bravest person he ever knew. You're undoubtedly the bravest one I've known."

Annie shook her head. "I'm not brave. I'm mostly scared to death."

Ingrid laughed. "All the bravest people are. That's why you're such an inspiration. As for Dhabi and me, we'll be leaving Georgetown soon. We're planning to take the Nightingale and scan the stars for others like you if that's possible. We'll get them on board with your uprising. Get them what they need. Bring them back here. Whatever it takes to keep Authority in check."

They reached the steps of the big house and lingered a little longer on the porch. Annie sighed and squeezed Ingrid's arm. "I can hardly imagine not having you near."

Ingrid squeezed back. "All you have to do is send a message, and I'll come running as soon as I can. Promise." She gestured to the door. "For now, we should enjoy our time together. You have some big, hard decisions to make soon. We all do. One thing I know for sure is that I have a family here. So no matter where in this galaxy I go, I will always have a place to come back to. I have a home."

Annie's shoulders relaxed as she threw her arms around Ingrid's neck and squeezed her into a tight hug. "This is our home, isn't it?"

EPISODE 22

Remember When the Music

Sunlight punched through the split in the curtains of Annie's bedroom window, falling over her eyelids and coaxing her awake. She didn't move for several seconds. Instead, she lingered in the warmth of the blankets. Today was the first big show in Georgetown. Maybe the last.

She had gone to bed pondering her future and even wrestled with ideas in her dreams. After her talk with Ingrid, she wondered if she dared to challenge Cody. To declare her independence. To stay or go. To enjoy the security of a home for herself and her animals or to remain in the protection of her brother. Her brain was worn, and her heart was torn. She had argued with herself all night, fighting both sides, unable to win.

All she knew for sure was that she couldn't take the horses back into space. And if it would be tough on them, it would be even worse for her dog. That meant if she went out with Cody, she'd have to leave them all behind. How could she give them up after fighting such a harsh battle for them?

She felt sure that Cody would object to her staying. But she was an adult. Annie could take care of herself. Just because she'd never had to before, didn't mean she wasn't capable. She looked toward the window again. It was time.

Annie launched herself from the bed with a manufactured enthusiasm. She would talk to Cody after the show. Explain to him that she was staying. She wouldn't give him a choice. It would be fine. Wouldn't it? Of course, it would. She was an adult.

Then why did her stomach ache?

Dressed in her work jeans and boots, Annie set out her fringed show costume and took a second to polish her bright red boots. She crept downstairs as carefully as the cast on her ankle allowed. Nobody was in the parlor or the small kitchen. Good. Annie grabbed her jacket and let Buffalo out of his kennel. He hurried to the front door and pawed until Annie opened it.

Annie let Buffalo do his business while she dropped a scoop of his food into his bowl on the bottom porch step. The dog lapped at his water and munched on his breakfast as Annie sat on the top step and looked around.

It was like her house back home. Trees, grass, dirt, clouds. Georgetown's terraforming had begun nearly three hundred years before, and the dirt was still black and rich from the ultra-infused nutrient formula. The clouds were thicker and pinker than back home. A little different, but not much.

Unlike her home on Earth, this was a working ranch, with young men and women hurrying from one place to another. Annie watched as several hands ran toward the pen behind the main barn. Another few seconds ticked away, and Annie realized that everyone was running in the same direction. She grabbed the leash from the porch rail and tethered Buffalo securely at her side. She needed to know what was happening.

The closer she got to the barn, the louder the commotion became. Ranch hands of every age chattered excitedly about a new arrival. Annie scooped Buffalo into her arms and found a little break in the crowd where she could see what was happening in the pen.

She leaned forward and saw a huge brown beast with darker, thicker fur like a mane. It had short curved horns on either side of its head. On one side of the animal were two ranch hands, and on the other was Cody, kneeling. It took just a few seconds for Annie to understand that this was a momma giving birth.

With Cody and the other men stroking the side of the momma, she lowered herself to the ground. That's when it really got serious. From the momma's narrow back end came a blob of something that made Annie's stomach lurch. It was followed by a red mass of fur and legs and big black eyes. Cody helped to clean the baby whatever-it-is and to make sure the momma was okay after the birth. Annie found herself crying at the sight, but not really sure why. She held tightly to Buffalo in her left arm and wiped her tears away with the back of her right hand. She swallowed hard and smiled when Cody nodded to the crowd. Their eyes met, and her smile broadened.

"Workin' at the crack of dawn?" she teased him, as he climbed over the side of the wooden pen.

"I figured I'd let you sleep in since today's your big show." Cody gave her a hug, and Annie inhaled a pungent musk she'd never smelled before.

"What is that thing? Some kind of cow?" Annie set Buffalo back on the ground as they followed Cody back to the barn.

"Sort of a cow. It's called a bison. It was once the official mammal of America. It was commonly called a buffalo, though technically, that's a different animal."

"Like my dog?"

"Yes, exactly. It's now extinct on Earth. Georgetown is the only place in the universe that has them." Cody pulled off his shirt and washed his hands up to his armpits in the barn's basin cabinet. "I'm glad you got to see the birth."

"I'm glad you were here for it, too." Annie sighed and tossed a towel from the counter to her brother. "What do they do with the bison? I mean, everything here seems to have a job. What do bison do?"

Cody laughed and waved to a ranch hand passing through the barn. "The bison help train the horses."

Annie blinked. "How?" She squinted, doubting his answer. "Are you kidding me?"

Shaking his head, Cody laughed. "It's true. The horses have to be able to separate the herds and flocks. Dividing them when necessary, or isolating an animal for protection or treatment."

Annie nodded. "Yeah, so?"

"When they train the horses to do that, they can't use cattle or sheep. Those animals get tired quickly and comply without much resistance. Then the horses only know how to manage easy animals." He paused until Annie nodded again. "But bison have more stamina. And they're stubborn. They fight being told what to do. So when a horse gets a bison under control, he's really learned how to do his job."

"That's amazing." Annie unclipped Buffalo from his leash to let him play with another dog. "So, the bison are like super-cows?"

Cody laughed. "The bison are like you. Not easily tamed."

"Speaking of me..." Annie plopped herself down on the stool next to the cabinet as Cody pulled a fresh T-shirt from the shelf and put it on. "I am not going back into space. For now, anyway." She waited for her brother to make eye contact again. "I'm going to stay here with the animals. Bull has said I'm welcome to stay in the guest house as long as I like."

Cody seemed unfazed. He simply nodded. "I was wondering what your plans were."

What? He not only wasn't angry, but he barely seemed to care. Annie swallowed hard. Was this being an adult? On Earth, one was legally considered an adult at fourteen, but she'd never been treated as anything more than a child. She had always lived at home, and Cody had decided everything for her since her parents passed.

Annie chuffed. "So you don't care what I do?" Heat rushed through her veins. "I thought you would be angry or try to tell me what *you* want me to do. But you don't even care?"

Cody shook his head. "Of course, I care. But you're grown. You're making good money now. You can take care of yourself. Look, I treated you like a child for too long. I should have given you more responsibilities. I shouldn't have protected you from everything in life."

Annie tucked her chin to her chest and glared at her brother. "You're just going to leave then?"

"Don't make it sound like that, Annie. I'm not deserting

you. I'll visit in-between trips. But you don't need me holding your hand anymore." Cody shrugged, as though his words meant nothing, but Annie detected a tug in his voice as he looked away from her.

She hopped down from her stool and ran to Cody's side. "I'll always need you. You're my big brother. You have to promise me that you'll come back every time you have the chance."

Cody hugged her tightly. "I'll be back so often that you'll forget I don't live here all the time." He released his grip and took a step back. "Now, you need to get ready for your big show. I already checked the horses over this morning. They all are healthy and ready to perform."

Annie gave him a quick squeeze again. "Thank you, Cody. Are you and Rebecca gonna be in the show, too? Please?"

He nodded. "Of course, we will. We have to train our replacements. What kind of show would it be without someone to handle the horses and someone to teach how to shoot? I mean, we're practically the stars." He paused for a second. "You are going to keep the show going after we leave, right?"

"You think I should?" Annie's heart pounded against her ribs. She'd been afraid to say the words out loud, but she wanted more than anything to continue performing with her horses. Cody's question gave her hope that it might be possible.

"You have to keep the circus going. It's what rallied everyone in the first place. It gave everyone—every oppressed soul in the galaxy—a means to fight back. You literally gave them a voice. You have to keep the show going. And we'll keep bringing you an audience."

Annie couldn't stop smiling. Not only did Cody respect her as an equal, he believed in her. "Thank you, big brother. I love you."

"Love you, too, sis," he said. "And one more thing."

"What?" Annie dropped her hands to her hips, expecting a sarcastic remark.

"Happy birthday."

Annie blinked in shock. In all her worry and hurry for the

morning, she'd forgotten that today was her birthday. "Thank you," was all she could manage to say.

She whistled for Buffalo, and he scurried to her side.

"I'll bring the horses over to the arena after I get all my notes taken and get myself cleaned up." Cody winked at her. "Rebecca is bringing lunch out, too. I'll have her get your show clothes if you tell me which ones."

"I set them out on my bed." Annie scratched Buffalo's ears. "I'm gonna go look for Jake."

Cody nodded and waved as Annie left the barn and headed in the direction of the arena. As she neared the gate, Phoebe drove up in her truck and parked. To Annie's surprise, Jake got out of the passenger side.

"There's the birthday girl!" Phoebe called out. "How can we help you get ready?"

Jake rounded the end of the truck and put his arm around Annie's shoulder. His face winced in pain when he raised his arm. "First things first. Here's a kiss for eighteen." Jake pressed his warm lips into Annie's forehead. He moved his face to Annie's ear. "And I'll have another present for you later," he whispered.

Annie noticed a glimmer in his steel-blue eyes, and felt a flutter, and then a sense of panic. What about Jake? She loved him. She knew that. And she was sure that he loved her. Would he try to convince her to leave with him? Was she strong enough to resist? Was she strong enough to let him go? Her mind flashed from one terrible scenario to another. She had too much to do without thinking about any of this right now. Her brain was in a fierce game of tug-of-war with her heart, and she had no idea which one would win.

And then there was that gleam in his eyes. Ugh.

Phoebe skipped to her side. "What's first?"

Annie looked back at the barn and then to the stables. "Cody says that the horses are cleared for the show, so we need to get them to the arena. But maybe we should get the guns together and check the ammunition. I want to use salt pellets again. No sense wasting the good stuff." Phoebe and Jake nodded and headed to the weapons room.

Annie's thoughts flashed back to the battle. How much ammo was spent on that? What was left? How would the audience react? Another cloud of worry crowded into her head.

The threesome gathered the pistols, rifles, and balloon targets for the show. Annie appraised Jake's injuries. "Are you gonna shoot?" she asked as he spun the empty chamber of a revolver.

"You think a couple'a scratches is going to keep me out of your show, Love?" He squinted as he rocked the chamber back into place. "I'm tougher than you think."

"This is more than a scratch," Annie said as she rested her hand over Jake's shoulder wound. "I just want to make sure you're okay."

Jake covered her hand with his. "I'm going to shoot just like you taught me. I think I've earned my sharp-shooter title."

Annie laughed nervously and whispered. "I already kissed you, remember?"

He whispered back. "I have something else in mind this time."

Swallowing hard, Annie looked up to see Phoebe blushing and averting her eyes. She turned toward the truck. I think we have everything we need here. We should get the horses loaded up and take all the gear over."

"I think your brother is doing that now," Jake said, gesturing to the rusted green pickup heading up the road, pulling the horse trailer behind it.

Annie loaded the guns and gear into Phoebe's truck bed and helped Jake raise his gear over the side, too. "Why is everyone being so nice to me?"

Phoebe coughed. "Maybe because you're our hero? Maybe because it's your birthday?"

"But I'm still just me."

Jake laughed and opened the passenger door for her. "I'm sure I'll infuriate you soon enough. Let's get to the arena and get set up. Do you have your costume?"

"Rebecca is bringing it." Annie slid into the center of the bench seat. "Where is yours?"

"Hanging in the dressing room." Jake got in beside her. "Everything is ready for your big show," he said as Phoebe hopped in behind the wheel. "Have you seen the poster?"

Phoebe giggled and reached behind her seat. "Yes! You have to see the poster." She pulled out a sheet of paper printed with bright lettering across the top. SHOOTING STARS TRAVELING CIRCUS. Below that was a pair of pistols, crossed at the barrels and a horse outlined in glittering stars like a constellation.

"Where did this come from?" Annie turned to face Jake. "Did you do this?"

"Not me. Dhabi gave us this one. Said he found these all over the com-boards. And there are a dozen other designs, too. I'd say you have some creative fans out there." Jake patted her knee. "Face it, Love. You inspire rebellion everywhere you go."

EPISODE 23

One Voice

It was showtime. Annie fidgeted in the great hall with her friends and the horses, wishing her boot wasn't quite so tight against her ankle cast. Jake's right hand rested firmly in the small of her back, setting off a mash-up of emotions within her. Even the horses seemed nervous.

Bull was speaking to the crowd, recounting the loved ones lost in battle and praising the names of heroes still fighting. Finally, he introduced the troupe, and Dhabi led the procession into the main ring. He called each performer by name. Nero, escorted by Cody, followed by Stubbs and Ingrid, and then Liza Jane and Jake. After everyone else was in place, Dhabi announced Jefferson, with Buffalo on his back, escorted by Annie Birchfield. The audience jumped to their feet and cheered.

As the horses circled the arena, Phoebe and Rebecca brought out Dhabi's sitar. He took his position at Annie's feet as Cody and the others led the horses out of the ring. Annie switched on her microphone. The crowd took their seats and fell nearly silent.

Annie felt just as she had the first night she sang for Andre at the Quail. Her tummy quivered as she drew a deep breath. She began to sing about cowboys and horses, realizing that Georgetown had a different understanding of what was and what was past. She did too.

After each song came a flood of applause. It was time to bring out the horses again. All four lined up to count, bow, and prance for their fans. Even Charlotte made a quick appearance and seemed to enjoy the sudden attention. All the horses looked to have much more shine and energy than when they'd been on the ferry.

Annie coaxed Jefferson to a kneeling position as Buffalo hopped down, circled the horse, and again jumped up to his bare back. While Annie sang *She'll Be Comin' Around the Mountain*, Jefferson pranced in time around her, and Buffalo posed on his hind legs, ending the performance with a spin and a tail whip as the song ended. More cheers. Annie scanned the crowd to watch the children respond, but she didn't see more than a handful of kids in the sea of people. She wondered why.

She sang another set of songs. One about her motorcycle, another about her home in Texas. More cheers. Annie's heart felt full. She was surrounded by all the people she loved. By her animals. By her friends. She didn't want to let them go.

Cody brought out her pistols as Rebecca set her balloon targets in place. The audience hummed with anticipation as Jake led Liza Jane to Annie in the center of the ring.

"Two of my favorite girls," Jake said with a twinkle in his eye.

Annie switched her microphone off. Leaning close to Jake's ear, Annie whispered, "I don't see many children in the stands. I haven't really seen many since we've been here."

Jake took her hand and helped her into the saddle. "Not many having kids here. Most are still afraid of Authority. Scared Authority might take an interest in the colony and start setting up rules, taxing and taking whatever they want. Just like everywhere else. Maybe the colony has been ignored in the past, but I'd guess Authority will take more interest from here out." He smiled up at her. "Are you all right, Love?"

"Yeah," she answered. Jake waited at her side a second longer before retreating to the edge of the ring. Annie turned on her microphone again. This was the part of the show she loved most, but it was also what she feared, so soon after the battle.

Her pistols felt comfortable in her hands. Were they too

comfortable? Doubt crept in and pawed at her thoughts. Wasn't she the reason for the bloodshed here and on the ferry? Wasn't she to blame? The face of Authority flashed before her eyes. Cruel. Overbearing. Power-hungry and hateful. That was him, not her.

Liza Jane shook her mane and startled Annie back to the moment. "Ladies and gentlemen...friends. I thank you for allowing me to come here and find refuge in Georgetown. You have welcomed my family and me to your colony without hesitation, even though we brought you trouble. More trouble than any of you deserve."

Annie held up her pistols to show the crowd. "You not only took care of us, but you fought alongside us. Our battle became your war."

To Annie's surprise, the crowd cheered at her words. Even before the applause settled, Annie could hear her heart pounding in her ears. She knew what she needed to say, though the words tasted bitter on her tongue. "And the war isn't over yet." The crowd grew silent. "No, not yet. We had a resounding victory, yes," she said as she led her horse into starting position. "But Authority will be back. Right now, our enemies are regrouping. Making plans. We have a treaty, but that won't be honored. Authority was humiliated, and they don't take kindly to that. They'll prepare for more. They're likely preparing now. Gathering resources."

A rumble rose from the crowd. Annie's confidence grew as she focused on the balloons around the ring. "Authority thought we'd be an easy target. Broken and begging before their first ship landed. But we were ready." Cheers erupted again. "And we will be ready when their soldiers return."

With that, Annie gave Liza Jane a gentle kick and squeezed her knees together to stay steady as the horse bolted forward toward the first balloon. Pop! Liza Jane zigged and zagged around the open ring. Pop! Pop! Pop!

Soon all the targets were gone. Annie holstered her pistols and took one last lap around the ring. Back in the center, with the audience still thundering, Annie swung her injured ankle over the saddle and did her signature flip dismount, landing solidly on her feet. A lightning bolt of pain shot up from her ankle and shook through her gritted teeth. She forced a smile and continued.

Everyone was back on their feet. Annie drew another deep breath and let it go slowly. She gave a humble bow to Liza Jane before Jake took the horse back to the hall. One more song and then the big finish.

"I'd like to thank you all again for allowing me to show what my horses can do. If it weren't for you, none of us would have survived to see this day." Annie glanced over her shoulder at Jake, leaning against the wall of the ring. She'd wanted to talk to him before sharing her decision with the colonists, but there hadn't been time. She hoped he'd understand.

"I also want to tell you all that I'll be having more shows here because while my brother and my friends will be leaving Georgetown, at least temporarily, I will be staying." She waved as the crowd cheered. "Thank you."

She again focused on Jake, who merely blinked at her announcement, then looked down and shook his head. Annie's heart ached. She would talk to him soon. Explain somehow. He loved her. He would understand.

She took a few steps forward and raised her chin to the colonists. "My momma, God rest her sweet soul, used to tell me that life was hard. That every day of my life, people would try to take away my dignity and trample my spirit to dust. She reminded me that she'd taught us right from wrong and that it was my duty to stand for what was right. She told me to put on my big-girl boots and stand my ground."

Dhabi joined her with his instrument and took a quick bow before sitting and waiting for Annie to begin.

I've got my big girl boots on,
I'm gonna stand strong,
Nothin's gonna get in my way.

I know what's right,
Ain't afraid to fight,
Gonna live to see a better day.

Annie had the whole arena swaying and clapping to the music. At first, it felt like the ultimate rebellion. Singing and dancing for the people. Celebrating. But there was something missing, and Annie couldn't quite figure out what it was.

Jake had said he had a trick for the show, but he never brought it up again. Maybe he'd decided against it. Her heart sank a little bit more.

She finished the song and watched as Cody and Rebecca set up the target for the over-the-shoulder shot. Ingrid brought out her rifle and placed it carefully in Annie's grip. "You're amazing, you know?"

"So are you," Annie replied. She prepared herself for the temporary deafness, knowing that this was the big finale.

The target was set, and she began her tease. "Do you think I can hit the bullseye from here?" Cheers. She took ten paces farther. "From here?" More cheers Ten more paces. "What about now?"

The crowd went wild. It was Jake's cue to come out with the hand mirror. She looked around but didn't see him. She shot a glance at Cody, who shrugged. After several seconds of panic, Jake emerged from the hall without the mirror. He approached her with his hands up in surrender.

"I can't find your mirror," he confessed. "I'm sorry to spoil your big finish, Love. But could I say something?" Jake wore a pleading expression. Annie nodded as Jake went on. "Since the moment I met you, I knew that you were trouble. You pushed back against every unjust law and rule you met. You championed your animals. You ached and empathized and sang and danced and shot and taught and dragged us all along for the terrifying and wonderful ride."

Annie wasn't sure whether to be flustered or flattered.

221

Jake continued. "And then you come out here and put on a fantastic performance for these lovely people." He waved his hands toward the crowd in a flourish. "You encourage them to fight back, however they can. Singing, shooting, tending animals, reading, writing books, building homes, marrying, having children. Creating families and communities."

Annie looked into Jake's eyes. She was confused. She wasn't sure if he was upset or disappointed or just what. Before she could respond, he continued.

"And this is the part of the show where I come out and give you the hand mirror and kiss you in front of God and everyone." He paused, and loud whoops rose from the stands.

A mischievous curl formed on his lips, and Annie prepared to be kissed.

Jake shook his head. "No, I'm not sure if I should kiss you now. I lost your mirror. All I could find was this." Jake reached in his back pocket and took a deep bow in front of Annie, holding up a ring. "Annie Birchfield, I know it's against Authority, but will you marry me and build a home here in Georgetown and have a baby or three?"

Annie stared at Jake, unable to breathe. She suddenly became aware that everyone in the arena was holding their collective breaths, waiting for her answer.

Her answer. She was still struggling to understand Jake's question, let alone form an answer. Before she had a chance to form the words, her head was already nodding furiously.

"Jake Stewart, since when do I care if something is against Authority? Yes, sir, I'll marry you and everything else." She didn't wait to put the ring on, but let her rifle drop to the ground. She threw her arms around his neck, smothering his lips with hers.

The audience bounced and cheered for several minutes before settling down. Jake took the opportunity to slip the ring onto her finger. Cody, Rebecca, Ingrid, and Dhabi all rushed out to hug them, and within a few seconds, the crowd was on their feet, singing *Amazing Grace* as loudly as they could.

The show was over, Annie thought, but there would be many more to come.

***

Back at the guest house, Annie sat on the steps next to Jake, watching Buffalo play in the grass. The sun had started its descent into the chilly night, causing Annie to shiver in Jake's arms. "I can't believe— I was afraid you were mad."

"Only mad for you, Love." Jake quickly pressed a kiss into her temple and waited several seconds before leaning away. He laughed. "Did you hear all the prepositions being asked after the show?"

"You mean propositions?" Annie asked with a chuckle.

"Over, under, around? I heard both prepositions and propositions." He winked at Annie. "Love, I believe you may have inspired the most enjoyable uprising in the history of humanity."

Annie shook her head as Jake's eyes twinkled. "I think that part of the rebellion is thanks to you."

He took her face in his hands and covered her lips with his. As they parted, Annie exhaled a deep, comfortable breath and leaned into his shoulder.

Jake nodded. "Then it will be my greatest pleasure."

The front door swung open behind them, and Phoebe led out a procession of revelers singing the birthday song. She carried a cake lit with sparklers.

Everyone took a sparkler and began waving it in the twilight as Rebecca started cutting and serving the cake. Dhabi sat on the other side of Annie and smiled.

"I'm happy for you both." Dhabi gestured with his fork. "When will you marry? Ingrid and I want to return for the wedding."

Jake laughed. "I'm going to build a house for us. We'll have the wedding as soon as it's finished." He scooped up a big bite of cake. "Shall we plan for a double wedding?"

Dhabi smiled and glanced back at Ingrid, Cody, and Rebecca. "Maybe a triple ceremony." He laughed as a napkin hit him on the back of the head. "You are inspiring change, Annie. You changed me."

Annie swallowed her bite in progress. "I don't think I should take credit for that." She tossed the napkin back to Ingrid.

Dhabi reached into his shirt pocket and pulled a small envelope out. "I have something for you." He handed it to Annie.

She took it and opened the envelope, sliding out a folded and yellowed piece of paper. She carefully unfolded the page to find a child's drawing of a brown horse with a pink saddle. At the bottom of the page was scrawled the name, *Liza Jane*. Tears immediately formed in Annie's eyes. "You kept it all these years? I can't take this from you."

Dhabi's eyes shimmered too. "You must take it. It's your birthday gift. And trust me when I say that I would be deeply hurt if you don't take it and keep it safe." His voice fractured and faded into another bite of cake.

Annie sniffed as she returned the paper to the envelope. "I will treasure this gift always, Dhabi. And before another person calls me a hero, you need to hear this. You are my hero. You gave up everything you had to save Cody and our animals and me."

"I'm not anyone's hero. I was going to take your money and leave you on Earth."

"But you didn't. Even with Authority bearing down. You had every reason to turn us over, but you didn't. Why not?"

The others joined them on the porch steps leaning close to hear.

Dhabi tapped the envelope gently. "My friend died when I was just a kid, and I knew it was Authority's fault. My mother told me there was nothing I could do about it. But she was wrong. From that moment, I started looking for an army to join so that I could fight back. I searched everywhere, but every army I found seemed to be under Authority control. Until I met you. I heard you sing. That first night you raised the army I'd been searching for."

Annie felt a lump swelling in her throat.

Jake laughed. "I told you she was trouble."

Dhabi nodded. "The very best kind. You don't ever give up the good fight."

Annie stretched her arms in both directions until she held tightly to everyone in her family. Buffalo climbed up the steps and plopped down at her feet. She squeezed them all together in one gigantic hug. "Neither will anyone in my army."

THE END

ABOUT THE AUTHOR

Kim Black is an award-winning author of novels,
children's books, and short stories.
She is an active member of the Texas High Plains
Writers in the Texas Panhandle.

Kim considers herself a genre mixologist, as she enjoys
writing all kinds of stories for a wide range of readers.
She surrounds herself with family, books, and her full-
time body-guard, Archie, a wire-haired terrier rescue.

For more information about Kim, visit her website:
www.kimblackink.com

www.ingramcontent.com/pod-product-compliance
Lightning Source LLC
Chambersburg PA
CBHW020107180626
46812CB00006B/2507